BOUND BY FATE

BOOK SEVEN OF THE WESTWOOD PACK

F.D. FAIR

Foundations Book Publishing
4209 Lakeland Drive, #398, Flowood, MS 39232
www.FoundationsBooks.net

Bound by Fate
Book 7
The Westwood Pack

ISBN: 978-1-64583-118-1

Copyright © 2023 by FD Fair
Cover by Dawné Dominique Copyright 2023
Book Formatting by Bella Roccaforte

Published in the United States of America
Worldwide Electronic & Digital Rights
Worldwide English Language Print Rights

Chapter One

Zeke–11 Years Ago

"I'm not like you, Axel!" I yell at my twin.

"I know you're scared, Zeke. Hell, I'm scared too, but this is what we were born for. This is what we've trained our entire lives for," he says, running a frustrated hand through his short brown hair.

"That's not it—" I begin but rethink my words. "Maybe you're right. Maybe it does have something to do with being scared. But that's not all it is, and you know it! This isn't what I want for my life."

"Damn it, Zeke! I know you've never taken this position seriously—" Axel starts, but I cut him off with a laugh.

"You think I don't take this position seriously? Axel, I want nothing to do with being an alpha. I never have. You know I'd be a horrible alpha; hell, the entire sleuth knows that."

I force myself to pause and take a deep breath before I say something I'll regret later. My brother is silent, but I can see the pain in his eyes. It is easy for me to read the face that mirrors my own.

"Axel, I'm not asking your permission," I begin, trying to soften my tone. "I'm going whether you like it or not."

He sits heavily in our father's chair—at our father's desk—and scrubs a hand over his face. The posture makes some of my anger fade. My brother and I are not small men by anyone's standards, but he still looks small when he sits in that chair. Physically, the chair and desk fit him fine, but my father's office will always instantly transport me back to our childhood.

How much time did Axel and I spend here with him? How many nights did we spend playing on the floor while he kept up with the long and thankless work of being an alpha?

A pang of loss flows through me at the thought of him. Our father was my hero. He was the biggest and toughest man I've ever known. He put himself in danger whenever the sleuth needed him, and everyone loved him for it. When he would go out in search of lost shifters, our people would worry for him—anxious for his safe return. I knew better than to worry though. Nothing could touch my dad.

The only time I worried about him was the last time he left. I had a bad feeling in my gut about that mission. As soon as the intel crossed his desk, I knew something was wrong. Someone reported that a young girl—rumored to be a tiger shifter—was living in the woods alone a few hours north of us. How did a tiger shifter end up all the way in Canada? How was she managing to live alone in Northern Ontario?

I begged him to take us along. Axel and I were eighteen and old enough to join him on his missions. He chuckled at how eager I was and clapped me on the shoulder. He walked out the door alone with a promise to be careful and take us along next time. Little did we know, there would be no next time.

That was the last time I saw my father. It was the last time I saw him alive—that is. The hunters who killed him left parts of him strewn throughout the forest, and his head was sent back to us with a warning that they were coming for the rest of us soon.

I wanted to launch an attack immediately. How dare they take my father from me? How dare they degrade his legacy by defiling his body? We needed to show them that their crimes could not stand.

Axel disagreed with me though. He let his fear rule him and decided that we needed to move the sleuth deeper into the forest for safety. When my mother agreed with him, I was overruled.

Heading toward Parry Sound was a simple choice. We had already been in contact with the coven there. The high priestess, Constance, was aware of our plight and happy to help. The fact that there was a strong pack of wolves nearby who were eager to make allies of any supernatural who could be persuaded was helpful in making our choice as well.

My brother vowed we would have nothing to do with the hunters ever again. It is why he doesn't want me to go, but it is also the exact reason why I must. Someone needs to make them pay.

"I can't lose you too," he whispers. His voice is so soft that I wouldn't have heard him if I wasn't a shifter.

I walk around the desk and place a hand on his shoulder.

"You won't lose me." I pause until he raises his head to meet my eyes. Looking at him is like looking into a mirror. We have the same green eyes, same brown hair, same stocky build, and same broad shoulders. We spent years decorating our bodies with tattoos —a foolish effort to differentiate ourselves from each other. Despite our efforts, our styles are too similar. Unless you pay close atten- tion to the designs we've chosen, our tattoos are little help in telling us apart. "You won't lose me, but you know that I need to do this."

He nods his head, but his shoulders slump in defeat. There's nothing else to say. There's no argument either of us will be able to put forward that will sway the other.

I take a deep breath, muster up all the courage I have, and walk away from my twin. I knew it would be difficult, but it is more painful than I had expected.

My brother and I share a unique bond. Identical twins are an oddity among shifters, but we are even more than that. We share our genes and our appearances, but we also share a soul that was split between us in the womb.

Shifters are always split in too many directions. They are both themselves and their animal counterpart, but they are also always searching for the mate who holds the other half of their soul. Axel and I are like that too. We each hold one-quarter of a soul. We are only a complete half when we are together. The other half of our soul belongs to our mate.

How the goddess found a woman who could be a perfect match for both of us is beyond me, but I trust that her judgment is better than mine. When the time finally comes to meet her, I have no doubt she will be perfect.

It's a complicated arrangement, and I wonder how our mate will take the news when she learns of it. It's uncommon, but not unheard of, for two shifters to share a mate. Axel and I have had the advantage of knowing since we were born that this would be the case. Even with all that time, I still struggle to imagine our future. That uncertainty is why I—unlike Axel—am not in a rush to find our mate.

For now, though, I am walking away from my twin—an integral and inseparable part of myself. The pain becomes bearable once I leave the office and fades slowly as I get farther away. I know already that it will not stop until we are together again. Like those cursed shifters who are at war with the animals inside of them, our souls will suffer and eventually fracture as time passes. Hopefully, I can get my need for revenge out of my system before I weaken us both by being apart for too long.

* * *

At first, I thought I could pick the hunters off one by one. I am only one bear shifter, but my supernatural abilities allow me to hide in the shadows. After six months, though, I have become sloppy while my prey has become wary.

At first, it was thrilling to hunt down the people who had stolen my father from me. I have managed to rid the world of more than a dozen hunters, but it has taken far longer than I had expected. I knew I was becoming careless, but I thought I still had plenty of time before they caught on to me. Classic Zeke—I was too confident and left a trail of bodies leading them straight to me.

It doesn't help that they've caught on to my tactics. The hunters are never alone now. They do not sleep alone, and they do not even go to the bathroom alone anymore. It's impossible for me to take any of them out without interference. They have stuck to my trail as if they are shifters themselves—which should be impossible. I feel trapped. I cannot attack them, and I cannot escape them.

I'm tired—so desperately tired.

I haven't slept well in days, and I just want to go home. It's not something I ever thought I would say. I have always been restless. My soul has always yearned for adventure; since my father's death, it has thirsted for revenge. Now that I have experienced this side of his missions—the running, fighting, and trying to stay under the radar—I finally understand why he wanted to protect us from this. I had romanticized the idea of going after the hunters—of being a hero like my father. I didn't understand the strain it would put on me. Even though the hunters are evil incarnate, each of their deaths by my hand has taken a small piece of me as well.

I'm currently making my way back home to Parry Sound. I know that I shouldn't be leading the hunters anywhere near my family, but I need to see Axel one last time before they catch up with me.

I need to tell my brother that I love him. I need to tell him that I'm sorry for everything. I need to warn him. Because of our connection, I know he is going to feel my death and suffer with me. That's what scares me the most. Not dying. Not being tortured. It is knowing Axel will feel everything.

If I stop to see Constance on the way, she may be able to help. If I have time to go to the coven, she may have a way to break the connection to protect my brother.

I know the pain he felt when our father died. I shared that pain in equal measure, and I cannot be the reason why he goes through it again. I cannot be the reason why he goes through it *alone*. If anyone can help, it's the high priestess of the coven of the moon.

I veer off toward the coven instead of my home. I've been running so long that I've lost track of time, but it must be near midnight. The moon is full and high in the sky.

I find Constance's house at the edge of the forest. It is the coven's first line of defense if an attack comes. As I step onto her property, I feel a tingle down my spine as I pass through the ward surrounding it. The wards recognize me as a friend, so they allow me to pass but alert Constance of my presence anyway.

The door to the workroom swings open, streaming light into the night as the woman herself fills the doorway. She's a petite woman with long, black hair and bright, blue eyes. The laugh lines around her gentle face make it seem like she's not a threat, but she's the most powerful witch I know. The only exception is possibly her own children.

"Zeke?" she calls out as I step close enough for the light to hit me. "What are you doing here so late?" Her eyes widen when they take in my appearance. I have only just now shifted back into my human form, and I haven't seen my own reflection in a few days. Still, I am sure I do not look my best.

"I need your help," I state simply, my voice rough from disuse. She ushers me inside, her eyes and hands immediately examining all the places on my body that are caked with dried blood. I don't tell her that not all the blood is my own. I don't need her looking at me like I'm a killer.

"I need—" I begin, but she shushes me with the kind of authority reserved only for those who changed your diaper when you were born.

"What you need is a shower and a hot meal," she says adamantly.

"But—" I begin once again. I need to warn her of the trouble I have led to her door.

"No 'buts.' Go shower while I make you something to eat. Then you can tell me what you need." Her words leave no room for argument, and she pushes me toward the bathroom with a towel and a set of clothes. I am not sure where either came from.

I close the door, turn to look at myself in the mirror, and wince. My hair and beard are wild and matted with caked blood and dirt. The deep brown has been stained a kind of rust color that is unfamiliar to me. I search the drawers and cupboards for some scissors to make myself presentable again, but I find none. I could probably ask Sebastian for some clippers or a razor, but he's only seventeen and not even a shifter. He probably hasn't even had to start shaving yet.

I turn the shower on and allow the water to heat up before I step inside. As I step under the warm spray, I watch as the clear water turns pink as it pools around my feet.

I spend more time in the shower than necessary, but I still don't feel clean. I'm probably going to need a dozen showers before I clean every drop of blood off myself. Now that I've had a moment to think, I am eternally grateful to Constance for the opportunity to wash myself before going to see Axel.

After pulling on a perfectly sized pair of jeans and a warm, flattering flannel shirt, I deposit my towel into the laundry hamper in the corner and walk out the bathroom door. The most amazing aroma hits me as I step into the hallway. If I had to guess by smell alone, I would say it's a perfectly cooked roast beef.

"Good," Constance says when she catches a glimpse of me. "You look much better."

"I feel much better. Thank you."

"All right," she says, gesturing to the table and a plate piled high with roast beef, mashed potatoes, steamed carrots, and even a Yorkshire pudding covered in gravy. "You need to eat, and we need to talk."

"This looks delicious," I tell her, my mouth watering at the sight before me.

I take my seat and dive into the food. I know I don't have long to tell her everything, but I do not pause to talk as I devour the meal. I must look starved, and I guess I may have been. This is my first home-cooked meal in months, and I didn't realize just how much I missed that.

When I finally raise my head after cleaning my plate, I find Constance watching me with a knowing smirk on her face.

"Sorry," I apologize.

She waves her hand, dismissing my embarrassment.

I watch as the now-empty plate hovers off the table and carries itself to the sink. My eyes widen at this use of magic. I've obviously seen her do magic before, but Constance has always been a stickler for not abusing magic. I've heard her tell her own children to do their chores with their own two hands countless times.

She lifts her finger to her lips in a *shh* gesture, and I smile.

"Tell me, Zeke. What it is that you need my help with?"

I clear my throat and muster up the courage to ask what I

need. My request is dishonorable—sacrilegious. Bonds—whether they are mating bonds or familial bonds—are sacred, and asking her this goes against everything I've ever been taught.

"I need you to block my bond with Axel."

"What—" Her mouth drops open in shock, and she pauses before she finds her bearings. "No. That is not what you need."

"Constance," I rush to explain, praying that my tone makes it clear that I am serious. "I'm in trouble. If something happens to me, I don't want Axel to feel it."

Her hard stare softens into one of compassion and pity as she registers the meaning of my words.

"Surely, you and your brother can face whatever this is together." Her tone is patient now. Even though I know I must convince her, it makes me wish I was a kid again and could leave all my problems for her to fix.

"No. I don't want him to have anything to do with this." I shake my head. "I did this, and I need to take responsibility."

"But—"

"Look, I really fucked up—sorry," I say, catching myself. Old habits die hard, so I amend the phrase. "I really screwed up, Constance."

"I understand, but blocking your bond may not be the answer. It's not something to take lightly."

"I know. Trust me. I know. I wouldn't ask if it wasn't necessary. We lost our father, and I left him to take care of the sleuth on his own. I can't do this to him too."

She must be able to hear the pain in my voice. She is still obviously hesitant, but she relents.

"How long do you want to block the bond for? Do you want it to be permanent?"

"I just need it to be temporary. A few months—"

I can't tell her the truth. I don't think I'll survive the week. After that, the block won't matter.

She runs a hand thoughtfully through her long, black hair, contemplating my request before standing and walking back to her workroom without a word. I follow her down the long hallway.

"Constance, I know this is a lot to ask—"

She spins, giving me a forbidding look.

"It is, indeed, 'a lot to ask.' Do you understand what you're asking me to do? Axel may not feel the bond break, but he will feel the lack of that bond. As soon as you drink the potion, it will be as if you don't exist. You are trying to protect him from pain, but you will only be causing him a different sort of pain."

I nod my head. I know what our bond feels like, and I am sure the lack of it will be less painful than feeling it snap entirely.

"I understand."

"And you still want to go through with this?"

"I have to," I say, working to keep the certainty in my tone.

She approaches me and raises a hand to my face. For a moment, I think she's angry enough to smack me, but she gently cups my cheek in her cool hand instead. Her gaze bores into mine, searching for something that I cannot understand. I let my certainty crumble and lean into her hand, allowing my eyes to drop closed.

"You're just a child," she says. She sounds frustrated, but her anger is no longer aimed at me. "I was there when you were born. I was the one who saw that your soul had been split. A rarity—a miracle—even among those who are accustomed to miracles."

She releases me and turns to her cabinet. I open my eyes to find her mixing ingredients. Her face is calm now as she creates what must be a rare and complicated potion with the ease of someone boiling water to make spaghetti.

"Your parents were worried about you," she explains in a pensive, faraway voice. "Parents always worry, but I assured them neither of you would suffer. What did I say? 'If only we all had someone to share half our trouble and half our joys.'"

"Did you get that from a greeting card?" I ask, unable to keep myself from making the joke.

She rolls her eyes, but I am pleased to see her exhale a laugh.

"All right," she admits. "I probably didn't say it quite like that, but it probably did sound that silly. Your mother—who had just given birth *twice*—probably wanted to slap me."

Her laugh turns to a somber silence, and we pass only a few quiet moments before she hands me a vial. The liquid inside is still warm.

"I'll only ask you once more, Zeke," she begins, watching my face for any evidence of hesitation. "Are you certain this is what you want to do?"

Without speaking, I quickly down the contents of the vial before I can change my mind. The potion is tasteless but thick on my tongue. I watch as Constance's face falls and her eyes fill with sadness.

Just as she warned, the bond between my brother and me fades. It slowly recedes until there is nothing but a gaping emptiness where it should be. Just like she said, there is pain. The pain is emotional—not physical—but its appearance is so sudden and intense that it makes my knees buckle all the same. Inside me, my bear roars. He is obviously feeling the same emptiness. If I do survive this, I will have to make my apologies to Axel and my bear as well.

"It will last for approximately three months," Constance says, her tone resigned. "It could be shorter because of the strength of your bond."

"Thank you."

"You can thank me by fixing whatever this is and coming home to your family," she says, wrapping me in a hug.

"I will try," I whisper. "I promise I will try."

I cannot stand to say goodbye, so I turn to walk out the door and into the night.

As I head away from the coven and toward my own home, my attention is pulled away by a sweet scent in the distance. It is like honey and lilacs, but it is unlike anything else I've ever smelled. My body turns to follow it of its own accord.

I hide in the bushes and watch as a group of women walk past. They are laughing and talking. I scan each woman, searching for the source of the scent that has entranced me. When my eyes land on the beautiful blonde woman with a perfect, hourglass body, and the face of an angel, my entire body freezes.

Mate, my beast growls in my head.

No. No. No. This can't be happening. I can't find my mate now.

I turn my body and start to run in the other direction, but my bear wrenches control from me and forces me to stop. I place my hands on the trunk of a tree and bend slightly, breathing heavily as I war with my beast.

Mate, he growls once again.

I know. But we can't stay. We will only put her in danger, I try to reason.

We protect mate, he huffs. To him, it is ridiculous and offensive to insinuate we couldn't protect her.

I am still weak from the prolonged separation from my brother and reeling from the new block upon our bond. My bear is clearly unhappy with me and unwilling to negotiate right now.

We can't protect her from the hunters. There are too many of them. Axel will have to take care of her.

No! We protect mate. Claim mate. Have cubs.

I never expected that impulse to appeal to me with such simplicity. After seeing my angel in the flesh, that's all I want. All I want is to settle down with that gorgeous woman and watch her stomach swell with my cubs inside her.

Despite that, I am ready to argue the point. I'm about to tell him why we can't have what we want when a voice rings out behind me.

"Hello," she says. Her voice matches the nickname I've already given her perfectly. She has the soft and sweet cadence of an angel.

I spin around and throw my back up against the tree. I fling my arms behind me, wrapping them around the tree—anything to keep me in place.

"Are you okay?" she asks and takes a tentative step forward. There is concern in her voice, and I want nothing more than to allow her to care for me for even just a moment.

Instead, I snarl and cling to the tree behind me.

"It's okay. I promise I won't hurt you." She takes a few tentative steps forward, and I watch as the moonlight reflects in her eyes and on her hair. She looks radiant. "I just want to help you. What is wrong?"

I want to run away. I am desperate to fight this connection. It is not because I do not want her. It is because I need to protect her.

The wind shifts and carries her scent straight to me.

"Mate," I growl the word, and it is both a question and an answer. I watch as her eyes go wide in shock.

She doesn't slow her movement toward me though. Her beautiful eyes are full of wonder as she brings her hand up to caress my cheek.

"Mate?" she asks, her voice full of curiosity.

On her lips, the word makes me lose control.

I have only one, final coherent thought before my beast takes over, ready to claim our mate.

I'm going to regret this in the morning.

Chapter Two

Opal—11 years ago

It's two days after my eighteenth birthday. My friends and I are walking home after a night of drinking at Supernatural. We could've taken a cab home, but where is the fun in that? It's a mild night, and we all feel at home in the forest anyway. Besides, I could use some of nature's energy right now. I didn't expect how hard being inside the packed club would be for me. Dancing is fun, but constantly brushing up against other people is just asking for trouble. I love my gift—I truly do—but sometimes it's more of a curse. I've also learned that it only gets harder to block my connections to others when I am drinking.

We are walking through the familiar forest—not far from the coven and our homes—when a tingle like electricity runs up my spine. I stop dead in my tracks and look around. Although I cannot see them, I know someone is watching me. Despite the secrecy, it doesn't feel malicious. It feels...like longing.

"Everything okay, Opal?" Jennifer asks.

"Yeah, you're not going to puke or anything, are you?" Jillian, Jennifer's twin sister, asks.

I release a nervous chuckle. "No. I'm just not ready to head home yet. You two go ahead. I'll meet you there."

Jenn—the responsible one of our trio—looks around. "Are you sure? It's late, and your mom would be pissed if we let you get kidnapped."

I laugh out loud at her antics. "Yes. I'm sure. Being around so many people tonight drained me, and I need to stay out here for a while."

"If you're sure..." Jenn sounds uncertain, but Jill is already grabbing her arm and pulling her toward the coven.

"See you tomorrow, Opal," Jillian yells behind her.

"Not too early," I yell back in warning. I hear them giggle as they walk away.

Once they're far enough away, I rush in the direction of the tingling. It continues growing stronger as I trek farther into the trees.

I know I am getting close to the cause of this feeling, but I am still shocked to find its source. It's a man. A beautiful man. His hair and beard are unkempt and a little longer than the average person would keep them, but it doesn't take away from his beauty. He's well over six feet tall with large, broad shoulders. I can't see much under his jeans and flannel shirt, but I somehow know that he's full of rippling muscles underneath those clothes. It's his eyes, though, that make my breath catch in my throat. Even after only one glance, I feel like I'm getting lost in them. They are twin pools of green that remind me of the moss growing on the trees. It's enchanting.

"Hello," I say as I walk toward him. He spins around and places his back up against the tree. He wraps his arms around behind him. He looks like he's scared of me, but that can't possibly be right.

"Are you okay?" I ask as I take another tentative step forward. He snarls at me, and I can immediately tell that he's some type of shifter. The sound should scare me, but it doesn't. Instead, it sends sparks straight through me and down to my core. He quickly moves to the next tree—farther away from me.

I hold up my hands to show him that I mean no harm. I know that shifters have all sorts of problems witches don't have to worry about. I have heard about wolves who went feral because they disagreed with their human's choices. Is that what I am seeing here?

"It's okay. I promise I won't hurt you. I just want to help you." I watch his eyes shift from left to right, looking for an escape route. There is no way that this huge, muscley guy thinks that little old me is a threat in any way. That would just be ridiculous.

Suddenly, his nostrils flare, and he speaks for the first time.

"Mate." His deep voice makes the throbbing in my core increase, and my knees go weak.

Wait...did he just say mate?

Witches don't instantly know who our mates are. Shifters only need one look into their eyes, a breath of their scent, or to hear a note of their voice to feel the pull of the mate bond. Witches do not have the luxury of that ease. I wish it was that simple for witches too. Instead, we feel drawn to our mates for no obvious reason. It is hard to tell if the person who gives you butterflies is your mate or just a cute boy. It's like the universe gives us a little push toward them, but we can't know for sure until we consummate the relationship.

I am studying his face for any clear sign of what I just heard him say. Once I'm close enough, I reach my hand up and rest it on his cheek. He closes his eyes for a split second, leaning into my touch indulgently. He rests there only a second before he takes control, spins me around so that my back is up against the tree, and merges his mouth with mine.

I moan in delight at the taste of him as he licks at the seam of my mouth and thrusts his tongue inside. Goddess above, his kisses leave me absolutely no doubt that I want his mouth everywhere on my body.

I pull back reluctantly, breathing hard.

"I'm Opal," I whisper. I want this man so badly, but I also at least want to know his name. I have enough self-respect that I've learned the names of my two previous partners prior to letting them fuck me silly. There's no question in my mind that's exactly what Muscles here is planning to do.

He blinks once—then twice. It seems like he's having a difficult time finding any words to use.

Finally, after what feels like an eternity, he says, "Zeke."

"Zeke," I whisper.

That's all the time I get to appreciate the feeling of his name on my lips before his mouth is once again on mine. I snake my arms around his shoulders, and he lifts me easily, allowing my legs to wrap around his thick waist.

As my core brushes up against him, I let out a gasp. If he's packing what I just felt—goddess help me—there is no way that thing will fit.

I open my mouth to say just that, but he distracts me by moving to gently lay me on the ground. He joins me there and moves his head beneath my dress. Within seconds, my panties are gone, and his tongue is sliding through my folds.

"Oh goddess," I cry out as his tongue thrusts inside. There's a rumble coming from his chest. It is deep and loud enough that the vibrations echo through me. I feel like I could orgasm simply from the feeling of his tongue fucking me. Before I can complete the thought, he moves to latch onto my clit and sucks the ever-loving fuck out of it. There is no way this is real. This amount of ecstasy is *impossible*. There is no one on earth who is this good at eating pussy. This must be a dream.

I open my eyes and look down to find his mossy green eyes

staring right back at me. I fall over the edge as he thrusts a finger inside of me.

"Oh, my goddess!" I scream. My legs are shaking from the force of my orgasm. I have never felt so euphoric.

I barely have a chance to breathe before he's kneeling before me, lining his length up with my core.

"Are you a virgin?" he asks in a gravelly voice that makes my core spasm once more.

My concerns about his size are long gone, and I am desperate to have him inside of me. I can't get the words out, so I just shake my head. That's obviously all the answer he needs, and he begins thrusting in and out of me. I feel so full. There is a slight pinch of pain at his first thrust, but it quickly dissipates. My body automatically adjusts to accommodate his girth like it was made for him. If he really is my mate, I guess it was.

His large, strong hands move under me to grip my ass firmly. He lifts, raising me to adjust the angle.

"Yes!" I cry as he hits the delicious spot inside me and triggers my orgasm.

I see his canines extend with the urge to mark me, and I feel my magic flare in response. I had expected to feel some hesitation, but I am ready.

Instead of marking each other as we should, Zeke pulls away from me with extreme speed. He flies backward and braces himself against a tree.

I sit up, confused. The space between my legs feels cold and empty with him suddenly gone. He called me his mate, and my magic confirmed it. Despite that knowledge, his suddenly pulling away—leaving me alone—makes me feel abandoned and angry.

"Zeke?" I ask as I adjust my dress and move to my knees. "Is everything okay?"

"I'm sorry," he growls through clenched teeth. His claws are digging into the bark of the tree, splintering it with the force of his grip.

"What are you sorry for?" I ask, standing up and walking toward him. My legs are still shaky under me. "Is something wrong?"

"I reject you," he whispers.

It takes a minute to recognize his words. He couldn't have—

My thoughts are interrupted by the pain. There is a sudden, burning pain in my chest, and the world seems to tip and sway beneath me.

"Why?" I cry, falling back to my knees.

"I can't—" he says. He is breathing heavily. Is he in pain too? I think I see a tear trailing down his face, but I cannot be sure with my own tears clouding my vision. There is no reason for him to cry when he's the one who just rejected me.

There, on the forest floor and covered in sweat from our love-making, I curl up into a ball and sob while clutching my chest. My mate just rejected me. The one person who was made specifically for me just walked away.

He was my mate. He was perfect for me. I felt it all in that moment. I would have marked him as my own, but it was over so fast. I should have had a lifetime with him, and now I am alone in this world after a few moments together. Where does that leave me?

Hours later, when the sky is beginning to turn pink and my tears have run dry, I pick myself up off the ground. I dust off the dirt and leaves that mar my light dress. I take the well-traveled path to my home, trying to harden my heart to the pain as I plan my next move. I can't stay here. I know that much. Every time I walk through this forest, I'll be reminded of this night—of my mate who doesn't want me. But where can I go?

That's when the thought strikes—Vivian. I can stay with Vivian. She's constantly inviting me to stay with her coven in California, but I keep declining. If I'm being honest, the way her coven is run has always intimidated me. This morning, going to an all-female coven doesn't seem like such a bad idea.

As I make my way home, the idea holds more and more promise. I first met Vivian through a pen pal program at school. Our teacher arranged for us to write letters back and forth with a student in the United States. She thought it would give us some insight into how people in different countries live. The first letter between us was a simple introduction, but I placed a secret message at the bottom using my magic. Only someone else with magic would know to answer. Surprisingly, although Vivian's life was different from my own, she did have similar magic.

Unlike the other pen pals in my class, Vivian and I kept in touch. It began with letters that later became emails and phone calls. Although we've never met in person, I would consider us close friends. It isn't like my relationship with Skarlyt or Drusilla, but we are close enough that I feel comfortable staying with her.

I hardly even register the walk to my house until I'm standing in front of it and my eyes begin to mist once more. It doesn't look much different from the other houses in the coven, but it's the little touches that set it apart. The boxes under the two front windows are filled with pink and purple petunias, the huge welcome sign stands to the side of the front door at a precarious angle, and the army of garden gnomes observe the lawn with good-natured smiles.

I rush inside and head straight to my room. I don't want to see or talk to anyone. I'll just break down again, and I've already cried far too much for my liking today. I grab the phone, quickly dial Vivian's phone number, and close my bedroom door.

"Hello," the melodic voice says through the phone.

"Is the offer to come stay with you still good? Just for a bit?" I ask, not bothering with pleasantries.

"Opal?" she asks, and I nod before I realize she can't see me through the phone.

"Yeah. You said that it would be okay if I ever wanted to come visit or maybe stay for a while—" I begin.

"Of course, you can," she cuts me off in her excitement. She doesn't ask for any reason or clarification.

"Okay. I'm going to the airport this morning and hopping on a flight. Will you be able to pick me up from the airport when I get there?"

"Yes," she squeals. "I will get a list of arrivals. What airport will you be coming from?"

"Toronto."

"Okay. I guess I'll see you in a few hours. I'm so excited."

"Me too," I respond. I try to sound excited even though I am certainly not feeling it and hang up the phone.

Packing doesn't take long. Other than my clothes, there's nothing here that I want to bring with me. Everything feels wrong. I know these things are mine, but it feels like they belong to another person. Someone who hadn't met her mate yet. Someone who hadn't been rejected. Someone who still had their entire life ahead of them.

Someone who is not me.

After writing a quick letter to my parents and another one to Matt, I call a cab to meet me at the edge of the coven. The letters explain where I'm going and that I am safe. I write them fast— trying not to think too much about my words and refusing to reread them before I seal them.

I don't want to wake anyone up to give me a ride for the same reason that I didn't want to see anyone last night. I know that it will only take one look from my loving mom, overprotective dad, or my best friend who also happens to be my brother for me to break down again. I also know that they will try to convince me to stay, and they would likely succeed.

With one last look at my childhood home, I head outside and quietly close the door behind me.

* * *

The drive to the airport and flight to California go by quickly. I'm in a haze of pain and forced inattention, and then I'm exiting the plane. I step into a new world of scorching California heat. I glance around, noting the palm trees and everyone's summery clothing, and smile. I think it is my first real smile since I met Zeke. The smile quickly turns into a giant grin when I catch sight of a vibrating redhead sprinting right for me.

Vivian looks exactly like her pictures. Her perfectly styled red hair is practically flying in the wind behind her as she runs toward me in her six-inch, stiletto heels, Daisy-Duke shorts, and red crop top. With her bright blue eyes, tanned skin, and cherry-red lips, she looks just like a red-haired Malibu Barbie.

"Opal!" she screams, and I drop my bag just as she launches herself at me.

"Hey!" I reply. My eyes mist again, but this time it is happiness. There's something about being near her that raises my spirits immediately. Her happy-go-lucky personality is infectious.

"Come on. I have so much to show you," she says, linking her arm with mine and giving me a second to grab my bag before she begins pulling me along to her bright red convertible. If I didn't already know red was her favorite color, it would be obvious now.

"First stop is the coven." I nod to her after placing my bag in the backseat and sliding into the passenger's side. "Like I told you, it's a little different than what you're used to."

"I think different is what I need right now," I admit, and she turns to look at me. Her blue eyes see a lot more than I want them to. She narrows her eyes slightly before turning back to the road.

"You don't have to tell me now, but I will want to know." I nod and don't reply, appreciating the fact that she's not demanding answers right now. I'm not ready to talk about it—not yet.

"As I was saying, the Coven of the Rose is different. There are no men—like I told you—only women are allowed to be members."

I chuckle. "I always wondered... how do you—you know?" I ask, wagging my eyebrows suggestively.

"Oh, we have plenty of opportunities for that. Our elders have just found that men usually cause an amount of drama that nobody wants to deal with. Instead, we live our lives with true freedom. No mates hold us back. No jealous men tell us what to do or what not to do. Anything we need to be done, we can do ourselves or hire someone for the day."

"What about when you decide to have kids?"

She waves her hand. "We find a male witch from one of the neighboring covens that would be suitable as a father, have them sign a solid legal agreement signing off any rights to any female children we birth, and that's that."

My mouth drops open in shock. "What if the baby is a boy?"

"The men take them," she says with a shrug as if that makes perfect sense.

"You mean they just give up their babies?" Suddenly, I'm not sure if I was right to come here. This coven seems a little too zealous for me.

"Yup," she says, popping the last *p*. "Only one in fifteen children born in our coven end up being boys, and only about one in a hundred women end up having second thoughts and leave the coven."

I nod along with her like I'm understanding everything that she's saying. In reality, my mind is reeling, and I am wondering if I made a huge mistake.

"Here, drink this," she says handing me a vial as we approach a small subdivision.

I take it from her hands, turning it around in my own.

"What is it?"

"It's a revitalization potion. We all take them to look our best," she says, and I look at her skeptically. "Here, watch." She pulls out a matching vial and downs it quickly. I watch as her skin seems to glow brighter and her hair becomes longer and healthier, and then I quickly down mine. I feel the changes as they overtake my body. My long, blonde hair seems to be almost white and is shining in the rays of sun. My normally milky complexion has a new glow that looks almost supernatural.

It turns out that the feeling of wondering if I made a huge mistake by coming here only lasts long enough for the first potion to truly kick in. Soon, I'm walking, talking, dressing, and acting just like the rest of Vivian's coven. By the time I finally explain my reason for leaving home, I've already become a completely different person. By the time I must retell the story, his rejection doesn't sting as much.

From there, I begin to plan. I know I don't want to live as they do in the Coven of the Rose. I do want a mate and a family some-day, but they have shown me I don't necessarily need my *fated* mate to have that. I can choose my mate the way they do, but I can decide to keep him in my life for the long haul.

I want to go home to my family and friends, but I know I need time to prepare.

Each night, I dream of a tall, broad-shouldered shifter with mossy green eyes and wake up to a pang of loneliness in my chest. Each morning, though, I morph him into someone else.

I remake him in another's image—someone who is completely different. Someone different enough that it doesn't hurt to look at him. Someone with a thinner build and black hair that's too long to be anything but a moody affectation. I picture clear, blue eyes and envision my life with him instead.

Sebastyn Moon is going to be my chosen mate; he just doesn't know it yet.

Chapter Three

Opal—Present Day

I wake to an alarm blaring next to my head and swipe my arm around wildly, attempting to get it to shut the fuck up. I didn't get much sleep last night. Drusilla and I had run to the twenty-four-hour drug store to get some supplies, and we didn't return until late at night. Then, like most nights, I crawled into my king-size bed, cocooned myself inside my covers, and cried myself to sleep.

After our shopping trip, I finally confided in Drusilla about my rejection. It felt good to tell her the truth, but telling the story brought all my worst emotions to the surface again. I thought I was finally making some headway with my feelings even though watching all the true mate couples and their newfound happiness is like a knife cutting deep into my soul.

Once I manage to locate the source of the offending sound—my phone—I swipe the screen mindlessly until the alarm finally stops.

I lay there, in my little cocoon, and review my life with a clarity I haven't had in years. Vivian told me her coven's signature potion was intended to encourage revitalization. I guess it may have been for that, but that's not all it did. It made me not care about anyone or anything except myself—not even my own parents. Looking back now, I cringe at the memories of how I treated them. Once I confided in Sarah, and I saw how merciful she was, I stopped taking it. Almost immediately, a fog lifted from my mind, and I was able to see how my vanity was hurting the people I once loved.

Soon, Vivian will mail another batch of the potion to me, and I will turn it over to Sarah and the coven for testing. Until then, I can't say for certain that it was the potion and not a spell that is transmitted through the potion that made me so shortsighted.

In retrospect, the fact that she insisted on making the potion and sending it to me should have been my first red flag. She wouldn't give me the ingredients or instructions, and that should have been a flashing neon sign telling me, "I don't do what you think I do." Maybe if I hadn't already been taking the potion regularly, I would have seen it.

After what feels like forever, I throw the covers off me and get ready for the day. Today is the day that we storm the hunter's compound in Orillia, and I need to go make amends with my parents before my father rushes into danger with the rest of the warriors. My mom is staying in the bunker with the most vulnerable members of the pack and coven, but my dad has opted to join the team that is heading to the facility. If the worst should happen...emotion clogs my throat at that thought, and I shake it away.

I can't think like that. Everything will be fine.

Before I have time to overthink it, I'm standing in front of my childhood home, trying and failing to figure out what I can say that will fix the damage I've done. There's probably nothing that will make everything better, but I have to try. I've avoided seeing them for long enough, but not even the shame of my actions can keep me away anymore.

As I walk up the steps, the front door flies open.

"Opal," my mom exclaims, crossing the distance between us in her fuzzy pink slippers, opening her arms, and closing them tightly around me. I tense up automatically as visions flash before me.

She is watching me walk out of the house and slam the door behind me. The memory is lost in the haze of my past, but I know I must've said something terrible to her before storming off. I can hear myself stomp down the stairs I stood on just a moment ago and watch my mother instantly drop to her knees. Her lithe body is wracked with sobs. My father bends to wrap his arms around her.
"What did I do?" she asks him, her voice breaking on the question.
"Nothing, love," he whispers into her ear. "She's just going through something. We need to give her time and space."
"Why won't she tell me?" She looks up into my father's eyes, begging him for an answer that he can't possibly have. "I know something happened to her. I thought she knew that she could tell me anything. What did I do to make her shut me out?"
"We'll give her some time, and she'll come back to us dear."
"I just want her back—"

As my mother releases me, the vision warps and disappears. I come back to myself with a gasp. I reach for my mom again and hug her back with everything I have. She should know that there was nothing she did or didn't do. It was all me. All the pain she felt and the tears she cried were all because of me.

"Mom..." I choke out the words, and sobs begin to wrack my own body. I feel her body tense momentarily before relaxing at my strangled voice.

"Oh, baby..." she whispers into my ear, her hands rubbing soft circles on my back. "Shh...It's okay. Everything's going to be okay."

I nod my head into her neck, and my tears soak into the collar of her shirt. She doesn't seem to care.

When I finally step back, wiping the tears from my cheeks, she is watching me with cautious eyes.

"I'm sorry, Mom. I'm so sorry for everything."

Her eyes widen in surprise before she waves me off.

"It's water under the bridge, my love." It is her signature phrase from our childhood—a promise of her forgiveness when we did something wrong.

"But..." I begin, wanting to tell her that she's wrong. It isn't "water under the bridge" because what I did to them is unforgivable.

She interrupts me by taking my hand gently and leading me into the house.

"Honey, Opal's here," she calls to my father.

I watch his entire body tense before he turns around and sees us together. Instantly, he relaxes and rushes around the kitchen island to wrap his arms around us both.

In the safety of their arms, I break down once more. I get my story out between sobs. I begin with Zeke and move on to Vivian and California. I try to explain the potion that I'd been taking for so long, and their eyes flare with an unfamiliar fury. I apologize for my actions—knowing that the blame is mine despite whatever the potion had done. Finally, I get to the part where Sarah helped me finally gain some clarity.

"My love," my mother says, placing her hands on either side of my face. "You have nothing to be sorry for. I knew something happened..." She shares a look with my father.

I know what's coming. I know she's going to blame herself, so I cut her off.

"I didn't want anyone to know at first. The longer I put off dealing with the pain, the longer I constantly took those potions, the less I could stand being in the same room as you two. My mind was warped. Watching your true mate bond should be inspiring.

To my poisoned mind, it was a stark reminder of what I'll never have."

"Oh, honey," my father says, placing a soft kiss on my head. "You deserve the world. If that fool wasn't man enough to love and cherish you the way you deserve, then I'm happy he rejected you."

My mouth drops open in shock, but my mother cuts in before I can begin dissecting his words.

"What your father is trying to say—" she says, stressing the word *trying* with a pointed look in his direction, "is that even true mates don't always deserve each other. Think of Skarlyt and Kirnon. She got a second-chance mate who was perfect for her. Maybe you will too."

I give them a soft smile, feeling hope for the first time in forever.

We spend the rest of the morning cooking breakfast, playing *Settlers of Catan*, and enjoying each other's company.

We will never be able to get back the time we missed, but I'll be damned if I don't do everything in my power to make up for my long absence.

* * *

Only hours later, our calm morning is a distant memory.

The triage tent is buzzing with activity as supernaturals of all varieties arrive by the dozen from the raid on the hunter's facility. It is already clear that we underestimated how many people they were keeping in that place. We had prepared more than a hundred beds, and they are already full.

We have already started moving the supes who are mostly healed somewhere else to make room for the ones who need immediate help. The variety of supernaturals in this makeshift shelter doesn't make our job any easier. It turns out witches, vampires, shifters, Fae, and even sea nymphs have vastly different medical needs. No one even knew sea nymphs existed outside fairy tales, so we can't even begin to guess how to treat them. Luckily, Constance thinks quickly on her feet and puts them in a tank with salt water. Once they were submerged, they were able to shift. Shifting seems to have stabilized them and sped up their healing.

Looking around, I can't help but wish that Phoebe and Sophia were able to stock up on some more tears before they left. Understandably, they took the small supply of tears they could collect to the laboratory. They knew they'd need something to help stabilize anyone who exited with wounds too severe to be teleported.

There's no way to know who was treated with the phoenix tears before being transported, but the condition everyone arrives in has me horrified. We are incredibly lucky to have one phoenix—let alone two—but we seem to be in desperate need of more healing magic.

Each person that arrives is not only starved and severely dehydrated but also covered in bruises and lacerations. Some of the wounds are so deep that I can see bone. If I had any doubt, the sight proves that those hunters were *monsters*.

I rush back to my workstation and continue dosing bottles of water with electrolyte packages and shaking them until the powder disappears. Even though we have so many witches on hand to help, it's still not enough. After all, many stayed in the bunker to take care of the children, and others joined the teams raiding the facility or those patrolling our borders.

I glance around the tent and find my brother moving from bed to bed with his tablet in hand and smile. He is collecting information: names, addresses, and descriptions. The data will be crucial as we try to reunite the families that have been separated by the hunters.

If anyone can help these people find their loved ones, it's him. He's the best hacker I've ever met. A small pang goes through my heart as I watch him. We used to be best friends as well as siblings.

When I was rejected, I pushed him away like everyone else. I abandoned him when I went to live with Vivian and her family. I allowed them to poison my mind against men for so long that I treated him horribly even when I returned. Now, I've pushed him away for so long that I don't know how to put the pieces of our relationship back together.

I wipe my damp face and secure my long, blonde hair in its high ponytail. The last thing these people need is to see me crying. They've been through too much already, and they need us to be strong for them. That's another reason why I shouldn't be one of the ones here trying to help.

My gift—my sight—means that it's extremely overwhelming to be surrounded by so many intense emotions. I made sure to wear gloves and cover as much skin as I could, but accidental touches still happen. Each person I touch gives me a glimpse of either their time in captivity or their future.

I have no control over what I see. The visions just come to me, and I cannot choose whether I see something helpful or horrible. I accidentally touched one small girl—she must have been around fourteen—when I pushed her hair away from her fevered brow. The vision I got was a glimpse of her future. I know now that she will take her own life. I don't know when—I never know when—but I do know that she will one day give up on this life. The knowledge is painful and impossible to confront. I want to hug her, take her home with me, and ensure that the future I've seen never comes for her, but I know that I cannot. If I did that for everyone I know will need it, I would need a bunker bigger than Alaric's to house them all.

For now, I can only treat her kindly and hope there's more to her future I haven't seen. Someone who will arrive just in time to help her and nurse her back to health.

I shake my head and try to clear my mind of the negativity. It is easier said than done, but I must try. The best I can do now is help them heal and perhaps talk to Skarlyt and Alaric about creating a program to help them. Maybe it would help to have a support group or a counselor for everyone we are saving. I know that Charleigh is a registered social worker, and she's already been working with shifters in the pack. With the help of a witch who could teleport her back and forth, she may be able to make house calls even after we are able to send these people back to their homes.

If we can do that, we may be able to prevent some of the deaths I've seen on the horizon today. I make a mental note to bring the idea up to her and Skarlyt later. Between the two of them, they'll have a plan in place by the end of the week.

I hear a squeal and turn in time to see River rush into the arms of the woman standing next to Skarlyt. I take in the woman, noting her bright, aquamarine eyes that are cutting twin rivers of tears down her gaunt cheeks. She drops to her knees, pulling River closer to her. My own eyes mist with tears as I realize that this woman can only be one person. This is River's mom. This is Andres' sister.

Nearby, Drusilla watches the interaction with a peaceful smile and wrings her hands together. I see her take a tentative step forward, but I cannot miss the insecurity evident on her beautiful face. My entire body itches to go to her, to comfort her the same way she comforted me so recently.

River's mom growls loudly, pulls River behind her, and bares her teeth at Dru. I take a step forward, ready to defend my friend, and see that Skarlyt is ready to do the same. We are not needed however. River leans back and explains who Drusilla is to her mother.

As the woman's—I think her name is Andrea—face softens, her elongated teeth recede into her gums. The tension I was holding in my body deflates as I recognize that there is no longer a threat. I watch for a few more moments until Dru guides them to a bed.

Although I have begun reforming my friendships, I'm still not completely sure where I fit anymore. Everyone seems to have forgiven me—some without even knowing the truth—but their forgiveness can't repair the damage I've caused. I glance over at Skarlyt and wish with everything inside me that I had never hurt her.

In the past decade, I didn't directly do anything to her—at least I don't think I did. However, I did purposefully put space between us and acted like an idiot when I finally returned. I ignored her and focused on her brother.

I know she would've understood, helped, and supported me if I had just told her about my rejection. I didn't tell her though, and I wince as she offers me a soft, impersonal smile and avoids my eyes. She looks at me like I'm a stranger, and I stare after her as she blinks away—probably teleporting back to the laboratory in Orillia.

I used to have a support system here. I had friends and a family. They could trust me, and I could trust them. Now...

I stop myself before I can go down the rabbit hole of self-pity. That pit of misery has become too familiar lately, and I try to turn away from it and toward something more useful.

As I walk to the next row of beds and start handing out the water bottles, a tingle travels up the back of my neck. It feels like someone is watching me. I've felt the same sensation throughout the day, but I am always unable to find its source. I try to avoid the memory the feeling triggers. It's the same tingling I felt right before I met the mate who would immediately reject me.

When I turn again, searching for the source of this feeling, I lock eyes with the man I am trying so hard not to think about. His green eyes still remind me of moss, and the dark circles around them only seem to make them glow brighter. In a flash, I'm brought back to that night. My heart hammers as my entire body locks up. I'm unable to move and unable to speak as the pain constricts around me.

As the memory fades, I'm finally able to gain control of my body.

"Get him the fuck out of here!" I scream. The words rip out of me with an unfamiliar fervor. Suddenly, I do not care who hears me. I do not care who I scare with this outburst. "Get him the fuck out of here! Now!"

I fall to the ground sobbing as the pain strikes again. Despite all this time, it is just as intense as it was that night in the forest. It feels like someone is taking a serrated knife to my soul, shaving off pieces of it in slow, jagged cuts.

I am vaguely aware as my friends surround me. Someone asks me if I am all right; someone else asks what I need. I search each of the faces swimming before me and settle on Sarah.

"It's him," I whisper. The explanation is simple, but I know she understands. The look on her face is one I know well. It's a look of pure fury. I've been on the wrong side of that look before, and I don't envy Zeke. He deserves every bit of her wrath.

I haven't known Sarah for long, and she has every reason to hate me. Still, she currently knows more about my past than anyone else, and I trust her to help me overcome this now.

It took me a long time to recover from what happened the night I was rejected. Looking back now, I know I didn't really recover after all. I simply invented a new version of myself who didn't care about anyone or anything and latched onto Sebastyn.

I knew he wasn't my mate. After all, my mate had already rejected me. Still, I made a fool of myself trying to forge a mating bond with him. I see now that I was just trying to cover the wound that Zeke left with Sebastyn. Thankfully, he and Sarah, his actual mate, were kind enough to forgive me. Sarah was the first person I told about Zeke. The first person ever.

She didn't pity me like I thought she would. Instead, she held me while I cried and told me everything was going to be okay. If only that were true. For a while, I thought she might be right. I've let my guard down, rebuilt some of my friendships, made some amends, and worked toward being the real me again. After seeing Zeke again—after feeling that pain again—I have a feeling all the work I've done has been for nothing.

I can hear the altercation and see the purple sparks coming from Sarah, but I just close my eyes and block them out. I am unaware of anything beyond the pain in my chest until I feel a pair of arms wrap around me protectively. I know exactly who it is— Sarah. She smells like the air right after a storm, and I allow myself to sink into her embrace.

Not long ago, I wouldn't have believed she would be the one to comfort me. Sarah, however, is an amazing person, and she inched her way into my life despite everything in our past.

I momentarily feel guilty for siccing my tornado of a friend on Zeke. I realize for the first time that the only reason he would be here today is because he was rescued from the facility with everyone else. How long was he there? Why was he there? What did they do to him?

I revisit the short glimpse I had of him, and my heart constricts with a different kind of pain. Now, there is pain for him also— sympathy as I wonder what he went through. I push those thoughts away.

It's the stupid mate bond. I can't take on his pain as well as my own. Not now. Not if I want to have a chance to come out of this with some semblance of sanity.

I let the visions come as Sarah brushes my hair away from my tear-stained face. I latch onto the visions I get of her and Sebastyn. I would usually pull away—the images are surely not meant for me. For a moment, though, they feel like a balm.

It doesn't last long. I am hit with the full force of the realization that I will never have the joy I see when I touch Sarah. The pain of my severed mate bond wracks me again.

I feel strong arms reach underneath me and lift me up. I know instantly that it's Sebastyn.

There was a time when I daydreamed about being in this position. I'm sane enough now to admit I was delusional to think that we would've made a good couple. Especially after meeting Sarah and seeing how perfectly they fit together.

As he walks, Sarah strokes my hair and murmurs reassurances that everything will be okay.

I knew I hadn't properly dealt with my rejection, but I thought the pain would subside after the initial loss. After what I just felt, I know that's not the case.

How am I going to live through this again?

Chapter Four

Axel

I am sitting at my desk and going over the sleuth's budget just like I have every night for the last decade. I knew what I was signing up for when I became the alpha. I trained for this. I wanted this. Still, there are days I wish I could just run away.

I drag my hand over my face, trying to scrub the blurriness from my eyes. I've been staring at the same page for the last hour and a half without making any headway. Everything I've done to take my mind off what's happening tonight hasn't worked. Alaric and his pack will be storming the hunter's facility soon if they haven't started already.

I push myself back from the desk, stand up from the groaning chair, and begin to pace around the empty office. The hunters are the only thing in this world that I truly fear anymore. I used to fear losing my family above all else. My father's death and brother's disappearance made that fear a reality though, and now the only thing left is the hunters. They are the reason for my father's death and, indirectly, my brother's disappearance. If they hadn't murdered my father, Zeke never would've felt the need to leave, and I wouldn't have stayed behind to become the alpha. I refused the call to accompany the pack to the facility, but I have more reason than most to hate the hunters. If it wasn't for them, my family would still be together.

I rub my chest absently, reflexively searching for the once-familiar bond I shared with my twin. Contrary to what everyone else thinks, I know Zeke is still out there somewhere. I'd know if he was dead. I would've felt his death. Instead, there is just a void inside me. It is like the strands of fate connecting us have worn thin—not severed.

"Axel, sweetheart. Are you in there?" a feminine voice calls through the door.

"Yes. Come in, Mom."

She slowly opens the door and steps through. Her eyes are already shining with tears. Like me, she is all too aware of the battle being fought in Orillia right now. Like me, she understands the pack's reasoning but is fearful. Who could blame her? The hunters have already taken so much from her. Even if Alaric and his group succeed, there is no telling who will be lost in the fight. If they fail—I do not follow that train of thought too far. If they fail, I know we won't be able to avoid the hunters much longer.

"Any word yet?" she asks with hope. I know she'll be unable to sleep until I can report to her that the conflict is over. Neither of us will be able to sleep until Trixie contacts me to let me know how it went.

If they eliminate everyone at the facility, we will at least have some time before others begin looking for the supernaturals who launched the attack. If they don't clear out the facility completely —if there's anyone left to follow them back to Parry Sound—we won't stand a chance. That is why I chose to keep my sleuth out of the fight and already have the more vulnerable members holed up in our bunker. My choice was made despite the insistence of some of the shifters—my mother included—that we should go with the Westwoods to Orillia.

"No. Not yet," I admit, slipping back into my chair. It's one thing for her to know how stressed I am; it's another thing entirely for me to show her. I'm the one who is supposed to be strong. I am the one she can lean on. I am the one who stayed.

"It will be okay, Axel." She takes a seat across from me. She's trying to put on a tough face, but I know it's just a mask. She's brokenhearted. She lost her mate and her son in quick succession, and both losses took a piece of her with them. The mother I grew up with was vibrant, bold, and outgoing. Now, there are days when she doesn't leave the house. There are days when she wouldn't eat if I didn't bring her food. In the beginning, I tried to convince her my brother was still alive—that he would come home someday. Eventually, I realized that just made her pain even worse.

"I know, Mom. Alaric won't allow anything to get near his family. We can trust him to take care of this."

"If you had agreed to help him, you could've made sure of it," she argues. It's the same argument we've had repeatedly for the past few days. She believes I made a mistake by deciding to stay out of this.

"What if we had gone with them? What if we had gone and failed?" I ask. I do not like to lead from a place of fear, but I know that my sleuth cannot withstand any more losses. "Who would lead if I didn't return? Who would fight if I lead the hunters back here?"

She lets out a deep breath and looks at her hands. She knows I'm right.

"I understand your reluctance. Truly, I do. What if the same happens to the pack or pride? What if us being involved could've prevented it?"

She stands, walks around the desk, and places a cool hand on either side of my face.

"You're an amazing alpha. You always take care of everything, and I trust your judgment." Her brows crease as she frowns around the next words. "This time—this time, I think you made the wrong choice."

"I was trying to keep us safe," I explain again, but my words lack any real conviction.

"I used to hate it when your father would go on those gods-damned missions. Do you know that?" Her tone is thoughtful, but I can hear the pain in her voice whenever she talks about him. "I was always so afraid for him, and it made me feel like a coward. Eventually, I asked him how he was so brave. He said he wasn't brave—he was always afraid." Her voice breaks, but she swallows the sob. "Being afraid doesn't stop you from doing what is right. 'Courage means acting in spite of fear.'" She quotes my father's familiar words back to me.

I let my eyes slip closed. I've repeated those words in my head over and over since I walked out of Alaric's kitchen. What if I have damned my friends by not having the courage to go with them?

"It's too late to change my mind now. I just have to trust in Alaric, Drake, Skarlyt, and Trixie. They can do this," I say with a sigh, opening my eyes again.

She nods her head and places a soft kiss on my cheek.

"I'm going to go make us some coffee and a snack while we wait."

I don't respond. I let my mind wander listlessly for a moment before I finally return to the documents set before me. There's no point in putting it off any longer. It's not like I can do anything else useful right now, and I need to figure this out.

Someone has been draining the general account bit by bit over the last year. I became aware of the problem while it was still small increments being removed at random intervals. The thief has gotten bold recently. In the last two months alone, more than fifty thousand dollars have been withdrawn without a clear explanation or destination. I don't know where the money is going or who is taking it.

My mom opens the office door, and I look up to see her balancing mugs and snacks on a small tray. I move to help her, but I suddenly freeze in pain. There is no warning. There is only excruciating pain throughout my whole body.

She drops the tray with a clatter and rushes to me as I collapse on the floor. Am I having a heart attack? Is this what it feels like?

I can see the coffee and pitcher of cream soaking into the rug in the doorway.

"What is it? What's wrong?" she pleads with me, roaming my body with her hands and eyes, searching for the source of my pain. After a moment, I realize there's nothing for her to find. It's not my pain that I am feeling—which means there's only one possible cause.

"Zeke," I whisper. My mother steps away from me quickly as if I just slapped her.

"Wha—What?"

"It's not me. It's Zeke," I grind out the words through the pain. Her hand flies to her chest, and tears flow from her eyes.

Just like that, the pain stops. For a moment, my relief is clouded by worry. Why is my twin feeling so much pain? Does this mean he is really gone? When I search for our bond, though, I can feel him. For the first time in a decade, I can feel my brother through our bond. I don't know how he blocked our connection for so long, but whatever just happened blew the locks off. I can feel him again. I know instantly that he is close and likely unconscious.

"Sorry, Mom," I tell her as I rush from the room, shifting immediately and charging in the direction of my brother. Charging in the direction of the Westwood pack.

I roar as I approach the clearing between the coven and the pack. It is both a warning and a welcome. The closer I get, the stronger the bond hums in my chest. After so long without it, the weight of it is unfamiliar and almost unbearable.

The area is busy with injured people and those trying to help them. Witches teleport in and out with more people constantly.

I do not see any evidence of my brother, and no one seems to notice my frenzy. I shift back quickly and scream as I run through the people gathered in the clearing.

"Where is he?" I can hear my own voice crack wildly, and I know I must sound crazed. "Where is my brother?"

A group of people rushes toward me, and I skid to a stop. My chest is heaving as Alaric moves to the front. I know Alaric means no harm, but any movement from the other alpha feels like a challenge at this moment.

"Axel," he says calmly.

"Alaric, I swear to all the gods that if you do not give me my brother right now, I'll slaughter each and every one of you," I growl, sounding feral and crazed.

"Your brother? Axel, he's been missing for years," Alaric responds without reacting to my threat.

"I know he's here. I can feel him," I growl and grab Alaric by the shirt. I know that I should try and control my temper—Alaric is my friend. Even though I knew that Zeke was alive, I had lost all hope of seeing him again. Now that he is so close—

Phoebe steps toward me, her hands already lit with flames.

"Axel, I don't care who you are looking for. If you touch my mate again, I swear on all the gods that you won't live to find them."

My eyes move to her briefly, and I release Alaric. The heat radiating from her does nothing to calm me, but I offer them a brief apology anyway.

"If we had your brother, we would have called you," Darren steps in to explain.

"He's here. I know he is."

"Maybe he's one of the shifters we rescued?" Drake's sister, Drusilla, offers this as an explanation, and my rage-filled gaze lands on her.

What the fuck does she mean rescued?

Another large male steps in front of her petite frame. With an inhale, I realize this man is very old, very large, and very dangerous. This is someone I don't want to fuck with.

"Rescued?" I turn my question back to Alaric and Darren.

"Yes. You may remember the rescue mission that you had no interest in joining?" Darren reminds me unkindly.

Again, I can't control myself. I snatch Darren by the shirt and roar in his face. I feel the heat radiating from Sophia, Darren's mate, and look to see her arms already engulfed in flames. She says nothing. She just waits a moment to see if I come to my senses. I quickly let go of Darren and back away with my hands raised. I'm in a rage, but I'm not stupid. I know that she can do a lot of damage to me before I even get the chance to shift.

"If your brother is here, we can find him," Alaric says. It's clear he's trying to calm me, but he's obviously trying to warn me too. "But you need to put some pants on and control your temper. The people in that tent have been held captive and tortured for years. They do not need to see you throwing a fit out here."

I slip on the pair of shorts he offers, and my rage fades a bit beneath the shame of my reaction. These are my friends. They have all been through a lot already today. I know that they would have called me if they had known where Zeke was. I let my rage blind me. I wasn't thinking straight.

I am steadying myself with a few deep breaths when I hear a voice—a lyrical, beautiful voice—cry out in awful pain. My ears perk up immediately, and I begin rushing toward the sound.

A moment later, the same voice shouts.

"Get him the fuck out of here! Now!"

I freeze, but the rest of the group rushes inside. I don't know what I just heard, but the sound of that woman's pain feels like being stabbed through the heart. I want to do anything and everything in my power to make it go away.

I stand frozen, caught in a whirlwind of different emotions. The bond with my brother reigniting, the frenzy of trying to locate him, the anger directed toward everyone, and now this grief for an unknown person. I am rooted to the spot, watching the entrance. I have no idea why that voice has affected me. My mind is running rampant. Is she part of my sleuth? Is she important to me in some way?

As I mull over the possibilities, Zeke stumbles through the entrance with his arms around Darren and Alaric. At the sight of him, I fall to my knees. I want to be the strong alpha that I was born to be, but the sight of him after eleven years has made me weak.

I search his body for evidence of trouble. His clothes are dirty and torn, his hair is overgrown and unkempt, and his exposed skin is covered in lacerations and bruises.

A pang of regret sparks through me. If only I had searched for him harder. Maybe I would have found him. Drusilla said these people had been rescued. Was my brother being held in that facility? Was he there for all this time? All those years I spent cursing him for leaving—maybe it wasn't his choice at all.

"Axel," he croaks out my name, and it sounds like he hasn't spoken in years.

The sound snaps me out of my stupor, and I jump up and rush to him just as he collapses into my arms. I pull him to me, wrapping my arms around his thin frame as we sink to the ground.

"I'm sorry. I'm so sorry," I whisper, tears streaming down my face. "I should have looked harder for you."

"Axel, we need to talk," Alaric interjects.

My eyes snap up to him. What could he possibly need to talk about right now?

"We can talk tomorrow," I snap at him and begin to stand. "I need to get my brother home."

"I understand. There are some complications—some things..." Alaric shares a look with his brother, and I can see them both struggling to find words.

"There are some things you need to know," Darren finishes apologetically.

"Zeke and I will come back tomorrow—once he's had time to rest." My tone makes it clear that their intrusion upon this moment is incredibly rude. I grab my brother as gently as possible and throw him over my shoulder. He settles against me, and I can feel him lose consciousness again. He's here, but he's in bad shape.

"That's just it," Alaric says, looking embarrassed. "Zeke is banned from pack and coven land."

"What?" I roar in response.

The brothers look at each other before turning back to me.

"Zeke rejected his mate eleven years ago; she is one of the witches in the coven. Seeing him here has caused the pain to resurface. Sebastyn's mate, Sarah, is a good friend to Opal and has banished him."

"How dare—Sarah has no right to banish my brother," I begin, unsure what piece of information to settle on first.

"We agree with her decision. Until Opal forgives Zeke, he is not welcome on our land." I open my mouth to interrupt, but Alaric raises his hand and looks at my twin. "I realize it was years ago. I realize he's already suffered. Zeke rejected the mating bond, and it caused a lot of pain. Until Opal is ready, Zeke is not welcome."

I am itching to defend my brother, but Alaric's words trigger a moment of clarity.

Opal.

If Opal is Zeke's mate, she's mine too. That's why the sound of her pain affected me. That's why I felt the need to rush to her defense. I didn't know the person she needed defense from was Zeke.

"Am I welcome?" I ask, uncertain what any of this means for me. "Would it be okay if I talked to her?"

Alaric and Darren exchange another look, and I know they are communicating silently.

"Axel," Darren begins, putting his hand on my forearm. "You are always welcome here, but you and Zeke look so similar—"

"We aren't even sure she knows you exist," Alaric explains. "She may think you are him."

The last thing I want is to cause our mate any pain, but I need to find a way to fix this. I desperately need to talk to my brother and find out what he was thinking when he rejected our mate.

"Call me when she's ready to talk. I don't care what time it is; I will come." I should explain that she's my mate too. I should tell them that I may be able to repair some of the damage my brother caused, but I don't. They know we are identical twins, so they may have already guessed. For some reason, though, I am unable to voice any of that.

With nothing more to say, I walk away toward my sleuth with my brother—still unconscious—bouncing against my shoulder. As happy as I am to have him in my arms, I'm fucking furious with him too. How dare he reject our mate? I will give him one day to heal before I expect answers.

Twin or not, I *will* get answers.

With a level of tenderness I don't know I'm capable of at the moment, I gently place Zeke on the bed in his room just as my mother rushes in.

His room is still furnished but ill-equipped for the ministrations our mother feels compelled to complete. She brings in water —warm and cool—and towels of various sizes. She brings bandages and ointments. Once Zeke is cleaned and bandaged, she rushes to the kitchen to begin baking.

Once she's gone, I settle into the chair next to the bed and try to digest everything I have learned in the last few hours. The fury I felt about my twin rejecting our mate abates as I watch his chest rise and fall in the even, measured rhythm of sleep.

He must have had a reason to reject her. He wouldn't have done such a horrible thing for no reason.

I just can't imagine what that reason could be or why he wouldn't have at least brought her to me beforehand...

Chapter Five

Opal

I wake in a panic, with pain radiating throughout my entire body. It's a pain I haven't felt in years. It's a pain that I, at one point, thought would never go away.

Eventually, it did. At least, it lessened enough that I could function. Now that it is back, I am not sure I'll be able to survive it again.

I curl into a ball and let the tears fall. This is too much. Never in my wildest dreams—or nightmares—did I imagine seeing him again. I knew it was a possibility when I returned to Parry Sound, but he never reappeared. Even then, I thought the pain was supposed to fade after the initial rejection.

Maybe I should ask Lennox about it. He spent years living in a pack with a mate who rejected him. He may have some answers or advice for me. I will seek him out soon—but not today. I'm allowing myself the next twenty-four hours to wallow in my pain. After that? No more wallowing.

I didn't give myself a chance to feel my own pain the first time this happened. I am not going to make the same mistake again. I am not going to let him ruin my life again.

"Are you hungry?" Sarah asks from the doorway of my room. The look of pity on her face makes my tears fall even harder. I know she's not trying to hurt me. I know I can be myself around her. Still, it's still hard not to slip back into my old habit of pretending to be a bitch.

I shake my head and roll over to face away from her. I feel pitiful and weak. I hate that I'm reacting like this, but I also don't have enough emotional strength to care.

Maybe I shouldn't have thrown out all the potions from Vivian. Maybe I should call and ask her to send more to me now instead of waiting months. I could explain the urgent need by saying the vials had broken or there had been a spill.

Even as the thoughts slip into my mind, I push them away. I can't allow that. The potion did help take my pain away, but the damage it did to my relationships is not worth it.

"I'll be here when you're ready to talk," she whispers as she leaves the room.

I curl into myself and sob.

* * *

I thought it was generous to give myself twenty-four hours to recuperate. It turns out I was underestimating just how awful I felt.

Three days pass, and I don't move except to use the bathroom. I only know it's been three days because Sarah has brought me food for each meal, forcing me to sit up long enough to eat.

I don't know why I'm allowing myself to sink into this depression, and I desperately want to stop. At the same time, I don't know how to change it. Each time I think I have gained enough strength to get up and shower, something in my brain flicks to Zeke. Then, I end up curled back under the covers with tears streaming down my face.

"That's it. Enough moping. Time to get up," Sarah says force-fully, storming into my room and ripping the covers off.

I panic and attempt to pull the covers back over me, but she stands and scowls at me.

"Nope. You're getting up and getting into the shower." Her hands are on her hips, her eyebrows pinched together, and her bright green eyes glowing. I can tell she means business.

"I can't," I whisper, hating how weak I sound. My eyes drop down to the floor.

"You can, and you will. I've given you three days. You need to get your strength back. I won't allow you to wither away in here."

I bring my eyes up to meet hers, pleading for her to just leave me alone. I can't do this. I thought I could get past it. I thought I *was* past it. Seeing him again—feeling this pain again—just makes it clear that I will never truly heal. There's no future for me without this pain. Tears begin to form in my eyes.

"None of that," Sarah says, her features softening. "I'm doing this because I care about you. Trust me, Opal. Once you shower and change clothes, you'll feel much better."

I know she's doing this for me. Because she's such an amazing friend, I can do this for her too. It may not be the miracle she's expecting, but I can at least try.

"Okay," I mumble as I climb out of the bed and make my way to the bathroom.

I let the water run for a moment. It steams the air around me while I debate whether or not to actually get in. Even the thought is exhausting, but Sarah will know if I abandon the effort now.

Once I step under the hot spray, I am forced to admit that Sarah was right. By the time I'm done washing my body and hair, I almost feel human again. The pain in my chest is still present, but it feels like I'm able to function normally—at least as close to normal as I can get.

When I turn off the water and reach out to grab my towel, Sarah is already standing at the bathroom door waiting for me.

"Are you feeling any better?"

"I actually do feel a little better," I admit.

"Good. Get dressed and come to the kitchen." She closes the door behind her without giving me the option to argue.

She hasn't been around long, but this imperious wellspring of elemental power is far from the sheepish, scared woman I first met.

Once I'm alone again, my mind wanders back to Zeke. I was devastated by his rejection, but that is a familiar hurt now. When I allow myself to think about how he looked in the triage tent, a different pain flows through me. He looked like absolute shit, and I can't help but wonder what he went through in that place.

Although I left in a rush, I was there helping the rescued supernaturals long enough to hear some of their tales. I know that nothing good happened in that place. As much as I loathe him for hurting me, I don't want to think about him being tortured.

That thought allows a flicker of hope to light in my chest. Maybe there was a legitimate reason for him to reject me. Maybe he knew he was going to be captured.

The hope is immediate and almost reflexive. I desperately want it to be true. I don't allow myself to follow that line of thought for long. If I let myself hope, I know it will crush me when I learn I am wrong.

Almost on autopilot, I go through the motions of getting ready. I want to throw on my sweatpants and hoodie, but I opt for my boho pants and a flowing tank top instead. I want to be comfortable, but I want to feel cute at the same time. I know I look hippyish—yet hot—in this outfit.

I make my way out of my bedroom for the first time in three days, and I'm immediately greeted by the scents of bacon and coffee. A small moan slips out of my lips at the decadent pairing, and I wander to the table where Sarah, Sebastyn, Skarlyt, Lennox, and Kayne are currently sitting.

I am accustomed to Sarah and, by extension, Sebastyn now, but the presence of Skarlyt and Lennox has me feeling momentarily embarrassed. I am not proud of my actions over the last few days. I try to remind myself that they have both experienced rejection before.

They are probably the only people I know who truly understand how I feel right now.

"Are you feeling any better?" Skarlyt asks, her eyes full of an emotion I cannot name. Someone else would probably mistake it for pity, but I know it's not.

"I'm not perfect, but the shower definitely helped," I admit. Lennox nods in understanding and scoops a forkful of food into his mouth.

"It will get better," Skar promises me.

"Thank you," I whisper.

"I'm happy to see you're on the mend, but I came here for something else too," she begins sheepishly. Sarah and Sebastyn both send her a scowl. It's clear they've already discussed putting this conversation—whatever it is—aside for now.

"What?" she asks, sounding wounded. "It's time-sensitive, and we only have a few people we can trust."

They groan but go back to their food, and I dig into my own.

"It's okay," I tell them. "I want to know. Maybe a distraction is just what I need."

Skarlyt shoots her brother and Sarah a triumphant look before turning her chair toward me.

"So, I have a brilliant idea—"

"Let's hold off on calling it 'brilliant' until we know if it works," Seb interrupts.

Skar shoots him a glare, but her smile is in place again when she turns back to me.

"As I was saying before I was interrupted..." She shoots one last look at her brother before continuing. "I have a brilliant idea, and I want to know what you think."

I nod at her. "Okay. What is it?"

"You know how we used our magic to make the structures in the clearing?" I nod again though I'm not sure where she is going with this. "We used the vines in the clearing, but what if we could do the same thing with dirt?"

She waits, and it is clear she's expecting a big reaction. She thinks I will understand what she's implying, but I don't. I look around the table, searching for a clue. My companions have nothing to offer, so I look back to Skar in confusion.

"I don't know where you're going with this," I admit apologetically.

She sighs in exasperation.

"I want to pull up earth from the bottom of the lake or ocean—wherever we decide—and make an island. I have it all mapped out already. An island just for supernaturals. It will be easier to keep us safe, and we can cloak it so that it can't be found. If the prophecy means that there is a war coming, it will be the best way to protect us."

"That's a brilliant idea. Well—if it works. Have you tested it at all? I don't understand what you want from me. You can all manipulate earth better than me."

"You may not be the strongest earth witch, but there aren't many people we can ask. We don't want to create a panic, and this idea will stress everyone out whether or not we succeed." I nod in understanding, and she continues. "So far, we have the four of us, my mom, and Ruth who can start today."

"Wait—today?" Seb asks.

Skarlyt nods her head.

"Today. Alaric has the location of five other facilities. He and his crew want to storm them and rescue everyone inside as soon as possible. If things go sideways, we need a safe place to go. It's going to be hard enough to coordinate five attacks at once. If we need to hide from five different hunter groups too..."

I am about to respond when Ruth and Constance walk through the door. Constance, being the mother hen that she is, rushes over to wrap her arms around me.

"Oh, Opal. How are you doing, my dear?"

I squeeze her back as much as I can from my sitting position. "Better."

She steps back with a smile. "Good." She claps her hands together and looks around the table with a large smile. "Are we ready to do this?"

We all nod and shovel the remaining food into our mouths as Ruth helps Constance clean up our breakfast.

It shocks no one that Lennox finishes eating first. He gathers Kayne up and gets him ready to go.

"I'm taking Kayne over to Alaric's for the day to play with Aurora," he announces, giving Skarlyt a kiss on the head and turning to leave.

"Lennox. Wait," I say, getting up and rushing after him onto the porch. "Can I ask you a question?"

"Of course," he says, turning back toward me.

I look down at the ground. I am not sure I have ever spoken to Lennox alone before. Although I know he is kind, I can't help but be a little embarrassed by the question I must ask him now. After a few breaths, I look up into his eyes again.

"Does it get easier? Seeing them—I mean?"

His eyes soften, and he adjusts Kayne in his arms so he can place one hand on my shoulder.

I tense under his hand as I am immediately bombarded with visions of Lennox's pain at seeing Olivia.

"It was hard at first. That's why I stayed away from my old

pack for so long. The pain didn't really fade; I just got used to it I guess."

That's not the answer I was hoping for, but at least it's something.

"Thank you," I whisper, and he gives my shoulder a small squeeze.

I lean over and give Kayne a soft kiss on his forehead. I gasp as images of the future cloud my vision.

Kayne is older. I am unsure how I know it is him because he is running through the forest in the form of a large, grey wolf. He is beautiful and strong as he weaves between the thick trees. Impossibly, I watch as magic seeps from his paws with each bounding step. As he lopes through the underbrush, he leaves a trail of blue magic in his wake.

The vision is gone as quickly as it came.

What was that?

"If you ever need to talk..." Lennox offers. I give him a thankful nod before he turns to head to the alpha house. It is clear he doesn't notice that I've seen anything. Years of practice have allowed me to mask my sudden shifts in emotion.

The wind whips around me softly as I stand on the porch, lost in thought. I don't understand how anyone could get used to this pain, but I'm sure I'm going to find out. I have a feeling that I will be seeing Zeke again sooner than I hope, and my feelings are usually correct.

Until then, I have other futures to worry about too. I'm going to have to talk to Skarlyt about what I just saw when I touched her son. It seemed like Kayne inherited not only the shifter gene but also her magic as well. It's incredible, but it shouldn't be possible.

The rest of our group meets me on the porch. I'm the only one who hasn't mastered teleporting, so I link my arm through Sarah's before we take off.

When I open my eyes, we are on a small floating dock in the middle of the lake. I'm glad I didn't attempt to teleport myself. Landing in a solid location is difficult enough; landing on a moving target would be impossible for me.

"Okay, we're only trying to create something small for now," Skarlyt explains, pointing to indistinct positions on the surface of the water. "Maybe from here to over there. We will start with our focus on the center. Once we build up a decent circle of land, we can each take a direction to spread it out."

We immediately get to work, each of us closing our eyes. I focus on sensing the earth beneath the water and pulling it up. It's slow and tedious work, but eventually I open my eyes to see a small patch of earth, maybe a foot around, surfacing in the lake.

The others must have felt me pause to look at our progress. They all open their eyes to take a breath as well. The small piece of dark soil remains.

"Okay," Skarlyt claps her hands together as if this is precisely what she anticipated. "We are going to try to spread it out on the surface of the water. Eventually, I would like to detach it from the bottom so that it can move if needed. Sarah, you take the north; Seb, take the northeast; Mom, take the east; Opal, you take the southeast; and I'll take the south. Ruth, you have the strongest earth magic, so you can take everything else." Skarlyt assigns our work and doesn't give us a chance to say anything before closing her eyes to get to work. I see the ground before her growing and expanding.

It's a lot easier to expand the surface than it was to create the base. Within minutes, we have created a semi-regular shape of the desired size.

"What now?" I ask.

"Now, we build it up," she says, the excitement of the endeavor evident in her voice. "We will make it thicker and compact it until it's strong enough to hold us."

Once again, we all get to work. Using my magic, I bring up dirt from the bottom of the lake and press it into the growing form as hard as I can.

The others finish before me, so they help me complete my section. I wasn't just being humble when I said I wasn't a strong earth witch. I have earth magic, but my sight seems to take up so much of my magic that any other power is negligible. My visions have become even more frequent lately, so it is safe to assume my earth magic may be even weaker than before.

"Time to test it," Skarlyt says. She doesn't wait before jumping straight onto the small island. Surprisingly, it holds her. It only bobs slightly as she jumps up and down in celebration.

"Wait. We need to make sure plants can grow on it before we get too excited," Seb says. Sarah and Ruth sweep their hands over the area, and small blades of grass begin to sprout in their wake.

I guess that answers that.

"See!" Skarlyt shouts, she pauses her celebratory dance only to point an accusing finger at her brother. "I told you it would work. Now, let's go talk with Alaric and Phoebe and start planning how our island should look."

Her excitement is infectious, and I feel myself smiling right along with her before long. This was a nice distraction after all. It feels good to be helpful, and it's encouraging to know someone is planning for the future.

Besides, the chances of me running into Zeke again are even smaller if I'm living on an island in the middle of some ocean, right? Unless they're going to invite him to the island too. Skarlyt did say the plan was to bring supernaturals there to keep them safe. I should probably find out what kind of shifter he is...just in case.

Rather than going with them to the alpha house, I ask Skarlyt to drop me off at home. I am not quite ready to face everyone.

"Skar..." I say once we pop into my living room. Skarlyt Moon moves fast, and I have to catch her before she takes off again.

"Yeah?"

I try to begin, but I am unsure how to word the news I need to give her. I catch myself biting my lip.

"Opal," she says, closing the distance between us and gripping my arms. "You can tell me anything."

The sincerity in her voice and eyes has me nodding.

"I think Kayne is a hybrid," I blurt out, instantly cringing at my bluntness.

Her eyes widen in surprise, but she seems more taken aback by my delivering the news than by the news itself.

"How do you...?"

I watch as her eyes turn accusatory. She is trying to calculate what it means for me to know this.

"I have visions," I blurt out again. Once again, my words shock her. "I have had visions since I was a child. Sometimes I see the future, sometimes I see the past. When I gave Kayne a kiss on his forehead this morning, I got a glimpse of his future."

"Tell me," she demands, all the amusement in her eyes lost to a mother's concern.

"He was running as a beautiful, gray wolf, but blue magic was seeping from his paws with every step."

"Blue? What shade? Bright blue? Or midnight blue?" she questions me feverishly.

Huh. That's not what I expected her to ask.

I nod. "Just blue. It was almost the same color as yours. Like an aquamarine. But I don't think you understand. This means he has both genes; he's a shifter and a witch..."

She begins to pace and waves her hand impatiently in my direction.

"I already knew that. In fact, I met another hybrid just yesterday. Blue...does that mean? Of course, it would be that..." She is mumbling to herself.

"Skarlyt," I say, gripping her shoulder to pause her rant. "Would you care to share with the class?"

She shakes her head to clear it. I had assumed the fact that I have visions regularly would at least give her pause, but she's taken that news in stride.

"I have always worried that Kayne would inherit some of Kirnon's wickedness. If his magic was aquamarine, it means he's still pure. How far into the future was this?"

"Uh..." I begin, trying to recall the image. "He was in wolf form, so it's hard to tell. Old enough to shift at least, and I guess he looked...adult sized?"

She nods again, and her body is practically vibrating with excitement.

"I have to tell Lennox and my mom..."

She is walking toward the door, but she turns back to me.

"Can you keep this to yourself?"

"Of course," I say.

As soon as the words are out of my mouth, she blinks away. The door is forgotten, and I know she's already somewhere far away delivering this news.

"Well, that was weird," I murmur to myself as I head to the kitchen.

I make myself a snack before plopping onto the couch and turning on one of my favorite movies.

Chapter Six

Zeke

I wake up with a groan and roll over on soft sheets.

Wait.

Sheets?

I open my eyes and look around, finding my old room. Then, the events of last night—was it just last night?—come back to me. I was rescued, I saw my angel, and I was banished from seeing her again. I know it's what I deserve, but I just wish I could explain why I rejected her. It wouldn't change anything, but I can't stand that she doesn't know how miserable it made me too.

I stretch my muscles and feel them protest. Still, I'm not in as much pain as I should be. I was in bad shape when we left the facility, and I wasn't much better when I was kicked out by my rescuers.

I throw the covers off and slowly sit up. Still, the dizziness hits me just as my mom walks in the door. As soon as her eyes meet mine, she drops the tray she was carrying and rushes to wrap her arms around me.

"Hi, Mom," I say, pulling her in tighter.

Sobs wrack her body as she shakes in my arms.

"Zeke...my baby...I thought I'd never see you again."

"I know, Mom. I'm sorry."

She sits back, lets me go, and slaps me on the arm.

"Why are you sorry? Did you intend to get captured and held in that horrible place?"

"No."

"Did you want to come home to me?" she asks.

"Of course," I say.

"Well, then, you have nothing to be sorry for. You weren't gone because you wanted to be, and you came home to me." She runs her hands over my face and arms as if she is making sure I'm real.

"I messed up, Mom," I tell her, my vision blurred by unshed tears.

"Shh. It will all be okay. You'll see," she says, pulling me back into her arms.

"You don't understand. What I've done—I can't be forgiven."

She pulls back once more to look into my eyes.

"So, tell me," she encourages, and I do.

I tell her everything about my night with Opal—well, the version of it that I'm comfortable telling my mom. I also tell her the watered-down version of my time in that facility. Finally, I tell her about last night—about the pain in my angel's voice when she saw me.

"Now you listen to me," she begins, pinning me with a glare I know well and thought I'd never see again. "If that girl is truly your mate, she will understand. I don't agree with what you did. I believe we could've fought this together, but we can't change the past. We can only move forward. Besides, your brother has been working on a plan to win over your mate while you've been sleeping for the past few days."

"Few days?" What the fuck?

"You've been asleep for three days, Zeke. Your body needed to heal."

Three days? Shit.

I try to get up, but her arms tighten around me. She holds me in place, and I let her. I sit there and hold my mom, and we cry. We cry until neither of us have any tears left.

"Oh, good. You're awake. We have some things to discuss," Axel says, walking into the room without further greeting.

"Axel..." My mom shoots him a warning about his tone.

"Don't 'Axel' me," he says, and I can tell it's a conversation they've already had. "He rejected our mate. He could've at least told me about her, so I could seek her out and take care of her. Then, to top it all off, he went and got himself captured."

"He's right, Mom. Axel is right to be angry. I hoped he and Opal would find each other while I was gone, but I should have told him about her at least. Besides, that's not the worst thing I did..."

I lower my eyes in shame. His accusations are correct, but he left out the worst thing I did. I blocked our bond. If I hadn't insisted that Constance cut us off from each other, this all could have been avoided. If we had our bond, I could have just sent him a message about finding Opal.

My mother *tsk-tsks* at us. She never did like it when we fought. This time, though, I don't think there is anything she can do to fix this. This is something that I'm going to have to do myself.

Reluctantly, she lets me go.

"For what it's worth, Axel, I'm sorry." I get up, testing my unsteady legs. When I pitch forward, my brother's hand shoots out to support me.

"I know you are," he says, but his eyes are still hard. "Go shower and shave. We can talk after."

I give my mom's shoulder a quick squeeze as I walk past her on my way to the bathroom. Let's see if I can remember how to make myself look presentable.

* * *

It must be nearly an hour later when I can finally step back and study my work in the mirror. After taking the clippers to my hair and beard and scrubbing myself until my skin felt raw, I'm finally starting to look like myself.

Sure, I've lost a lot of muscle mass, my cheeks are sunken, and my eyes are a duller green—all obvious signs of starvation and malnutrition—but the bruises and lacerations are gone. Although only a minor visual improvement, it's a step in the right direction, and I'll take it.

I leave the bathroom and head to the office—where I know I will find Axel. I know this is going to be a fight, and I am trying to prepare myself for it. Axel has every right to be pissed at me, but it doesn't mean I'm looking forward to it. I'll let him get in as many hits as it takes for him to forgive me. After all, I deserve them.

I walk into the office and find a tired-looking Axel sitting in the chair behind the desk with his head in his hands. As he looks up, the dark bags under his eyes show me just how much sleep he's gotten: close to none.

"Talk," he growls as he meets my eyes, sits back in the chair, and crosses his arms over his chest.

I run a hand over my face as I sit in the chair opposite him. At one point, he would have been thrilled to have me home. I know that he still probably is. Now that he knows I rejected our mate, though, his happiness is tainted with something else. Knowing my twin, he's warring within himself.

"First, I want to say I'm sorry," I begin. Axel just growls at me, so I push on. I don't have to ask what he is so impatient for me to talk about. I already know he wants to know what happened with Opal.

The pain flows through my chest at the reopening of this wound. My bear—already feral—lashes out at me each time I even think about her. I haven't shifted since the night I rejected her; he won't allow me to. I've tried to reason with him so many times; I've tried to explain that she's safe because of the rejection, but he simply growls at me in response. In his mind, it's simple: he's big and strong and could've protected her. I know that's not the case. She would've been captured along with us. At least she was free to live her life this way.

"I was coming back home to see you eleven years ago when I met Opal. The hunters weren't far behind me. I knew that it was my last chance to say goodbye, so I took the risk and came back. Obviously, I didn't make it to you like I'd planned. That is because I saw her."

If he is surprised by this admission, he doesn't show it.

"I went to the coven—to Constance—and begged her to block our bond. She didn't want to, but I needed to stop you from feeling the pain of my death." I pause, taking a shaky breath. "The hunters were on my trail, and I assumed they'd kill me as soon as they found me. I was on my way here to say goodbye when I saw her. She was perfect. She was an angel. I couldn't stop my bear from trying to claim her. If I'm being honest, at that moment, I didn't want to stop him...But after it was done, reality came crashing down on me, and I rejected her and ran. I know you think I was wrong, but I was taken by the hunters less than two hours later. They caught me and dragged me to that facility, and I was trapped there for the last eleven years. That's how I know I made the right choice: she didn't end up in there with me."

My tale complete, I watch his face for any sign of his reaction. I can see a level of understanding in his eyes, but there is no forgiveness.

"What about your bear?" he asks after we sit in silence for some time.

"What about him?"

"How does he feel about the rejection?" I hear it in his tone; he already knows the answer.

"He's pissed. I can't shift—haven't been able to since that night. He doesn't even talk to me now; he only growls when I try to reason with him. I only survived the last eleven years because he sent me some of his strength when I needed it. As pissed off as he is, he must understand to some degree."

My bear takes that opportunity to growl at me once more. He knows I'm being honest. If he thought I was lying about my reasons, he would've let me die in that facility. Hell, he probably should have let me die. Maybe he was trying to torture me by keeping me alive to feel their torture and experiments.

Axel's eyes drop down to his desk as he lets out a big breath. "I know you think you did the right thing, Zeke, but you're wrong. We could've protected her. We should've protected her. Because of your selfish decision, we missed out on eleven years with our mate. Who knows what she went through in all that time."

"Selfish?" I yell. "What I did was the furthest thing from selfish. I kept our mate safe from the hunters. I kept you safe from the hunters. I could've led them here. We would've been slaughtered, Axel. *Slaughtered*. The hunters that were after me were sick and twisted—they got off on torture for the pleasure of it."

"I understand why you feel that way, but you're missing my point of view altogether. You thought they would follow you here, but what if it were the opposite? What if you brought her here and we could've kept her safe? Kept you safe? What if all you went through was for nothing?"

I get my breathing under control as much as I can. I don't want to fight with my brother. I've missed him so damn much. For the first time in eleven years, I'm safe. I won't be cut into over and over again. I won't be forced to take all kinds of drugs to try and trigger a shift that will never happen.

"I know how you feel, Axel, but you weren't there. You don't know what they are capable of. It's better for her to hate me than to have been trapped in that place with me."

He nods. I rise from my seat to embrace him, but he stops me with a hand.

"I'm glad you're home, Zeke. I truly am. I missed you more than you will ever know. But...you kept my mate from me, and I don't know if I can forgive that."

"I am sorry, Axel. I honestly thought you would've found one another by now. I trusted in fate to bring you together in my absence."

Tears brim in my eyes. That is the biggest regret I have. I wish I didn't have to reject Opal, but I don't regret it. No matter what anyone says, she's alive right now because of that. What I regret is not telling her to find Axel or somehow telling him to look for her.

He scrubs a hand down his face once more and whispers, "I know you did, but we never crossed paths. I've missed out on eleven years with my mate because of it."

I nod, trying to think of what to say. I know there's nothing that can make it up to him or change the past, but I have to try. Somehow, I must earn his and Opal's forgiveness.

I'm about to promise him I will find a way to do just that when his phone rings.

"Yeah," he answers gruffly.

I can't hear what is being said by the other person. My bear doesn't feel like helping me hear any better, so I sit back down and wait.

"Right now?" he asks in an impatient tone. After listening and nodding a few times, he agrees. "Fine. I'll be there in twenty."

He hangs up and slams his phone down on the desk.

"I have to go to the pack," he explains.

"Is everything okay?" I ask. Normally, I would offer to go with him. After the scary storm woman banished me, I wouldn't dare try. She is terrifying.

"I don't know. Alaric wouldn't tell me over the phone. I just know that he wants me there and reminded me that you are not permitted on his lands until Opal gives the word."

"How am I supposed to convince Opal to revoke the banishment if I can't even see her and plead my case?" I ask.

"That isn't my concern right now. You're just going to have to find a way." Tears rim his eyes as he finally meets mine across the desk. "If you can't find a way—" He clams his mouth closed, halting any further words.

Still, I know what he was going to say. If he must choose between me and our mate, he will choose our mate.

My face freezes with shock momentarily before I nod in understanding. If I was given that awful choice, I would make the same one.

"I'm sorry, Zeke. I hope you're able to repair the damage you did—for all our sakes." He pulls me into him, wrapping his arms tightly around me for the first time. He holds me as if he thinks I'm going to disappear, and I cling to him the same way. He gives my shoulder a small squeeze on his way out the door, and my shoulders slump once he's out of sight.

I do not know much about my future, but I know this: I will either earn the forgiveness of Opal and Axel, or I'll die. There is no alternative. I refuse to live in a world where my mere presence hurts the two people I love most.

Chapter Seven

Opal

I need some time to decompress from the activity of the last few days, so I settle into my couch, sip my tea, turn on the TV, and start *Twilight* for the millionth time.

Yeah, yeah. I know. This movie is wrong in so many ways, but I love it. There's something comforting in the inaccuracy and—now that I've rewatched it so many times—familiarity. I'm at the part where Bella first sees Jacob shift into a wolf when Sarah walks into the room.

I press pause on the movie and turn to her.

"Hey, I thought you'd be gone longer. Want to watch *Twilight* with me?"

She rolls her eyes at me and smirks. I am well aware that Sarah doesn't understand how these movies can interest me.

Why would a vampire sparkle in sunlight? Why do the vampires act so high and mighty about only drinking animal blood when there are obviously shifters—who look just like animals—next door?

"I have to go back, but I need to talk to you for a minute—" she begins, but I cut her off. I can see the concern in her eyes, and I know where this is headed.

"Listen. I'm okay." I stand and walk over to her. "I promise. I'll get there. Today was exactly what I needed to snap me out of the funk I've been in."

I pull her into a hug, and she sighs.

"I know, Opal." She pulls away from me, studying my face with an apologetic look. "That's why I'm here. I need to tell you something..."

"Sarah, is something wrong?"

She pulls away from me and begins to pace.

This can't be good.

"I'm headed back to the alpha house. We are meeting with all the faction leaders to talk about the island. Alaric wants the entire team there so we can give them details."

"Why didn't you just say so?" I say, turning toward my room to change out of my sweatpants. "I said I didn't feel like going there, but this is different."

"Wait. That's not all." She spits the words out, rushing to follow me to my room. "Axel will be there—"

"Okay," I say, nodding. Her anxious tone is confusing me. "That is the bear alpha, right?"

"Yes. Well, it turns out..." She pauses again, and I turn to face her.

"What?"

"It turns out Zeke is his twin brother." She grimaces at the words, and a fresh twinge of pain flows through me at the sound of his name.

Shit. I guess that answers my questions about what type of shifter he is and if he'll be invited to the island with us. I take a step toward my bed—needing to sit down as this revelation washes over me.

She rushes over to me, but I back away. If she hugs me right now, I'll cry. If I start crying, I won't stop. No. I won't let Zeke ruin anything else for me.

"Okay," I say, swallowing my pain with more strength than I feel.

"Okay?" she questions, and I nod. "When I say they are twin brothers, I mean they are *identical* twin brothers. They look exactly the same, Opal."

"I'm sure they aren't exactly the same." She shakes her head. Shit. Of course, twins will look alike, but I assumed they would not be truly identical. Does this mean that seeing Axel will hurt just as much as seeing Zeke even though he's not my mate? Can I do this?

I turn to look at myself in the mirror. I can see the vulnerability written all over my slumped shoulders and drawn face. I'm just exhausted. I just want a break.

I pull my eyes away and give myself a pep talk. I am a strong, independent woman. I've lived on my own for the last eleven years. Being rejected didn't kill me, so this won't either.

I raise my eyes back up and meet my own hardened gaze in the mirror. I refuse to let Zeke take anything else away from me. He already took the happily ever after I was owed, and I pushed all my friends away when he broke my heart. My life is just now starting to get back to normal. Just today, I was part of a project that will help keep our entire pack and coven safe. I finally felt like I was where I belonged. He will not take being part of that away from me too.

"Let's go," I say after a deep breath. Sarah looks at me in shock before gesturing to my clothes.

I look down and realize I'm still in my comfy clothes.

"Oh, right." I rush over to my closet and throw on my ripped jeans, fitted tee, and hoodie before slipping on my flats and walking to her. "I'm ready."

The words are barely out of my mouth before her slim hand is on my shoulder and we're landing on the porch of the alpha house.

F. D. Fair

"Are you sure?" she asks, reaching for the door handle.

"Yes," I tell her, blinking away the brief confusion that accompanies teleporting so suddenly. I breathe deeply, making the decision and pushing the door open myself.

It seems that Sarah waited until the last moment to let me know because everyone else is already assembled. Most of the people are familiar, and I'm greeted warmly by everyone in attendance.

When I get to Axel—I know immediately that it *is* Axel—I freeze. Sarah steps in front of me, and he growls at her. I am not sure if *growl* even really describes it. The sound is so deep and menacing that it shakes the floor.

It doesn't scare me. In fact, it does the exact opposite.

"Axel..." Alaric moves to stand in front of Sarah. "Is there something you want to tell us?"

Axel growls again, and I have the urge to walk around the people trying to protect me to comfort him. I know he won't hurt me.

"Alaric," Axel says, a barely controlled warning. "You need to get away from my mate."

Mate? Oh, gods. Not again.

I peek around the wall that Sarah and Alaric form between us and meet his gaze. When I look into his eyes, there's nothing but love staring back at me. There's no hate—no menace. Just undiluted longing. Sarah was right, he does look almost identical to Zeke. His tall frame is covered in muscles, his deep brown hair is a little longer on top, and his eyes shine a mossy green.

"Excuse me?" Sarah shouts. "You are not her mate."

I walk around my friends, dodging the hands that reach for me. When I reach Axel, I place my hand on his arm. He sucks in a shaky breath, and the tension drains from his body.

Without looking away from my eyes, he takes a deep breath to explain.

"My brother and I share a unique bond. You were all born with half of your soul, but we share that one half. We are meant to share that soul and the mate who would complete it."

I take an involuntary step back. Two mates? That's not possible. Besides, Zeke rejected me. Surely that has already ruined any bond the three of us were intended to share.

"I..." I begin, but I am unsure of what I want to say.

Do I want him? Of course, I do. Just like Zeke, he's sexy as fuck and makes my entire body vibrate with need. Am I ready to be claimed? I don't think I am.

Being close to him does make the now-familiar pain of rejection hurt less. Even though they are identical, seeing Axel brings me no pain.

"I know you're not ready, and I would never try to rush you," he says solemnly. He brings one large, freckled hand up to gently brush my hair behind my ear. "I am not my brother. What he did to you was wrong—even if he does think he had a good reason."

"Wait," I cannot stop myself from interrupting him. "He thinks he had a good reason for rejecting me?" I try to keep the hurt from my voice, but I know I fail when I see him flinch.

"We can talk about that another time. When we are alone," he nods meaningfully to the crowded room around us.

I nod, implicitly agreeing to be alone with him at some point in the future. Given the way my traitorous body is reacting to his presence, I may be demanding his mating bite by the time that meeting is over.

"Okay," I whisper. My hand tightens on his forearm, and my vision flashes.

I'm looking at a younger version of Zeke and Axel in their bedroom. They look about thirteen. Even then, they were extremely handsome.

"I wonder what our mate is going to be like," Axel asks. I am not sure how I can tell them apart, but I can.

"She's going to be perfect," Zeke says with conviction as he throws himself on his bed. "She'll be strong, smart, and loyal. Everything we could ever dream of and more."

"You don't think the 'two mates' thing will send her running for the hills?" Axel sounds self-conscious.

"Nah," Zeke promises with a smirk. "If your nerdy books don't chase her off, nothing will."

Axel picks up a pillow and tosses it at his brother. Zeke, already laying down, is defenseless as it lands across his face.

"I can't wait to meet her," Axel says with a sigh. "I wonder what she's going to look like."

"Like I said," Zeke reassures his twin, "she's going to be perfect."

The vision twists immediately into another.

This time, Axel is alone in some sort of office. His eyes are red rimmed with dark bags under them. He's scouring a map that is laid out on his desk.

"I don't understand," he whispers to himself. "Where are you, Zeke?"

He frantically looks over the map. I recognize it as a map of our area, but there are others piled underneath. A woman walks into the room. Their features are so similar that I can instantly tell this must be their mother.

"Any luck?" she asks, her own eyes showing the same exhaustion.

"None yet. I'm not giving up. I can't." Axel doesn't look up from the map. She nods and walks back out of the room, her shoulders slumped in defeat.

"Come on, Zeke. Give me a sign," he curses. "Two years is too long for you to be gone."

Time seems to flash before my eyes, and I see Axel sitting behind the same desk going over paperwork. He still has bags under his eyes, but he looks healthier than he did.

"Axel," Alaric says, poking his head through the open office door.

"What is it?" Axel asks. He sounds impatient, but he motions for Alaric to come in and sit down.

Alaric takes the seat opposite him.

"I was informed that you've given up searching for Zeke."

Axel's eyes snap up to the other alpha's with a growl.

"What of it?"

Alaric's eyes widen in shock. "But why?"

"Not that it's any of your business, but it's been four years. Zeke left on his own. If he wanted to be found, he could've called."

"Are you sure this is what you want?" Alaric sits forward, leaning closer. His voice is full of concern.

"Listen, this is none of your business," Axel's teeth are clenched. "I think it's best if you leave. I don't come to your office and question your decisions about your family."

Alaric stands up and walks to the door. Before he leaves, he turns. "All I'm saying is...if it was Darren, I would never give up."

I watch Axel scrub a hand down his face as Alaric walks out of the door.

I shake myself out of the vision and turn back to my friends who are all staring at us with their mouths hanging open. I'm going to have to wait to process everything I just saw until I get home.

Sebastyn is the first one to recover. As always, he resorts to pretending as if nothing happened at all.

"I'm going to get Drake and Rayne," he says, clearing his throat awkwardly before blinking away.

"Shit. She's going to be so pissed she missed this," Phoebe says, and Skar agrees.

Before anyone else can speak, Sebastyn reappears with Drake and Rayne.

Rayne looks at everyone with a smile of greeting before she registers the looks on our faces and realizes she must've missed something big.

"What is going on?" she asks, her face falling as she anticipates trouble. "What did I miss?"

I look around at everyone, hoping someone else will take over this explanation. I've grown to love Rayne, but she can be a little scary sometimes.

Skarlyt steps in to save me.

"Apparently, Opal here is one lucky bitch, and she's got two mates."

If I had any concern that this odd arrangement wouldn't be accepted by my friends, it is thrown out the window by her statement and the nods of confirmation from the other women.

"I apologize—but—I thought her mate rejected her?" Drake asks. I know he doesn't mean to be an asshole—or maybe he does—but his words send a pang of pain through my chest.

"He did. Well...one of them did. Axel's twin brother, Zeke, rejected Opal. Apparently the three of them share a soul. Oh, and Zeke apparently thinks he has a good reason for rejecting her eleven years ago," Skarlyt finishes her retelling simply, but her last statement elicits a round of growls and snarls from the group. My heart swells. The last few days have left me feeling vulnerable, exposed, and in need of support. To find that support in the same people I spent eleven years pushing away makes me feel so thankful. If I could turn back time, I would stop myself from becoming bitter and lashing out at everyone. My only option now is to be thankful that my friends gave me another chance.

"Okay," Rayne looks at me and takes a moment to absorb all this new information. "So, we will probably need a girl's night to sort all this out?"

Several of the women cheer, and I see Skarlyt assuring Lennox that her mother can help with Kayne that night.

"Girl's night," I agree, smiling despite myself.

"Fine," Alaric says grudgingly. He turns toward Axel before he continues. "You and I will be having a conversation tonight as well."

I can hear the hurt in Alaric's voice. If I hadn't seen the vision moments ago, I wouldn't know why. Alaric and Axel were friends, so he probably feels hurt—possibly even betrayed—right now.

"All right," Sarah brings us back to attention with a clap of her hands. "If we're all done planning tonight's entertainment, we did meet here for a reason."

Although this meeting started with far more excitement than we expected, we can begin our discussion without any more distractions. Well—I may be a little distracted.

As Skarlyt explains the idea of the island and our progress in actually creating it, my eyes keep drifting toward and then darting away from Axel. By the end of the meeting, we have settled on a location for the island—an otherwise uninhabited part of the Pacific Ocean. Alaric and the other alphas create a crude map of what the island will become. It is only a rough drawing of outlines and notes, but there's a section set aside for each of the factions. Skarlyt and Sarah assign a few witches to work with each of the factions as they develop a plan for the location.

As expected, I am assigned to work alongside the bear shifters. I'll be visiting their sleuth to discuss their needs. Axel promised me and everyone else assembled there that I wouldn't see Zeke. It's a relief, but I also don't want to force him to leave his home while I'm there.

"As long as the island is complete, the bears will join you when you raid the rest of the facilities," Axel says to Alaric and the rest of the group.

"Some of our new friends in the Amazon have agreed to help too," Phoebe adds.

"I know you wanted to move quickly, Alaric, but I'm not sure it's feasible to get this all done in a week," Skarlyt says, studying the sketch of the island.

"We need to make it feasible," Alaric says with the confidence of someone who has experience making impossible things happen. "Matt—Opal's brother—has been able to decode some of the chatter coming into the Orillia lab. He thinks the hunters at the other facilities are getting suspicious."

"He thinks we won't have long before they come to investigate themselves," Rayne confirms. Rayne looks worried. If Rayne looks worried, the rest of us should be terrified.

"Shit," Skarlyt says, meeting Rayne's eyes. "If that's the case, we need to recruit everyone. Everyone can have two days to get their designs completed before we leave. Axel, can you have a team of your best builders ready to leave by then? We are going to need a lot of houses built in a short time."

"I will make it happen," Axel nods.

I don't know much about the sleuth's alpha, but I heard he was hesitant to join the raid on the Orillia facility. I am relieved to find him so willing to help us prepare the island. It's clear the others feel the same relief.

With our assignments in place, we disperse for the evening. The others are still distracted with their planning when Axel slips my hand into his and tugs me out the patio doors.

Although the gesture is familiar, it is clear as soon as we are alone that he isn't sure how to address me.

"I..." he begins, stepping away and starting to pace. He is so tall and large that each step takes him so out of my reach before another brings him back.

"It's okay, Axel. This situation is...different, but I know you're not like Zeke."

"I appreciate that," he says. "I know this must be difficult."

"I do have a question," I begin.

"Anything," he promises, taking my hands in his.

"Are you—Are you going to reject me too?" My voice is small and laced with fear. I hate sounding so weak. "I just need to know before—"

He pulls me into him and wraps his arms around me.

"I will never reject you. I can't wait to claim you as my mate," he whispers into my ear, and his breath tickles my neck.

My heartbeat speeds at his words and proximity. He's not going to reject me. He wants to claim me.

I pull back from his arms to look into his eyes.

"Can I kiss you?" I ask.

He doesn't answer. He just closes the space between us until his lips are pressed firmly against mine. Heat spreads through my entire body. Our kiss deepens, and he licks my lips. I know he is requesting entrance, and I grant it instantly. Our tongues tangle together and his grip around my waist tightens. A moan issues from deep in my throat.

I wrap my arms around his neck even tighter. My legs lift off the ground, and I'm not sure if he lifted me or caught me. Either way, I wrap my legs around his waist. My entire body is screaming at me, desperate to get closer to him.

Axel is breathing heavily when he forces himself to break the kiss.

"Angel, if we keep this up, we'll end up doing something you're not ready for."

"What if I don't want to stop?" I ask. My entire body is

buzzing with need. Am I rushing to make this man mine before he has the chance to change his mind? Is it just that I've gone too long without sex?

"I don't want to claim you in Alaric's back yard."

A small, irrational part of me feels like this is a rejection. I let my legs slip back to the ground and look toward the ground so he can't see the tears brimming in my eyes.

Axel places a hand under my chin and turns my face up toward him. "This is not a rejection, Opal. Never. I want you more than I have ever wanted anything. But I know my brother hurt you. I don't want you waking up tomorrow morning and regretting anything."

He places a soft kiss on my lips to solidify the words.

"Besides," he smiles and uses the pad of his thumb to outline my lower lip. "We'll be spending a lot of time together over the next few days. If you wake up tomorrow and still want to claim each other, we will."

"Okay," I whisper against his mouth and, once again, merge my lips with his. It's not as hot and heavy as our first kiss, but it is slow and sensual.

We break apart when we hear someone clearing their throat behind us. I turn to see Alaric standing in the doorway with his arms crossed.

"Until tomorrow, angel." Axel gives me another soft kiss on the lips before following Alaric out to the dock.

I am left staring after them with my heart still racing.

I want nothing more than to claim him as mine, but I know he's right.

I need to be sure.

Chapter Eight

Axel

Grudgingly, I walk away from Opal and follow Alaric to the dock. Each step away from her feels more and more difficult.

"What the fuck, Axel?" Alaric growls at me once we hit the dock.

I run a hand through my hair and begin to pace. I know Alaric is probably feeling betrayed because I didn't tell him that Zeke and I share a mate.

In hindsight, I'm not sure why we didn't tell Alaric before. There was a time when Alaric was like another brother. We shared everything. He spent plenty of time with Skarylt, but we spent our fair share of time at the Moon household as well.

After Zeke left—or, I guess more accurately, was captured—I pushed Alaric away as I dealt with my grief. I wish I had reached out to him, and I know he would have dropped everything to help. My pride didn't allow me to let him back in.

Instead, I did the only thing I know how to do: focus on the sleuth and dedicate myself to it. I would say I dedicated my life to it, but I know I didn't really have a life. I ate, slept, and took care of the sleuth. Rinse and repeat. I repeated it every single day for the last six years—ever since I stopped searching for Zeke.

"I don't know..." I try to find the words, but they fall flat. What do you say to the man who was once like a brother to you after you've spent years pushing him away?

"Why didn't you tell me? I understand not wanting to broadcast it to everyone, but I thought we were friends."

I can hear the vulnerability in his voice, and it proves what I already know. When I pushed Alaric away, he felt like he lost both me and my brother.

"I guess—when we were younger, we were worried what you would think. It's not exactly common for shifters to have multiple mates."

"Really?" He is incredulous. "You really think I would have been judgmental? I may have been curious about how it would work, but—come on, Axel—we were best friends. At least, I thought we were."

I stop my pacing to look at him.

"We were kids, Alaric. We were embarrassed of anything that made us different. Now that I'm older, I know you would've been supportive, but I can't change the past. You know now."

Alaric lets out a frustrated growl.

"Yes, I know now. But it would've been nice to know before we brought Opal into our home and sprung this on her. I'm sure she would've appreciated a warning as well."

"You're right." I blow out a breath. "But do you think that Opal would've agreed to be in the same room as me if she did?" I question and he opens and closes his mouth like a fish, narrowing his eyes at me. "For the record that wasn't the reason I didn't tell you or her before today. But now that I'm thinking about it, I have to wonder if the reason I couldn't bring myself to tell her earlier was because of some grand scheme fate had planned..." He stares at me in contemplation, tilting his head as if he's mulling over my words. I step up to him, "Listen, I'm sorry, Alaric. Not only for not telling you tonight, but for pushing you away. I have no excuse for it, only that I wasn't in my right mind."

He claps me on the shoulder.

"You don't have to apologize for pushing me away. I get it. When Darren was taken, I lost my mind. I didn't know what to do. I had Phoebe to help keep me sane, but I would have much rather shut myself away until we got him back. Darren was only gone for days, and Zeke was gone for years. I know it's not the same, but I am closer to understanding what you were going through now."

He's worked through some of his frustration now, and he sounds more like his normal, patient self. I nod my thanks for this admission, but my throat is too clogged with emotion to speak.

"We both made mistakes. I could've fought harder to stay in your life, and you could've reached out to me," he continues. "We're both at fault, but I need to know if you have any more surprises in store for me. Opal is a guest in my home, and she's been through enough already."

I sigh but nod my agreement before walking to the edge of the dock and taking a seat.

"Zeke didn't want to reject Opal. He did it because he thought it was the only way to keep her safe at the time. He knew the hunters were closing in on him, and he assumed they would kill him *and* her if they found them together. He says he hates what he did, but he's glad he kept them from taking her too. A part of me is ecstatic to have my brother and my mate in my life. There was a time when I didn't think I'd find either of them. Another part of me is furious with Zeke and wants to keep Opal as far away from him as possible so he can't hurt her again."

Alaric says nothing, but he comes to sit next to me on the dock and lets his feet hang down over the water.

"I feel like I'm going to have to choose between them..." I pause and take a deep breath. It's hard to admit out loud, but it's the truth. It's been a long time since I've opened up to Alaric, but I know he won't judge me. "I would choose Opal. I know that. I don't want to be placed in that position though. I just don't know how to fix this."

"That's a lot to unpack," he says, taking a deep, steadying breath. "Why does Zeke think Opal would have been captured if she was with him?"

"He was captured two hours after he left her. He said he was coming home to say goodbye to me when he ran into her." I recite what Zeke told me, wondering what Alaric makes of it. Normally, I would have told Alaric that it was Zeke's story to tell when he is ready. I have always tried to respect the privacy of others, but this is chewing me up inside. I need to let it out.

"Well, he could be right. They could've captured them both. They also could've been safe with the sleuth, and we could have beaten those hunters years ago. We can't know for sure, and we can't change the past. Zeke needs to work through that with Opal. You can't force her to forgive him, and you can't force her to stay away. The Mother intended for the three of you to be together. Her will doesn't change because of something stupid your brother did a decade ago."

I go to interrupt him, but Alaric continues. Alphas have a thing for giving advice. It's natural, and I let him get it out.

"You need to talk to Zeke about what he wants. Make sure he is certain about that before you bring Opal anywhere near him. I'll be honest—Opal hasn't always been my favorite person. She's changed a lot in the last few months though, and I guess her attitude makes more sense now."

"What do you mean by that?" I ask, unsure if I am offended on my mate's behalf or not.

"Well, for years, Opal was horrible," Alaric says simply. A growl escapes me as I decide that I am, indeed, offended on my mate's behalf. "She was awful to everyone except Sebastyn, and she acted like she knew they would be mates even though there was no indication of that—even after it was clear he and Sarah had a connection."

Another growl slips from my mouth. I am unsure if I am jealous or just angry at Alaric's tone.

"Calm down," Alaric chuckles. "It was all an act. Now that we know about Zeke, it makes more sense. She didn't take the rejection well, and she latched onto Sebastyn even though—maybe *because*—he wasn't interested. At the time, it seemed like she was punishing herself by throwing herself at this man who didn't want her. I guess she may have been trying to punish herself after all."

I am unsure how to respond to this new information. Alaric lets me settle into the silence. We sit and stare out at the water, and neither of us say anything for a long while.

"Your mate? Your pups?" I probe. We both know I was aware of his mating even though I didn't come to the ceremony, and I have met Phoebe a few times now. However, this is the first casual conversation we've shared in a long time. I am rusty from lack of practice. "You are happy, aren't you?"

"I am," he says with a chuckle. "I really am. Just wait until you meet the boys. They're so smart and strong—so much stronger than they should be at their age."

"What do you mean?" I ask. As he begins explaining, I almost wish I hadn't asked for the story. My bear surfaces, ready to go to battle for those two little boys and, of course, Phoebe. Supernatural or not—mage or not—an abusive husband and father are two things no one should ever have to deal with. The fact that they made it here and are thriving is miraculous.

A pang of guilt hits me as Alaric explains the battles they've had to fight against mages and then hunters, and I internally berate myself.

I've been a shit friend.

Alaric should have been able to depend on me showing up for

him. What did I do when he finally asked for my help? I turned him down. I told him I wanted no part in storming the facility in Orillia.

"You deserve every ounce of happiness, Alaric." I mean every single word that I say once he finishes telling me about their daughter, Aurora. His eyes are still alight with excitement and joy.

"You deserve happiness too, Axel."

"The jury is still out on that one, but I'm going to try to deserve it."

"You will," he says adamantly, and I nod. I do not quite believe him, but I want to.

"I have to go talk to Zeke," I say, and we both rise to our feet.

"I think that's a good idea," Alaric says, patting me on the back as I turn to walk away, feeling a thousand times lighter than I did when I got here. Even though the conversation I need to have with Zeke is looming over my head, getting some of that off my chest was freeing. For the first time in many years, I feel like I have a friend I can depend on again.

As I walk, I think about Opal and the way my body practically vibrated under her touch. I think about how her silvery-blonde hair fell down her back, how her sapphire-blue eyes sparkled in the lights, and how her plump, pink lips popped open when I announced I was her mate.

I have never wanted anyone this much in my entire life. I'm not a virgin, but the way my body reacted to Opal had me feeling like a teenager. The way her petite frame fit perfectly against my large one was like two puzzle pieces fitting together.

How could Zeke have rejected her? I had trouble ripping myself away from her tonight, and that was with the promise of continuing our conversation later.

My mind flits back to what Alaric said about my conversation with Zeke. I need to find out what he wants before I try to force anything to work between all three of us.

Is it fair of me to hope that he wants a second chance with Opal? Is it selfish that I don't want to be forced to choose between the other pieces of my soul?

I still think Zeke was wrong to reject our mate, but I can't discredit the fact that he at least believed he was doing the right thing. After all, he is right. A shudder flows through me at the thought of the hunters kidnapping them both. He hasn't shared much about his time with the hunters, but I am smart enough to know it was worse than he's letting on. Imagining Opal there beside him makes my heart constrict.

I shake those thoughts away and send a silent prayer up to whatever god is listening.

Please don't make me have to choose between the other parts of my soul.

Chapter Nine

Zeke

Axel has been gone an awfully long time.

I wonder if he saw her. If so, is that why he's been gone for so long? Are they claiming each other right now?

Pain shoots through my chest at the thought. I know it is pain that I deserve. It isn't that I don't want them to be together—I do. It is just the thought of being left out that leaves me feeling hollow.

"Zeke? Are you in here?" Axel calls from the front door.

"I'm here," I call back, rushing to meet him at the door. "Did you see her?"

There's a big, stupid grin on his face, and I don't have to wait for him to say yes.

"And?" I prod. It may hurt, but I want to know everything.

"Let's go to the office and talk," he says, avoiding my question. "There are a few things we need to clear the air about." The smile fades from his face as he walks past me.

Great. This is it. This is the moment I lose my brother. I don't blame him. I know he feels like he must choose between Opal and me, but I won't force him to do that. They both deserve to be happy. If they need me to disappear again to make that happen, they can consider it done.

I follow him into the office, and he takes a seat.

"Opal will be visiting the sleuth tomorrow."

"What?" I exclaim.

"I promised her that you wouldn't be here while she was. She's not ready to see you. We're working on a project together. It's a project I think would normally be right up your alley. Until you make it right with her though, you can't be a part of it."

"A project? What project?"

He dives in, explaining the goal of creating an island where we can all be safe from the hunters. I'm not shocked when he says it was Skarlyt's idea. Something that wild and imaginative could only have come from her brain.

After a few probing questions, Axel realizes that I missed out on the whole concept of the prophecy—which is the reason for these preparations. He doesn't know everything, but he explains what he does. It's terrifying. An old enemy? Time for supernaturals to come out of the shadows? What does this mean? Things are changing—not just for supernaturals.

"Shit," I exhale the curse as a sigh. "That is...a lot. You're right; I would love to be a part of it. But...back to Opal. How is she? Is she okay? Do you think she would talk to me?" I spit my questions at him, and he chuckles. That's the first time I've heard him laugh since I got home. Opal is already making him happier, and he's only known her for a few hours.

"She's perfect!" He gets a faraway look on his face, and it makes me both happy and heartsick. "We talked, but we were in a large group. There wasn't much time for us to be alone. I plan on having a conversation with her tomorrow about how we move forward. Before I do that, I need to know what you want."

"What *I* want? What do you mean?" I ask in shock.

Surely, I have nothing to do with whether or not they mate.

Hopefully, they'll both be able to stand being in a room with me someday, but I have no illusions about my place in their pairing now. There is no way Opal wants me now. Not after the pain I put her through—not now that my body is covered in scars.

"I need to know where you stand. If you were given the chance to make things right with Opal, what would you do? She can't go through that hurt again. I won't allow it. If you plan on sticking to the rejection, you'll have to leave."

I can see how hard it is for him to say the words. Honestly, I had expected him to just tell me to leave. I didn't expect him to give me a chance to make it right.

"If Opal can find it in her heart to give me another chance, I will spend the rest of my life making it up to her. I will do everything in my power to be worthy of being her mate," I swear solemnly to him. He can hear the honesty in my voice and the corners of his mouth tilt upward.

I guess I said the right thing.

"That's exactly what I wanted to hear. I'm not saying it's going to be easy. You're going to have to work, but Opal asked about your reason for rejecting her. I would like to explain it to her if that's okay with you. I don't think you were right, but I do understand your perspective. Maybe hearing it will bring her some peace."

I nod in agreement, but I don't think I have many options. Did I do the right thing? At the time, it seemed like the only way. Both Axel and my mother seem convinced that we could have protected her together.

"Let's go for a run. It's been too long since our bears were together," Axel says, sounding genuinely excited for the first time since I was rescued.

"Uh..." I begin. "About that..."

"What?" he asks, concern lining his features. "You said your bear wouldn't let you shift, but I figured he would reconsider now that you've admitted you want to make things right with Opal."

93

"It's maybe worse than you're thinking it is," I admit without meeting his eyes. "I'm pretty sure that my bear is feral. If I shift—more like if he *lets* me shift—I won't be able to control him. He will probably destroy anything in his path, and I don't think I'll be able to shift back."

"You said he wouldn't let you shift. You didn't say anything about him being feral," Axel raises his voice.

"In his mind, I've kept him away from his mate and caged up for eleven years," I whisper the words to counter my brother's shouts and pray our mother can't hear. "I was ashamed. I hurt my mate; I destroyed my bear. Those are the two things I'm supposed to protect and cherish. I don't know how to fix it. I don't get anything from him except growls and snarls."

"You're going to shift, and I'm going to talk to your bear." Axel slams his hands on the desk as he stands. I go to interrupt him, but he holds up an imperious hand to stop me. Despite the situation, it reminds me achingly of our father. "We will shift in the cells, so you can't hurt anyone. We share a soul; our bears share a soul. I don't think it's possible for yours to hurt mine. Besides, being home may just be the thing to fix him."

Although I don't have much faith in this plan, it does make sense. More than that, it is the only option left for me. I nod and follow him downstairs.

My mother always insisted the cells in our basement were an unnecessary precaution. There's always an occasional rogue shifter who can't be trusted or children who cannot yet control their shifting who need somewhere to go for everyone's safety. It's evident that these cells haven't seen much use in the last eleven years, but they have been kept clean and free of dust. I had worried that hearing one of those heavy doors locking behind me would trigger panic, but these cells are so different from the ones the hunters used that I am able to ignore the similarities.

Once the door is closed behind me, I try to calm myself

enough to attempt the shift. It's like there is an atrophied muscle there I have forgotten how to use. I try to remember how it once felt to shift, and I try to focus on that memory. Now that we are in the safety of our own home, the change comes easier than I expected. Still, it comes at a high price.

Just as I had feared, my bear immediately pushes me to the background and takes complete control. I am cut off from the world around me. I can't see or hear anything that is happening because my bear has sole use of my eyes and ears.

When a shifter takes the form of their animal, both halves are usually present. Neither man nor animal has complete control unless it is freely given. When we hunt, the human will hand the reigns over to their animal because a bear is better at grabbing mouthfuls of fish from a stream. For normal shifters, both elements are always present.

I, however, am about a decade past "normal." When I shift, my bear effectively pushes me to the back of his mind and seals me up behind a brick wall.

All I can do is pray that he doesn't hurt anyone.

Chapter Ten

Opal

A night with the girls was exactly what I needed. I haven't had that much fun in years. It got off to a rocky start because I had to explain my history with Zeke. Only a few of my friends had any clue about it before the meeting at the alpha house.

"But Axel—the good twin—said that Zeke—the possibly evil twin—had a good reason for rejecting you?" Rayne clarifies once I am finished with my retelling.

"He said Zeke *thought* he had a good reason," Sarah corrects. "He didn't say it actually *was* a good reason."

"There aren't many reasons I would judge good enough," Sarah adds, crossing her slim arms.

They begin throwing out reasons why Zeke may have rejected me and ran away, but none of them seem to fit the little bit that I know. Did he choose to reject me once he realized I was a witch? Some shifters are weird about that. Was he not willing to settle down in Parry Sound? Skarlyt—who knew the twins when they were young—verifies that Zeke was always eager to travel far from home and chafed under the idea of taking on the alpha role later in life.

"He ended up at the Orillia facility, right?" Charleigh asks. "Do we know when?"

"I could probably locate the information when I get back." Rayne shrugs her slim shoulders. "Hunters are shit at keeping records, but they do try occasionally."

"You think he rejected his mate because he knew he was getting kidnapped soon?" Sarah does not sound impressed with this idea, but I try to imagine the situation anyway.

Charleigh just raises her hands in a peaceful gesture.

"It's just an idea," she says. "I wouldn't want hunters anywhere near my mate—whether or not I had just found him myself."

Could I forgive Zeke if this was his reason? He knew he was in danger, so he needed to get away from me. When he got taken by the hunters, we wouldn't have had a chance to return and explain. If that was the case, why didn't he just leave? Why did he have sex with me first?

The more I revisit that memory, the more I realize that he may have been trying to leave. He tried to get away from me, didn't he? I remember seeing him clutching the tree behind him like an anchor. Was he trying to get away before the mating bond could hit us both with its full force? I was the one who kept walking toward him. I was the one who had put my hand on his face and practically dared him to kiss me.

I have to stop revisiting this train of thought. I'm indulging the hope that his rejection was justified, but there's no real evidence that is the case. I'm already acting as if there was some noble reason behind his actions. Until I speak with him or Axel, though, that is nothing but a wild hope that will crush me when I realize it's impossible. No, until I speak to either of them, I'm not going to allow myself to hope. Not when it comes to Zeke.

My friends must have seen my mind wandering toward these unfriendly waters because they try to distract me after a few minutes of conjecture and reflection. They were quick to change the subject to happier things. It turns out, Rayne and I are the only ones who are not knocked up, so we are the only ones who can actually drink. The others still enjoyed themselves, and they seemed to find us to be more and more hilarious the drunker we got.

Even my hangover this morning can't dim the happiness flowing out of me. For the first time in what feels like forever, I'm happy. Truly happy. The pain from Zeke is still there, but the anticipation and excitement of being near Axel drowns it out. Today, I get to spend the entire day with him.

As I shower, the question I wasn't ready to answer the night before burns in the back of my mind. Do I still want to claim Axel? After an evening of drinking with the girls—well Rayne—and a night full of X-rated dreams starring a certain alpha, the answer is yes. A thousand times, yes. Given the circumstances, it may seem sudden, but the events with the mages and hunters have shown me life is too short.

As I am stepping out of the shower, a knock on the door startles me.

"One minute," I yell, quickly wrapping myself in a towel and rushing to the door.

I have a full day ahead of me, but I'm not expecting anyone. I peek through the peephole, expecting to see someone from the coven or pack. The last thing I expect to see is Axel, made small and distorted by the glass, pacing back and forth on my front porch.

"Hi," I say, swinging the door open and greeting him with a genuine smile.

He turns to look at me, and his mouth drops wide open in shock. He doesn't respond. His eyes just roam my body, his gaze full of a hungry heat. I glance down, realize I'm still only wearing a towel, and giggle.

My laugh seems to snap him out of his trance, and his eyes snap up to mine.

"Uh, hi. Sorry, if I interrupted you." He shuffles from foot to foot, looking nervous.

"No worries. I was just getting ready to come see you." I open the door wider and gesture for him to come inside. He looks unsure but ultimately decides to follow. I head to the kitchen and start preparing a pot of coffee. I'll have a moment to get dressed and dry off while it's percolating. "Is there a reason you came over? It's fine, but I know how to find the sleuth."

"Yes...well...the thing is..." Axel stumbles over his words.

When I hear just how much he's struggling, I place the coffee back on the counter, walk over to him, and place my hand on his arm.

"You can tell me anything," I promise.

He glances down at my hand and back up to my eyes, before pulling his other arm up to rub the back of his neck. For such a big, burly man, he sure is cute when he's nervous.

He clears his throat. "I was hoping to ask for your help. Now that I'm here, I don't know if it's a good idea."

"Of course, I will help you with whatever you need," I tell him honestly, feeling a little concerned. What could he possibly need my help with? Why is he so hesitant to ask?

He steps back and begins to pace again. "I know, but—it's for Zeke."

The sound of his name doesn't hurt as bad as it did yesterday, but it still sends a pain shooting through my chest. I take a few deep breaths to center myself.

"What's wrong? Is he okay?" I am pissed that he rejected me, and I want to hate him. Still, after the conversation with Axel last night, I just can't find it in me to let him suffer.

"It's his bear. He's gone feral." Axel blows out a deep breath and stops pacing to take a seat on one of the stools at the counter. He places his head in his hands. "He warned me that his bear had gone feral after rejecting you—he warned me that he couldn't control him, but I didn't listen. I convinced him to shift last night. He was right. His bear immediately took over and tried to attack me. I've never seen anything like it. Because we are both alphas, I couldn't even do anything to stop it."

Axel looks both heartbroken and guilt-ridden. It's clear he was certain he had the situation under control. Holy shit, though, he did not.

I know shifters can go feral if the human makes a decision the animal doesn't agree with. That is what happened to Kirnon after he rejected Skarlyt. He could barely force himself to shift, and his wolf had become sickly and weak. Honestly, it hadn't even crossed my mind that the same thing could be happening to Zeke.

"What can I do?"

Axel looks up to meet my eyes; he is clearly surprised at my answer.

"You really are an angel."

I feel a blush creep up my neck at his words, and I wave him off.

"I'm no angel," I assure him. "No matter what Zeke did to me, his bear doesn't deserve to be in pain because of it."

I try to justify my need to help him by saying it's for his bear's sake. If I am being honest, though, I want to help the man too. Zeke looked so broken the last time I saw him, and—rejected or not—it hurt my heart to see him like that. If I'm going to cement the mating bond with Axel, I need to get used to seeing his brother. I would never make Axel choose between the two of us.

"I was hoping you would have a potion or something that could calm his bear long enough to let Zeke shift back."

I jump at his words.

"Wait. Do you mean Zeke is still a bear?"

"Yes. He's locked in the cells, so he is not a danger to anyone. Well—anyone but himself."

I rush around the counter and sprint to my room. Once I close the door behind me, I drop the towel and use it to dry the excess water from my legs and torso. I had planned to dress sexy for Axel today, but I don't have the time now that I know Zeke is in trouble. I throw on whatever clothes I find laying around and pull a brush through my still-wet hair.

"Come on," I call out to him as I open my bedroom door and head to my workroom in the back.

He follows me and exhales his admiration when he takes in the room. My workroom is nothing special—definitely not as amazing as Constance or Skarlyt's, but it's mine. I don't do nearly as many experimental or crucial spells, so I have the luxury of keeping this room cozier and more comfortable than either of them.

The back wall is lined with bookshelves that are filled to the brim. To anyone else, it would look like they are just haphazardly piled together, but I can find anything I need in those books. A long counter runs through the center of the room, adorned with a variety of beakers, scales, measuring spoons, and mortar and pestle. The other two walls are lined with plants and ingredients—both fresh and dried—that I may need.

I select one of the books that specializes in shifters and flip through the pages. I don't know exactly what I'm looking for, but I'll know it when I see it.

Out of the corner of my eye, I watch as Axel walks around the room, trying to take everything in.

"Ah-ha," I say as I find exactly what I'm looking for. "To tame a beast."

To tame a beast. Heal a disconnect between human and shifter.

- *Dandelion Root*
- *Rose Petals*
- *Butterfly wings*
- *Honey*
- *Lavender*
- *Oregano Oil*

Bring water to a slow boil.
Blend all ingredients together thoroughly with mortar and pestle.
Slowly add dry ingredients to boiled water.
Let simmer for fifteen minutes. Infuse it with your magic and intent.
Strain into a cup using cheesecloth.
Do not discard strained ingredients. For best result, the shifter should ingest the entire contents of the cup and then chew on the herbs. Potion should be effective within minutes and last at least twenty-four hours.

I begin gathering supplies and begin heating the water. At first, Axel seems anxious to help, but he eventually realizes he doesn't know where anything is and settles into a chair by the window.

I crush all the dry ingredients before adding the oregano oil and honey. I mix the combination until it becomes a paste. Once the water is boiling, I use a spatula—it has long been repurposed from kitchen use—to add in the contents, turn my burner down to simmer, and let it combine.

"We have to wait about fifteen minutes until this is ready," I tell Axel.

"Are you sure this will work?"

I give him a small smile. Do I know this will work? No. But I'm hopeful.

"Any real witch will tell you nothing is ever certain. I've never done anything like this, but it should work."

"It won't hurt him, right?" he asks.

"It shouldn't hurt him," I try to sound reassuring. "If it doesn't work, it will only stay in his system for a day. Then, we can ask Constance or Skarlyt for help. The hardest part is going to be convincing a bear to drink it."

"I didn't think about that." He begins to pace again, his earlier nervousness returning with a vengeance.

"Don't worry about it," I instruct. "I have a plan."

I do have a plan. Is it stupid? Absolutely. Could I get hurt? Probably. Will it work? I'm pretty confident it will.

"What is your plan?" Axel asks, sounding suspicious.

"Well—his bear is upset because he rejected me, right?" I ask and wait for his nod to continue. "Then, theoretically, he'll be on his best behavior in my presence. Hopefully, it'll last long enough for one of us to pour the potion down his throat."

"No! Absolutely not," he looks aghast by this suggestion. "I'm not going to let you get anywhere near him in this state."

I walk over to Axel and place my hands in his.

"I trust you to protect me, and I need you to trust me. I believe this will work." He doesn't respond, but he pulls me into him and wraps his strong arms around me.

After a few moments, I step away.

"I have to stir the potion," I explain regretfully.

I walk back to the cauldron and stir the contents, letting a steady stream of magic seep out of me. I focus my intent on wanting Zeke to get better—even if it is just so he can tell me his side of the story.

I then think of Axel—not Zeke—as I pour more positive magic into it. I could try to focus on Zeke, but I am sure some measure of negativity would taint my magic. Even a small amount of negativity during the infusion could be disastrous. No. Instead, I think of Axel. The way tingles slide up my arm when he touches my hand. The heat and longing in his eyes when he gazes at me. The way my heartbeat races when he's nearby. The way he is desperate to make his brother better.

I open my eyes as the timer goes off and proceed to carefully strain the potion. I take a small whiff, and I'm glad to find the oregano oil seems to be effectively masked by the sweetness of the honey. Honestly, that may be its only purpose in the spell.

"Okay, we're ready." I tell Axel as I finish sealing the potion in a thermos and spooning what is left of the damp, loose ingredients into a container.

Together, we head out the door and begin our trek to Axel's home.

"Is there anything I should know before we get there?" I ask.

"Only that my mom is extremely excited to meet you and will probably want to keep you all to herself," he chuckles.

"Do you think she'll like me?" I hate how vulnerable I sound. The version of myself that I spent the last eleven years building would never have asked that question. The real me—the me I am trying to be now—is absolutely terrified of making a bad impression.

He stops in his tracks, takes my hands in his, and waits until I meet his eyes.

"She's going to absolutely love you."

"There's something I should probably tell you too," I say and look down at the ground.

I don't give him the option to respond before spitting it out. "I can do earth magic, but my real gift is the sight. When you touched me last night, I caught glimpses of your past." He looks a little panicked, so I push forward. "I didn't see anything bad, but it's not something I can control all the time."

He relaxes a little, but there's a tension between us that wasn't there before. Hardly anyone knows about my visions, but this is the same reaction I get from most people. Nobody wants someone in their head.

"What exactly do you mean by 'the sight?'" he asks.

"It's hard to explain, and it's a rare gift. If I touch a person or object, I may catch glimpses of their past or future. I can't choose what I see, and I can't really choose when I see it. I spent years training so I could stop invading the privacy of my family and friends, but I've been losing control lately. Last night, I saw three visions of you in the past." One in his beautiful eyes lets me know he's feeling violated. Whether or not it's intentional, no one wants their privacy invaded like that.

"I'm sorry," I whisper, releasing his hands and looking down at the ground.

A couple heartbeats later, his hand moves to my chin, bringing it up so our eyes meet.

"It's all right, Opal. I was a little shocked, but I trust you. It's strange, but I feel like I've known you forever and trust you with my life. I guess that's what happens when you meet your mate. I only ask that you tell me what you see so we can discuss it. There are parts of my past...I would prefer you not to see."

"I feel the same way about you, and I promise I'll tell you about anything I see." I go up on my tip toes and place a soft kiss on his lips. "There are parts of my past I'm not proud of either, so I would never judge you."

"The past is the past. All that matters is our future. Whoever you were—or I was—in the past doesn't matter."

"Thank you," I say, my heart overflowing at his understanding words.

As we turn and continue toward the sleuth, I describe my visions from the night before to him. Although the one with Alaric causes him to wince, my description of the scene between him and Zeke when they were kids makes him laugh.

For the first time since Zeke's rejection, I don't fear seeing him. I know it's still going to hurt, but I finally feel strong enough to get through it.

Was it only four days ago that I thought I wouldn't survive seeing him again? It's incredible how much has changed in such a short time. For the first time in eleven years, I'm looking forward to my future—a future that includes a caring mate and possibly even children. They're two wonderful things I thought I would never have. All we need to do now is claim one another.

"By the way, I do still feel the same way this morning," I say with a small wink in his direction.

He looks confused for a moment before he seems to realize my meaning. "Really?"

I stop once again and turn to face him. He looks wary but full of hope.

"Really," I assure him. "I've had time to think about it, and I am sure. Let's go take care of your brother. Then, we can try to sneak off somewhere private."

A low growl escapes him before he kisses me, lifting me off the ground and backing me up against a tree. It reminds me of my time with Zeke, but that memory brings hope instead of pain in this moment. Maybe I can replace that bad memory with a good one.

I wrap my legs around his waist, grinding against him as we kiss. Soon, we are pawing at each other's clothes. We are both desperate to feel the other's bare skin.

Way too soon, he's pulling back.

"As much as I hate to say this, we really need to go help Zeke."

I nod and lower my legs. He supports me for another moment before making sure I drop to the ground gently.

"We do," I agree with a smirk. "But after..."

"Immediately after," he cuts me off with the promise. "Immediately after, I'm whisking you away to somewhere we will not be disturbed."

He places one last kiss on my lips.

With a reason to hurry, we speed toward the sleuth.

We've got some work to do before I can make this man mine.

Chapter Eleven

Opal

I am not sure what I expected when Axel told me about Zeke's condition, but I am not imaginative enough to have anticipated the huge, feral black bear throwing himself against the bars of the cell. Although the walls seem sturdy, he is attacking them with self-destructive fervor that makes me nervous. He is either going to seriously hurt himself or break through the bars that contain him. I am not sure which will happen first.

I stop in the doorway, staring at the scene before me. I wish I could say I am unafraid, but it would be a lie.

The bear begins growling and snarling through the bars as soon as we enter the room, but his attention seems to be focused on Axel. After a moment, he raises his snout and sniffs the air curiously. He spins away from his brother and locks eyes with me. I suck in a breath when I see how much pain is in his gaze.

Without my permission, my body begins to move.

"Wait," Axel says, grabbing my arm and pushing me behind him. Although I cannot see beyond Axel's broad back, the growls and bangs coming from the cell indicate that Zeke's bear doesn't seem to like that at all.

"It's okay," I assure him. "He won't hurt me. Don't ask me how I know that—because I have no idea."

Axel looks at me skeptically but nods.

I reach up and place a kiss on his cheek before I walk around him and toward Zeke. When his eyes find mine once more, he calms. The feral glaze in his eyes begins to fade.

"Hey, big guy. You're not going to hurt me, are you?" I say softly, keeping my arms out in front of me. It is the same way I approached Zeke that night eleven years ago.

His big, meaty head shakes from left to right, and I shoot a triumphant look in Axel's direction. Once again, the bear growls as soon as my attention is pulled away.

"Now, you stop that," I scold him. "That's your brother."

The bear lowers his head slightly as if he is sorry. Since he is a bear, I can't be sure how sorry he actually is. I get close enough to the cell that I can feel the hot air huffing out of his mouth and nose with each breath before I stop.

"I need you to do something for me," I say to the bear, maintaining eye contact. Although my instincts are begging me to run, I can't help but admire how beautiful his large, intelligent eyes are. He tilts his head in question, and I continue. "I need you to give Zeke back, please."

I figure it's worth a shot, but the bear just swipes a paw on the ground and lets off a low growl.

Guess that's a no.

"You are beautiful and strong, but I can't understand you. You want to fix what Zeke broke, right?" I ask. I'm not even sure that is what I want, but I think this is a line of thought the bear will understand. I know each hour spent trapped inside his feral bear makes it less and less likely Zeke will ever be able to shift back.

The bear inclines his enormous head in agreement, but he shows no signs of shifting back.

"If Zeke doesn't come back, I will never be able to understand you," I explain. I reach my hand through the bars and am surprised to see how violently they are trembling. I hear Axel suck in a breath at my movement, but I don't stop. The bear looks at my hand and back at me before rubbing his face over it. "I need to give you a name. I can't keep thinking of you as just 'the bear.'"

I take a moment to enjoy the feeling of his coarse fur under my hand as he encourages me to pet his cheeks and ears.

"Can I call you Shadow? Because your fur is so black it almost blends in with the dark?" He must like the name because he sticks out his tongue and licks my hand, leaving a glob of saliva behind. "Ew, Shadow, that's gross." I pull my hand back and wipe it on my pants.

"Since you won't give Zeke back, will you take this potion I made for you? It will make you feel better." Shadow looks at me with something like confusion before making a humming sound that I think is agreement.

With slow, calculated movements, I reach into my bag and pull out the thermos. I pour some of the potion into the cap and hold it out to him.

"You may not like the taste," I warn apologetically. "But I tried really hard to make it for you."

He makes a few tentative sniffs, and I wonder how far I can push his desire to not offend me. I don't know what the potion will taste like, but I know bears don't tend to eat a lot of lavender and oregano. He looks at me again before he dives in with his huge tongue, lapping up all the contents.

It's not long until the potion starts to work. The bear's body slowly sinks to the ground—becoming tired and calm—and transitions back until there is only Zeke left, naked and alone, in the cell. I can see now what I had guessed before. He has lost some weight during his time with the hunters, and he looks weaker than when I last saw him. Still, seeing his body makes mine light up with lust.

"Opal," Zeke whispers weakly and reaches a hand toward me.

I knew this would hurt, but my name on his lips triggers something with an intensity I had not expected. I step back from the bars like they've burnt me. I thought I was ready to hear his side of the story, but I guess I was wrong.

"I can't—" I begin, turning to Axel with tears springing to my eyes. "Let him out and take me home. Please."

As if he expected this, Axel is already stepping forward to help me get up the stairs and away as quickly as possible.

"Opal, I'm sorry." Zeke's voice is desperate and pained as he calls out. I turn to look at him one last time.

"Zeke," Axel growls a warning to his brother.

"I'm not ready," I explain. "I can't talk to you—yet. Please, leave me alone until—it hurts too much to look at you."

I do not know what I want or what I am capable of living with, so I cannot tell either of them what I need coherently. I turn to the door and head back the way I came.

Once I am outside, I take a moment to breathe in the clear, fresh air and center myself. I know Axel will need a minute to release Zeke. I'm sure Zeke will want a shower and to sleep in a bed—not a cell. Besides, I am not ready to speak to Zeke; that doesn't mean Axel needs to ignore his brother.

"Ready, angel?" Axel asks, coming up behind me a couple minutes later.

"More than ready," I agree. With that, we walk hand in hand toward my home. We were meant to spend the day with the sleuth, compiling a list of requirements for their part of the island. I didn't anticipate how seeing Zeke would affect me though, and I no longer have the energy or mindset to do the work.

Before I know it, we are walking up the front porch to my house. The trip through the woods passes so quickly that it may have never even happened. My mind is completely void of every-thing and anything. I guess that is better than me focusing on what just happened with Zeke.

While I punch the code into the door's electric lock, Axel shuffles quietly behind me. As I open the door and turn to him, I can see the uncertainty written all over his face. Should he come inside? Should he just tell me goodbye?

For a moment, I consider those options too. Do I want him to stay? Or do I want him to go? That thought causes a wave of loneliness through me. I definitely don't want him to go.

"Do you want to come in?" I ask, walking through the door and leaving it open for him.

"I wasn't sure if you'd want me to." His voice is low and devoid of his usual confidence. Do I somehow have the ability to make this big, strong alpha unsure of himself?

"Of course, I do. Besides, we are supposed to be figuring out what the bears will need on the island." His shoulders slump, so I quickly continue. "Working together will give us a chance to get to know each other better."

I give him a bright smile. He returns it, but it doesn't quite reach his eyes. I feel guilty, but I know in my heart that it's not my fault. He's just feeling frustrated with the situation that we find ourselves in.

Taking his hand in mine, I lead us toward the kitchen, and he gently kicks the front door closed with his foot.

"Would you like something to eat? I'm sure I have something." I busy myself searching the cabinets. Being in such close quarters with Axel makes my body burn with desire. Proof of it is lining my panties, and I'm sure he can smell my need with every breath he takes.

I quickly gather boxes of crackers from the cupboards and bricks of cheese and packages of deli meat from the fridge.

"Here let me help." He comes around the kitchen island, closing the minimal space between us and taking the cheese, cutting board, and knife. He slices the cheese as I place the crackers on a tray and separate and roll the deli meat. Within minutes, we have filled the tray. I wonder briefly if we'll be able to finish it all. Who am I kidding? I've seen shifters eat before. I know this will all be gone soon.

"All right," I begin, grabbing a pen and notebook while Axel moves the tray to the table. "If you had to pick, what's the one thing the bears need on the island?"

"Honestly, we don't need much." He shrugs his broad shoulders. "Obviously, an area that is densely covered in trees would be best. A stream or river with running water would be nice."

I write that down with some stars beside it.

"How many bears are in your sleuth? How big of an area will you need?" That's the part of Skarlyt's plan I am the least sure of. If she plans to eventually bring all supernaturals to the island—which I know she does—we're going to run out of space.

"We have two hundred and fifty-two adults and twenty-three cubs right now. A few of our women are pregnant, so that number will grow." He pauses and runs a hand over his beard. "I would think about twenty acres would be enough...That way we have room as we expand."

My eyes go wide at that thought. Twenty acres is a sizable chunk of land. If each of the factions need that much space, the island would have to be massive.

"Do you think the rest of the shifters are going to need that much space?"

He nods as he sandwiches pieces of cheese between two crackers.

"Probably. We are all used to having plenty of space. In all honesty, we're going to need an island approximately the size of Cuba—if not bigger—to accommodate everyone. I thought Skarlyt was crazy when she brought it up. I've been thinking about it though, and I think it could work if we design it right."

"Okay," I prompt. "How do we design it right?"

He takes the pen and paper from me and begins to draw an outline.

"Well, if we figure that each group is going to need approximately twenty acres...The smartest thing to do is design the island to have at least five acres of farmland between each faction. We will need the space to grow our own supply of food, and it will leave a buffer area between everyone when we get fed up with each other."

I watch as he draws a large shape and uses lines and circles to break it up into equal sections. His hand moves confidently across the paper, and I can tell he knows what he's doing. He even makes marks to show where each small village could go.

"I am assuming we'll be able to continue altering the island after we get there?" He waits for me to nod before continuing. "I don't know much about geography or geology, but we'll need some kind of variation—hills, valleys, and mountains—to keep us from washing away each time it rains."

I watch in complete awe as he continues. He seems to get lost in it. He pencils in notes about how thick the land would need to be—some vampires prefer to live underground—and where fresh-water streams could begin.

"This is amazing, Axel. Where did you learn to do that?"

He blinks up at me in surprise.

"It's what we do for money," he explains. "We run a construction company. We mainly build for other supernaturals. Human builders don't know about some of the things we need. Vampires need secure basements; bear shifters need larger and wider doorways."

"I didn't realize. How many homes do you think you can build in the time we have?"

He looks down at the drawing and calculates for a moment.

"If we have all hands on deck and work section by section, we can at least have temporary housing for everyone within the week.

It won't be perfect, but it'll keep us safe. We can complete the rest once we're safely on the island." He looks back up at me. "What we really need to focus on is making sure the basics are covered for the—more-human among us. We need to ensure there is running water, plumbing, and solar electricity. Most supernaturals would be able to survive in tents for an extended period. The vampires and witches would probably not enjoy it though."

"You're amazing," I say, rising and stopping in front of him. He glides the chair backward, giving me room to wrap my arms around him.

He grabs my waist and pulls me forward. I accept the invitation and straddle him, a leg on either side of the chair. He leans into my neck and takes a deep inhale.

"So are you," he whispers, pressing a light kiss on my neck.

My entire body shivers at the touch. I pull my head back, not giving him a chance to say anything before I merge my lips with his and snake my tongue out to taste him. A low moan rumbles between us, and he pulls me closer.

I remove my arms from his neck, sliding my hands down his chest. I savor the feeling of each hard, well-defined muscle as my touch travels across his torso. When I reach the bottom, I grasp the bottom of his shirt and raise it, breaking our kiss just long enough to pull it over his head. Now that I have a clear view of his physique, another shiver rolls through me. My tongue darts out to lick my lips, already anticipating tracing each muscle and tattoo on his body.

"Your turn," Axel says, pulling my shirt up and over my head.

Funny. I didn't even feel his hands move.

I watch his eyes flare with heat as he takes in the upper half of my body. Instantly, his open mouth connects with my breasts. He pulls my bra to the side, capturing my nipple in his mouth and sucking. My back arches—my body begging me to get closer to him. Each flick of his tongue makes my core throb with need.

I grind against him with vigor. The expert use of his mouth on my nipple has me increasing my speed.

Breathless, he breaks away.

"Where's the bed?"

I can't seem to find any words, so I point to the bedroom. He lifts me easily, so I'm still straddling him as he carries me to my room. Once we are inside, he kicks the door closed and gently lays me on the bed.

"Beautiful," he says as he reaches for the waistband of my pants. He shimmies them down with ease.

Once they're off, he throws them into the corner and begins kissing and licking up my leg. More wetness pools in my panties as I anticipate him reaching the apex of my legs.

"Is this all for me?" he asks, his words rumbling against the fabric covering my core.

Still unable to speak, I nod my head yes.

He hooks a finger under my panties and swipes it through my folds before bringing it to his mouth.

"Delicious. Just like I knew you would be." Watching him suck my juices off his finger has me wishing that it was me he was licking rather than his finger.

Before long, my wish is granted. He uses his teeth to rip the panties off my body. They may be ruined, but I don't mind. He acts as if the material is his enemy, so it is mine as well.

"Are you sure you want this, angel?" he growls at me. He is near enough that I can feel his words teasing my skin, but he has yet to kiss me the way I need him to.

I nod my head.

"Words, angel. I need your words. Once I start, I will not be able to stop until you are mine in every way."

Goddess, if that is not the hottest thing I've ever heard.

"Yes," I pant. "Please. Yes."

As soon as the word is out of my mouth, his tongue reaches my center. He slowly thrusts it in and out of me. One hand supports my leg while the other rises, his thumb finding and slowly circling my clit.

A feeling of pure euphoria hits me, and I begin to move my body in time with the thrusts of his tongue. My hands ball into the fabric of the bed under me.

I scream his name as my pussy clenches his tongue, coating it.

He waits until the spasms slow, before rising and removing his pants. As his cock springs free, I lick my lips. Goddess, this man is perfect. His cock has a slight curve upward, and it excites me beyond belief knowing that he's going to hit my G-spot with each thrust.

He lines himself up with me and pauses, leaning forward to meet my eyes.

"Last chance, angel."

"I want you, Axel. Make me yours," I whisper.

He enters me without further preamble. He sheaches himself to the hilt in one thrust, and I cry out. He stays buried inside me for a long moment. He does not move, allowing me to acclimate to his impressive size.

Goddess, I need him to move. I shift my hips and the muscles inside, trying to push myself up and down his cock. He lets off a low, warning growl.

"I need you to move," I snarl, sounding just as animalistic as he does. I am delirious with the need raging inside of me.

He places his lips on mine for a couple of heartbeats, before fulfilling my request. He begins hammering in and out of me like he's possessed. It's as if he's in a trance—unable to stop until he's made me his.

With each thrust, his perfectly shaped cock hits my G-spot, quickly pushing me over the edge again and again.

I feel my magic rise, tingling as it forces its way to the surface. For a moment, I am panicked. This is when Zeke pushed me away.

I look up into Axel's eyes as I place my hands on his chest. I watch as his canines elongate, ready to claim his mate. I let my head fall to the side, giving him access.

As his teeth break my skin, my magic flares, marking him as ours, and we both tumble over the edge one last time.

As the mating bond snaps into place, I feel an emptiness I was unaware of begin to fill. There's an immediate comfort and familiarity that settles between us.

Axel pulls his teeth from my neck, licking the mark, and my entire body trembles. Even after the mind-altering sex we just had, my body is ready for more.

"Mate," he growls.

"Yes. Mate," I whisper back, giving him a soft kiss on his lips.

He removes himself from me and rushes to the bathroom. He returns with a wet washcloth. After cleaning me up, he climbs into the bed behind me, wrapping his big arms around my body.

I can feel that hole inside of my soul become less gapingly empty. Still, it is not entirely full. It's as if there's a space reserved for Zeke.

I finally have my mate.

But not the only one. A small voice filters through my mind.

As I drift to sleep, nearly content in the arms of Axel, my final thought before closing my eyes is about Zeke.

Can he fix what he broke? If not, will this hole be a permanent fixture in my soul?'

Chapter Twelve

Zeke

I watch Opal walk through the doorway and up the stairs. To say I am surprised to be back in my human form is an understatement. My bear pushed me so far down that I thought it would be impossible for me to regain control.

The fact that Opal was here to see me shift back is even more shocking.

Shadow, my bear says through our bond. I almost weep when I hear him speak. It's been years since he has done anything except growl at me.

Shadow? What is that? I question.

He sighs in exasperation. It's clear he still isn't too pleased with me.

Shadow is the name my mate gave me. His chest puffs out with pride.

What? When did she give you a name? I am so confused and still reeling from shifting moments ago.

He allows me to see his memories from the time I spent insensible inside him. He shares his memories of Opal, and jealousy rises inside me. She touched him—petted him even. She didn't flinch when he growled, but she does each time she hears my voice. He's telling the truth; she even gave him a name. It means he has a name she can say without a tremble in her voice, and I do not.

I know it's irrational to feel jealous of a part of myself, but I've been without my bear for so long that it's hard to feel like *he* is still *me*.

I need to fix this, I tell him.

Yes. Mate doesn't like you. He says this simply, as if it is well-known. If hearing him say it breaks my heart, he doesn't seem concerned. He curls up in the corner of my mind and goes to sleep with a peaceful look on his face. It's the most settled he's been since that night eleven years ago.

"Are you okay?" Axel's voice startles me, and I open my eyes to find him at the door of the cell with a ring of keys.

"I think so," I nod. "I feel like myself, and my bear seems to be content for now."

He watches me for a moment before placing the key in the lock.

"I need to fix this, Axel. I know she said to give her time but..." I begin, but he fixes me with a glare.

"You have hurt her deeply. It will be a miracle if she even allows me to bond with her..." He looks defeated, and his shoulders slump.

"She will. You didn't hurt her. She knows that. Just promise me that you will take care of her."

"I will," he says with determination before walking out of the room.

With the cell unlocked, I am free to leave, but I don't want to. I slide down the bars and settle on the cold, concrete floor. What if I can't fix what I broke? What if Opal will never forgive me? I place my head in my hands and cry until my eyes are red and puffy.

"Enough of that," my mother scolds from the door. "Stop

feeling sorry for yourself and show your mate why she should bond with you. No one wants a mating bond with someone wallowing in self-pity. No one can fix this but you."

I raise my eyes to find her sitting on the bottom stair patiently. I do not know how long she's been there waiting for me. Part of me is glad the years haven't changed my mother much. She's equal parts comforting and challenging. There is part of me that wants my mother to sympathetically pat my back and bring me cookies, and there is a part of her that will. Still, there is a larger part of both of us that needs her to challenge me, point out my failings, and push me forward.

I am the only one who can fix this. Opal said she's not ready to talk, and that's fine. When she is ready, I need to make sure that I am strong enough to explain everything without breaking down.

"You're right, Mom," I say and get up off the ground. I give her a kiss on the cheek and a hand to help her up as I pass.

She gives me a soft smile and follows me up the stairs.

"First order of business," she announces, handing me a towel. "Shower. You stink."

"Yes, ma'am," I say, turning to the bathroom.

"When you're done, meet me in the kitchen and we will see what we can do," she calls just before I close the door.

With a little extra pep in my step, I go through the motions of grooming and cleaning myself. I wasn't in that cell for long, but I'm still covered in dirt from the floor.

Once I'm clean, I step out of the shower and look at myself in the mirror.

"Come on, Zeke. You can do this." I mentally prepare myself for the work ahead of me. First order of business, gain some weight and get some sleep. I need to be healthy if I'm going to have any hope of winning Opal back.

I get dressed quickly and follow my nose to the kitchen. My mother seems to be cooking up a feast. I stand in the doorway and watch her for a few minutes. Her long, brown hair swings behind her as she floats from station to station with a huge smile on her face. The vision in front of me is one of those that kept me alive while I was imprisoned. In eleven years, I only prayed for three things. I wanted to see the people I love one last time. My mom, Opal, and Axel. It seems like someone was listening.

She turns, seeing me standing in the doorway, and her green eyes shine with love.

"Come on, then. You need to eat." She places a large plate of pancakes, bacon, and hashbrowns on the counter in front of me.

"I don't think I can eat all this, Mom," I tell her as I take my seat. She simply waves a hand in the air as if I'm being ridiculous.

"You will clear your entire plate. You know there are starving children..." she begins.

"In Africa," I finish for her, and she nods. It's what she always said if Axel and I didn't want to finish our dinner—usually the vegetables. It's a silly, throwaway phrase that is mostly incorrect. Still, her eyes mist over as if she didn't believe she would ever get the chance to say those words to me again.

"So." She claps her hands, rests her elbows on the counter and leans toward me. "What do you plan to do to win your mate back?"

My mouth gapes open and closed.

I try to form a response, but I have no idea what I'm going to do or say to convince Opal to give me another chance.

"Men," my mother says, rolling her eyes. "This is what you're going to do. You're going to get yourself healthy." She gives me a pointed look because I have already stopped shoveling food into my mouth. I obediently stab another piece of pancake. When she is satisfied that I'm eating once more, she continues. "You're going to give her time and space, but you will still be present. You need her to see you and remember you are still waiting for a chance."

"How do I give her space but not too much space?"

She shakes her head at me as if that is the stupidest question that has ever been asked.

"You don't talk to her or pressure her to talk to you. You just need to be nearby. When she's ready, you need to be there, ready and willing."

I nod my head, beginning to understand. Women are complex creatures.

"You need to plan something incredible for when she is ready. What does she like?"

"I...I...don't know," I admit. I realize for the first time that, although my soul feels like it has known her forever, I literally know nothing about her.

"Well, there's your first problem," my mother says, clucking her tongue. "How are you supposed to woo someone when you don't know what she likes?"

"You're right." I stand abruptly and stride to Axel's office.

"What are you doing?" she asks, entering the room a few steps after me, as I search through his rolodex. I find the number I need and dial the office phone.

"Axel?" A masculine voice from my childhood comes through the line. Emotions clog my throat. With everything going on, I didn't stop to speak to Alaric the last time I saw him. Now, though, I'm questioning if this was the right call to make.

"Axel?" he says again.

I clear my throat.

"Al," I call him the name only I ever dared to call him. He hates it—or hated it—with a passion. He constantly corrected anyone who dared call him that.

"Zeke?" He sounds shocked, and I nod my head before I realize he can't see me.

"Yeah, its me."

He sucks in a shaky breath as if he's warring with his emotions.

"Damn, it's good to hear your voice."

"I sound like shit, and we both know it," I chuckle. "It's good to hear you too."

"Listen, about the banishment..." he begins. but I cut him off.

"Don't worry about that. I understand."

"You do?"

"I do. I don't want to cause Opal more pain than I already have. That's why I'm calling."

"Who is it?" I hear a feminine voice in the background. I hear Alaric put his hand over the microphone as he has a quiet conversation with someone.

"Sorry about that," he says once he comes back.

"No worries. I'm assuming that's Mrs. Al?" I chuckle, and he growls at me.

"Her name is Phoebe, and I have a feeling you two will get along splendidly once she sees how effectively you wind me up."

My chuckle turns into a laugh.

"Laugh it up, chuckles," he says, trying to sound fierce. I can still hear the smirk on his face through the phone.

"So, listen. I fucked up with Opal and need to fix it, but I don't know how," I blurt out the reason for my call, thankful that we can pick up right where we left off eleven years ago.

"I'm happy to hear you say that, and I'll help however I can. I'll admit, though, I'm not sure how."

"Well...I was thinking I would try to do something nice for her..." I begin, and my mom clears her throat. "Sorry, Mom thinks I should do something nice for her. But it turns out that I have no idea what she likes or dislikes."

"Uh..." I can picture him pacing and rubbing at the scruff on his chin in discomfort. It's his signature move when he feels like he's been put between a rock and a hard place.

"Listen, I'm not asking you to do anything other than give me a hint of something I can do to show her that I want to fix what I broke," I add. I know he feels like he's betraying a friend by telling me anything about Opal, and I hope to assure him I just need to be pointed in the right direction.

I hear a rustle on the phone before a feminine voice replaces Alaric's.

"Zeke, is it?" Her voice is warm and honey-sweet, and I am terrified of the woman on the other side immediately.

"Uh...yeah?"

"I'm Phoebe. I have to say that I don't like you on principle—girl code and all that. I care about Opal. If you want to try and make her happy, then I'm willing to help you."

I breathe out a sigh of relief.

"I'll do anything," I swear.

"Good. She loves the outdoors, hates big crowds, and her favorite movie is *Twilight*," she says, and I groan.

"I know. I know. All you shifters think that movie is horrible, but she loves the fact that they got so much wrong. She thinks it's ironic or something."

I haven't seen any of the *Twilight* movies because I was in captivity, but even the hunters would laugh about the things that series got wrong.

"Thank you," I tell her, not needing anything else. Plan something outdoors, away from crowds, and maybe watch *Twilight* for ideas.

"You're welcome. This is your one chance with me. Hurt her again, and I'll fry your ass."

My mouth drops open in shock and Alaric comes back on the line before I can respond.

"Did you get what you needed?"

"I think so..." I pause. "She wouldn't really fry me, right? Could she?"

"Oh, yes. She would, and she certainly could. My phoenix mate is anything but subtle. Don't worry, though. It would hurt, but it wouldn't be bad enough to kill you. She's been practicing."

"Okay, then. That's good news." I am now even more afraid of Alaric's mate. Did he say *phoenix?*

Alaric wishes me good luck, and I hear him chuckling as he hangs up the phone.

"Well, that was terrifying," I whisper as I place the receiver back on the cradle.

"What was?" Mom asks, walking over to me.

"Alaric's mate." She nods in understanding.

"Phoenixes are fiercely protective of those they care about. Did you get what you needed?" she says, changing the subject.

"Wait... I thought phoenixes were extinct."

"It was a shock for us too. We don't spend as much time with the wolves as we used to, but a phoenix in the pack quickly becomes everyone's news. The only supernaturals we spend much time with as a group are the mountain lions. They are a small group nearby, and that's the only reason why.""

I take a seat on the leather love seat in the corner of Axel's office and pat the open spot beside me.

"What happened with the pack?" I ask. "Why did you stop running with the pack?"

Tears swim in her bright green eyes as she looks at me. She places her palms on either side of my face and gives me a soft smile.

"I wasn't the only one who missed you. Axel was inconsolable. He would lash out at anyone who said that you were dead. For years, he searched for you. By the time he stopped searching, he didn't have many friends left."

"Alaric wouldn't turn his back on Axel," I tell her adamantly.

"You're right. He didn't. Alaric was worried about him. Axel decided it was time to stop searching for you, and Alaric came to talk to him—warned him that he may regret the choice."

"So, what happened then?"

"Well, Axel didn't take kindly to being told that, kicked

Alaric out, and told him to mind his own business." She wipes a tear from her eye. "Your brother didn't know I was listening, but I was just in the hallway. I saw Alaric's face when he walked out. He was crushed. Once Alaric was out of the picture, Axel threw himself into working with the sleuth. He worked day and night to make us safe. Somewhere along the way he lost himself."

"What do you mean? He seems mostly the same."

"Once again, you're right. Having you back and then meeting Opal has changed him. Before that, he didn't socialize, didn't go out, didn't leave the house unless it had to do with work. He would go to job sites, check on the status, do the quotes, come home, and do the paperwork. He didn't have a life."

"And what about you?" I ask. We've spent all our time talking about Axel, Opal, and myself, but my mother is sitting right here in front of me. I know nothing about how she's spent the last decade.

"What about me?" she asks.

"How are you doing? Are you okay?"

She looks at me in surprise.

"You know. I don't remember the last time someone asked me that and truly meant it. Everyone asks how you are, but they very rarely want the honest answer."

"Well, I want the real answer, Mom."

"I'm doing okay. I'm not great, and I'm not bad. I am so happy you are home—that I can hold you in my arms again. I am so proud that you and your brother have met your mate." I move to remind her that I still need to win her back, but she puts her hand over my mouth. "She will forgive you. Of that, I have no doubts."

I nod, wanting to believe that.

"You don't happen to have the *Twilight* movies here, do you?" I ask.

Apparently, my mother doesn't share most people's opinion

about that series. It turns out she does own a copy of the movies, and she is happy to spend an evening watching them with me.

With a giddy smile on her face and an extra bounce in her step, she leads me to the living room. She instructs me to prepare popcorn while she locates the movies. There are four!

I fall asleep before the end of the sequel, but I have no doubt my mom is going to make me watch the rest when I wake. I dream of vampires that sparkle in the sun and brag about drinking deer blood.

Chapter Thirteen

Opal

It feels like I only just fell asleep when loud knocking startles me awake. Judging by the darkness of the sky outside, it's been hours. I try to roll over, but I am pulled back into a hard wall of muscle. I sink into Axel, reveling in his body heat. I'm about to sink back into sweet oblivion...when the knocking starts up again.

"Who is it?" Axel mumbles.

I chuckle at the sound of his voice, heavy with sleep.

"I don't know. I'll be right back." I place a soft kiss on his head and shimmy out of his arms and off the bed. I throw on my fluffy bathrobe, ensuring that everything is covered, before heading to the door.

The knocking gets louder, and I call out to my impatient visitor.

"I'm coming!"

I open the door to find my brother, Matt, standing wild-eyed on the other side.

"Thank the goddess," he says, grabbing me by the arms and looking me over from head to toe. "Drake and Rayne told me about this whole mate thing—which I'm insanely pissed at you for not telling me about by the way. Are you okay?"

"I'm okay. I promise," I tell him as he pulls me into a hug.

"Good. That means you can explain why I didn't know about your mate rejecting you." He pushes me away so I can see the determined look on his face, and I can't help but laugh. My nerdy, little brother, complete with the glasses and slicked-back hair, is attempting to look fierce. Maybe I have miscalculated him though. As I watch him now, I realize that he's grown to be at least a foot taller than me. His shoulders are broad, and the arms he crosses in front of him in a gesture of anger are noticeably muscled. To me, he will always be my brother who likes taking things apart and putting them back together more than people.

A low growl comes from the direction of the kitchen, and Matt's back snaps straight as he peers over my shoulder.

"I would not talk to her that way right now if I were you," Axel growls.

Matt immediately drops his hands, and I spin around to face Axel.

"Axel, this is my little brother. Matt, this is my mate," I introduce them. Axel seems to relax at the knowledge that he is my family, but Matt is still tense. I usher Matt inside and guide him to the couch in the living room.

"I—What...When did this happen?" Matt stammers.

"Today," I respond, turning to walk over to Axel. "Can I have a few minutes to talk to my brother?"

Axel runs his hands up and down my arms before placing a soft kiss on my lips.

"I'll go take a shower."

With that, he turns back in the direction he came, and I take a seat on the couch opposite Matt.

He just looks at me in confusion, and I know the explanation I owe him is long overdue. I take a steadying breath, and I tell him everything. I start with Zeke's rejection just after my eighteenth birthday and finish on my mating with Axel today. Although I'm still uncertain of it myself, I include Axel's explanation that Zeke supposedly had a good reason for what he did. Matt is somewhat appeased by the knowledge that he wasn't the only one who didn't know about my rejection, but he's still pissed that he is the last one to know now.

"It makes so much more sense now. I thought you just became a bitch for no reason—no offense." I wave my hand in a gesture of 'none taken.' "I always wondered if there was another reason. One day, we were best friends; the next, you left home without a word to anyone. When you came back, you didn't want anything to do with anyone except Sebastyn."

I wring my hands in my lap, and I can't meet my brother's eyes. He's right. We were close. After Zeke's rejection, I pushed him away along with everyone else.

"I just couldn't stand for you to look at me as 'poor Opal who got rejected by her mate.' I was miserable and didn't know how to tell you—or anyone—what happened. So, I did what I thought would make me strong. I faked it until I made it and turned myself into an uncaring, cold bitch. I'm so sorry I hurt you."

He's at my side in seconds, wrapping his arms around me.

"I never would've looked at you like that. I would've helped you find him and cut his dick off." We laugh at that thought. "You did nothing wrong. He did. No matter how noble he seems to think his reasoning is."

I can see the fire in his eyes. It's a family trait. Our blue eyes glow brighter when we are angry, almost as if there are small, hot flames simmering behind them. One of our teachers had expected us to excel in fire magic, but we ended up with a form of earth magic instead. Mine is weak, and his is tied more to metals and, therefore, electronics. Calling either of us earth witches is a stretch.

"I know. I truly do. I wanted to tell you so many times, but it was like another person took over my body."

He leans back and nods toward the bedroom door before whispering, "So that's Axel?"

I wipe the tears from my eyes, happy for the distraction.

"Yup. He's amazing." I look back at the hallway to see Axel, now fully dressed, running a hand through his still-damp hair.

He walks over and shakes Matt's hand, properly introducing himself, before turning to me.

"I'm going to head home to check on Zeke and let you catch up with your brother."

"Okay," I say sadly. I don't want him to leave, but I am also curious how Zeke is fairing after the potion. I remind him that there's more of the potion left in the thermos and give him a kiss before he walks out the door.

"Wow. Is that what it's like when you have a mate?" Matt asks.

"What do you mean?"

"The way you two look at each other. It's like you'd die if you were apart." He has a dreamy look on his face.

"I never thought about it that way, but I guess you're right. Axel is now the center of my universe. If you weren't here right now, I'd be miserable because he left."

I don't know how else to explain it. There's already a hollow feeling forming in my chest, and he only just left.

"At least you two are better than Drake and Rayne. Those two don't know the meaning of privacy, and I swear they have made it their mission to fuck on every surface of every room in that gods-damned lab." A disgusted look crosses his face, and I laugh. "It is not ideal working conditions."

"That sounds like Drake and Rayne. Want to have a movie night like old times?" I ask.

"Sure. First, I want to hear about this new project you're working on with Skarlyt and Sarah. Rayne told me it is 'classified,' and apparently I can walk in on her and her mate five times a day without getting clearance for classified information." He tries to look hurt but ends up laughing.

I begin making snacks for our movie night while I describe the island to him. I even pull out the drawing Axel made and explain what all the markings mean.

Before I can forget, I take a picture of the drawing with my phone and send it to Skarlyt and Sarah. Their responses are immediate:

> Skarlyt: OMG. That's amazing! Tell Axel he's moved up to head designer.

> Sarah: Wow! That guy is talented. Glad I didn't banish him too.

> Me: He really is.

> Skarlyt: Okay, enough with the island...I have to know...is he that good at other things too? *Wink wink*

> Sarah: Skarlyt Moon! You can't just ask whatever you want because you put a *wink* behind it.

> Me: Ha ha. I can verify that he is good at several things.

> Skarlyt: I need all the details. Wait. I'm putting Kayne to bed. Then I will come over.

> Sarah: Let me know when. I'll meet you there.

> Me: I'm having a movie night with Matt. We can talk in the morning. Come over for breakfast.

Skarlyt: Fine. I'll probably be grumpy though.

Sarah: Rayne and Phoebe will be mad if they don't get an invite.

Me: If you can pick them up, they are welcome.

Skarlyt: On it. See you then.

Sarah: Bright and early.

"He literally just left," Matt says, impatiently watching me text back and forth with the girls.

"It's not Axel," I explain. "Sarah and Skarlyt wanted to come and interrupt our movie night, but I told them to come for breakfast instead."

With that, we grab our popcorn and blankets and get comfy on the couch. After a few minutes of indecision, we agree to try *Encanto*, the newest Disney movie.

As I snuggle into my cocoon next to my brother, suddenly my life feels almost perfect. I cemented the bond with my mate—*one* of my mates—and I am getting my friends and my little brother back. The only thing that is missing is the mate who rejected me eleven years ago. I'm going to have to talk to him soon. I had planned on making him sweat it out, but my awareness keeps turning back to the hole in my mate bond. I know instinctively that it's a hole that only he can fill.

Worst-case scenario, I don't like what he says and have to live with this missing piece forever. Ideally, whatever his reason is will make sense, and we can complete our bond.

"Matt..." I pause the movie and turn to him on the couch.

He's already falling asleep, and his eyes are nearly closed, but he perks up at the sound of his name.

"Yeah?"

I bite my lip, contemplating what to say.

"You know I'm sorry, right? For leaving, for pushing you away, for how—how I treated you, Mom, and Dad."

He wraps his arms around me.

"Of course, I do."

I nod and sniff, and tears leak from my eyes. *Encanto* got magic all wrong, but watching the family turn on each other reminded me of how I treated my own family for years.

"You know we don't hold anything against you, right?" I shrug my shoulders noncommittally, but he waits until I meet his sapphire blue eyes. "Seriously, Pal. We knew something happened, and it was hard to watch you suffer without being able to help. We all knew that wasn't truly you, and we prayed for you to come back to us."

The use of his old nickname for me—Pal, because he could only catch the second syllable of anything for a few years—leaves me sobbing. He wipes the tears from my cheeks with his thumbs.

"We all love you. Obviously, our prayers worked," he says as he motions to the room around us, the empty bowls of popcorn and the blankets piled high around us.

The vulnerability on his face makes me snake my arms around his waist and rest my head against his chest.

"I promise I'll never become that girl again."

"Even if you can't fix everything with Zeke?"

His question surprises me, but I mull it over seriously.

"Not even then," I promise. "I understand what it costs to push everyone away now, and I'll have Axel to keep me balanced. Though I do wonder if I'm strong enough to survive his rejection again."

"You are," he whispers.

He falls back on the couch and pulls me with him. He puts one arm over my shoulder, and I lay my head on his arm. Normally, I would be weirded out by fully-grown siblings snuggling like this, but right now I'm thankful to be cuddled up with my little brother just like when we were children.

He grabs the remote and turns the movie back on. It only takes about one musical number—less than ten minutes—for him to fall asleep. I gently slip off the couch, pull a blanket over him, take off his glasses, and kiss him on his head.

As my lips touch his forehead, I see flashes of him from the past few years.

Matt is young—still just a kid. He is up late at night—illuminated by the blue light of a computer screen—searching for any answer to why I have acted so erratically.
He studies me with confusion. He's trying to find clues or detect symptoms. He takes notes and searches some more.
He approaches my friends—Skarlyt and Dru—to ask for advice. They have no help to offer him.
"I know I am only one of your children," Matt prays to the goddess. "I know there are others who have greater need than I, but I really need my best friend back. Something is wrong with my sister. Please, I'll do anything to get her back."

I wipe the tears from my eyes before returning to my side of the couch.

My thoughts turn once again to Zeke, and I wonder if it's possible to fix the fissure between us. As the movie ends, I switch back to *Twilight*. I already know every word, so it's easy for me to fall asleep with it playing.

When I sleep, I dream of what life would've been like if Zeke had claimed me on the night we first met.

I would've met Axel later that same night. I could've spent a decade with them instead of being all alone.

I never would've felt the grief that caused me to push away my family and friends.

When I stop to think about it, I probably would've even had a couple of beautiful bear cubs by now.

Chapter Fourteen

Opal

I wake up surrounded by heat. I try to roll over and rip the covers off me, but I can't. The heat is nearly unbearable. It takes a minute for me to realize that it's not the blankets making me so hot; it's an arm and a leg.

I turn my head as much as I can to find Axel snuggled into my back. I glance around. I'm fairly sure I fell asleep on the couch with Matt. How did Axel get in? How did I get to my bed?

"Good morning, angel," he rasps, still mostly asleep.

"Good morning. When did you get back?"

"You fell asleep on the couch, so Matt let me in. I carried you in here." He places a soft kiss on my neck, and tingles spread all over my body. I twist to face him, and this time he lets me. I eagerly bring my lips to his. Damn, I can't believe this sweet, sexy man is all mine. I lose myself in the kiss until I notice laughter and the smell of bacon coming from the kitchen.

"Who—" I begin, and Axel chuckles.

"The girls have been here for about half an hour," he explains. "I told them to wait for you to wake up."

"Shit. I better go help before one of them comes in here," I say, wiggling out of his hold.

"Too late," Rayne says from the door. "I heard you talking."

Of course, she did.

"Damn vampire hearing," I grumble under my breath.

"I heard that too," she sings as she turns back to the kitchen.

"I'm going to head home for a bit this morning," Axel rubs the sleep from his eyes and begins stepping into his jeans. "Zeke is feeling much better now—thanks to you."

"I wanted to ask if it would be okay for me to talk to him at some point today. I had some time to think about it, and I figure putting it off will only make it more awkward."

Axel stops pulling his shirt over his head and turns to look at me in shock.

"I didn't know if you would want to...He asked me about it last night, but I told him I wasn't going to bring it up to you."

I close the distance between us.

"Is it an issue for you? If it is, I won't go. You're my mate first and foremost..."

"But he is also your mate. I just want to make sure you do not feel any pressure from either of us." He studies my face for any sign of hesitation. "You don't have to worry. I will never be jealous of you spending time with him. If you decide to cement the bond with him as well, I will support you. Zeke and I have always known we'd share a mate and are prepared for it. I will also support you if you don't feel ready or decide not to bond with him at all. I still hate the fact that he hurt you, and it will take time for him to prove that he won't do it again."

I place a soft kiss on his lips. "It will take time for me to trust him as well. Without knowing his reasons, I don't even know how I feel about it yet."

"I'll be back in a few hours to pick you up. You enjoy breakfast. That'll give Zeke time to prepare his groveling," he says with a wink. When he walks out, I hear him greet the girls before the front door shuts behind him. Immediately, there is an army of pounding steps coming toward me.

Somehow, Skarlyt is the first through the door.

"Oh, my gods!" She emits a high-pitched squeal and wraps me in a hug.

"Can't breathe," I wheeze.

"Sorry," she steps back. "It's just—I'm so glad you finally found a mate who deserves you."

"He does deserve you, right?" Sarah asks, sounding skeptical. I step into the bathroom to brush my teeth, but I leave the door open so I can still hear.

"Pssh. Of course, he does. Look at her, she's practically glowing. He must have a wicked tongue or an enormous d—" Rayne starts, but Phoebe wraps her hand around her mouth.

"Did you just lick me?" Phoebe shrieks, ripping her hand away and wiping it on her pants.

"If you don't want your hand licked, don't put it that close to my mouth," Rayne explains simply.

Sophia snickers, and her twin gives her a glare. Sarah just rolls her eyes and shakes her head in disapproval.

"You always act up when Dru isn't here."

"I like it," Skarlyt says. "Just think about how much more fun our lives have been since Rayne got here." Rayne preens under the compliment before sticking her tongue out at Sarah.

"No way. Keep that thing away from me," Sarah says, holding the other woman at arm's length.

A normal person—a sane person—would close their mouth when presented with a frighteningly powerful witch who can shoot lightning out of her eyes, but normal and sane are not words I'd use to describe Rayne.

Instead, Rayne proceeds to stick her tongue out further and chase Sarah all the way back to the kitchen.

The breakfast conversation is normal by our standards. We laugh and joke, and I avoid plenty of questions about how Axel is in bed. Of course, I don't answer them. A girl should never kiss and tell—unless you're Rayne or Skarlyt, and then you tell anyone who will listen.

"I heard you say you're going to talk to Zeke today," Rayne says.

A round of questions circle the table before everyone watches me in shock.

I narrow my eyes at Rayne. Like I said, damn vampire hearing.

"Axel says that Zeke believes he had a good reason for rejecting me." Sarah goes to interrupt, but I hold up my hand to stop her and continue. "Axel has made it clear that he supports my decision either way. After Axel and I completed our bond, I feel a hole in my soul where I know Zeke is supposed to be. If I ever want the chance to be truly happy, I need to talk to him and let him explain." I take a deep breath. I didn't intend to have the conversation steered in this direction, but now it is, and I might as well get it all out.

Everyone nods in understanding. To her credit, Rayne even looks a little sorry she brought it up. I'm sure it won't last long.

Once they are done getting the details about my love life, we begin discussing the plan for the island. I show them Axel's sketch, and Rayne explains that Matt has already helped Drake locate a spot in the ocean that should be safe for us. Skarlyt formally excuses me from a coven meeting I didn't even know about because I am "obviously busy tonight." Everything is moving forward so quickly that it barely feels real.

We are saying our goodbyes when Axel returns.

I see Rayne open her mouth, but Skarlyt grabs Axel's attention before she can say anything too dirty. Sarah silently claps a hand on Rayne's shoulder and teleports her away.

"Axel, you are just the man I wanted to see," Skarlyt begins. Axel, wisely, looks nervous, but she doesn't give him time to object before continuing. "Opal showed me your design, and I wanted to ask you to take charge of designing the island...and also...possibly... have it ready by sometime tomorrow." She mumbles the last words to obscure just how heinous the request is, but Axel's eyes widen in shock.

"Do you know how much work that is?" he asks.

"The designs don't have to be complete. We just need to know how to build the foundation. Even if the rest of the details aren't ready, we can at least have a base ready."

She has her puppy dog eyes and pouty lip on full display.

Axel rubs the back of his neck. It's clear he's uncomfortable, but he sighs in defeat.

"I will see what I can do."

"Yay!" Skarlyt jumps up and kisses his cheek before quickly teleporting away with Sophia and Phoebe before he can say anything else.

"You're such a pushover," I laugh.

"Did you see the look she was giving me?" My mate looks shell-shocked by the interaction. "I don't know how Lennox ever says no to that woman."

"I don't think he does," I admit. "I need to take a quick shower before we leave."

"I'll clean up the dishes," Axel says. I look around at the mess the girls made cooking and wonder how I didn't notice it while they were here.

"Don't worry about that. I can clean it when I get back," I call behind me.

I hear him grunt in response, but I hear dishes clanging together in the next room before I even turn on the water.

Who am I to complain if he wants to clean?

Less than an hour later, I'm trembling from nerves just outside Axel's house.

Am I ready to talk to Zeke? No, probably not. Should I talk to Zeke? Definitely. My hesitation must be clear on my face because Axel takes my hand in his.

"Breathe, angel. You don't have to make any decisions today. If you need to walk away, you walk away. Zeke will not try to stop you, I promise."

"Lead the way," I tell him, going up on my toes to give him a light kiss.

Axel leads me into his office where Zeke is already waiting in one of the chairs. He stands as I enter the room. Axel leads me over to his side of the desk and guides me to sit in his chair. I know it is a power move intended to let me know I am the one in control. If it bothers Zeke, he doesn't show it. He simply nods at his brother and sits back down in the chair across from me.

"I'll be in the kitchen if you need me," Axel says, leaving the room and shutting the door behind him.

"Opal."

"Zeke."

We each say the other's name at the same time and then simultaneously gesture for the other to go first. It makes us both laugh, but the situation is too tense for the humor to last long.

"You go first," I say.

He takes a deep, unsteady breath.

"I guess I don't really know where to start..."

"You've had some time to think about it," I begin. I want to snap at him, but I can tell that he's nervous. I have every right to be angry, but acting angry will just make this harder. "How about starting with what you were doing the night we met."

His eyes meet mine, and he nods.

"You're right. That makes sense, but I'll have to start further back than that. After all, that's where it truly begins, and I really need you to understand."

His gaze lowers to his lap for a beat while he collects his thoughts, then his focus returns to me, and he begins.

"My father was murdered by hunters. He ran a construction company, but his real job was going out to rescue lone shifters all over Ontario. He loved building things, but saving people is what he was passionate about. We were just eighteen when he left to follow a lead that I thought sounded suspicious. I was right, but I wish I hadn't been. A week after he left, his—his head arrived in a box with a note letting us know they were coming for the sleuth next."

I suck in a breath at his words. I already knew that their father had died, but I didn't realize it had been so violent and awful.

"Axel and I gathered up some of our strongest men and followed his trail to where it happened. It was a bloodbath; they tore him apart. We gathered—we did what we could to give him a proper burial."

Tears prick my eyes as I imagine them finding their father's body like that. What kind of monsters would do that to a person? What kind of monsters would make sure his family found him that way?

"After that, Axel was convinced that the only way to keep us safe was to move the sleuth somewhere closer to witches who could conceal us. I didn't understand Axel. I wanted to take the fight directly to the hunters. Dad was my hero, and I wanted revenge. So, that's what I did. I left and went to get my revenge."

I nod my head. Safety is important, but I know I would seek

retribution for far less. Although I already know, it didn't turn out the way he planned.

"At first, it was fine. They didn't know what hit them. I didn't know who had killed my father, but I wanted to wipe out as many as I could before they could hurt anyone else. I messed up though. I had followed them too close for too long, and they figured out how to track me. I knew they were getting close. I knew I didn't have long."

His gaze lowers to the table again, and his body radiates tension. I want to lean forward and take his hand in mine, but I can't make myself do it.

"I had been running for days by the time I first saw you. I was on my way to say goodbye to Axel. When I saw you..."

His eyes flick up to mine, and our gazes lock. I can see the raw emotion there. Whatever he says next, I know it will be true, and it will be the thing that broke his heart. I nod solemnly, giving him permission to go on.

"When I saw you, it was love at first sight. Gods, you looked like an angel. You touched my face, and—for a few minutes—I fooled myself into believing it could be all right. I knew I needed to get away from you, but I was desperate to stay—desperate to keep you. The urge to claim you as my mate was so clear and strong that it brought me a moment of clarity."

His hands, large but slender, are wringing in his lap. I can hear in his voice the proof that this night hurt him too.

"The hunters were coming. I knew they were close. I knew I wouldn't be able to leave if I was near you, and I knew staying would put you in danger. They would have captured you too, and they would have been merciless experimenting on a bonded pair."

A shudder runs through me at that thought. I saw the people we rescued from the Orillia facility. I spent hours nursing them back to health. I know the hunters can be ruthless and inventive in their tortures. When Axel said Zeke believed he had a good reason to reject me, I wasn't expecting to hear he'd done it to protect me.

"You are saying you rejected me because you wanted to keep me safe from the hunters who were chasing you," I summarize and wait for a nod from him to continue. "Why didn't you just tell me?"

"It all happened so fast," he explains, sounding hopeless. "I would have died for you the moment I laid eyes upon you. If you felt the same about me, I wouldn't be able to send you away somewhere safe. You would have followed me, and you would have been killed or kidnapped with me."

"How long?" I ask. It is a pointless question. He *thought* the hunters were breathing down his neck. If he had really been a day or two ahead of them, there was no way for him to know that. Still, I need to know. "After you left me, how long did it take for the hunters to catch you?"

"Two hours."

I suck in a sharp breath. Holy shit. He's right. Two hours? If he hadn't rejected me, we would have still been in that clearing, celebrating our mating, when the hunters caught up. Trying to explain without rejecting me would have taken too long. Gods know I wouldn't have listened to his warnings without putting up a fight. Even though it's been eleven years, knowing how close I came to danger makes my heart race. The only reason I wasn't locked in a cell next to Zeke is because he rejected me. He hurt me in the worst possible way to save my life.

"Do you believe me?" he asks, sounding hopeful and desperate. He leaves his chair and comes to crouch next to me. He pauses there to watch my reaction. He is close enough that I could reach out and touch him but far enough away that I won't feel crowded.

"I do," I say. I turn the chair to look into his eyes. "Yes. I believe you."

He lets out a deep breath, releasing some of the tension in his shoulders.

"Thank the goddess. Do you think I could ever have a second chance?"

Everything I've believed for the last eleven years—every ounce of hate I've harbored for this man—was for nothing. I've spent years hating the one man who truly sacrificed himself for me.

With shaky hands, I reach out and grab the sides of his face. I allow my thumbs to caress his cheek, and his eyes slip closed as he brings his hands to rest atop mine.

Instead of giving myself time to reconsider, I lean forward and capture his lips with my own. It feels like coming home—like the hole inside me is getting smaller with each brush of our lips. I explore the seam of his mouth, wanting to deepen the kiss. Just like the first time I kissed him, it's all consuming. It's like a fire is raging and the only way to extinguish it is to complete the bond.

Suddenly, my mind is no longer on the kiss and the man on the other side of it. I pull back with a gasp. My vision goes dark before the room around us is replaced by unfamiliar scenes. They flood in and overwhelm me.

I watch Zeke and Axel find the clearing where their father had been ripped to pieces. Then, Zeke leaves home—leaves his brother—to seek revenge. They both feel like he's abandoning Axel, and they are both miserable because of it.

The vision skips forward, and he's already running from the hunters. He's breathless and checking over his shoulder at every turn. He's afraid of them catching up, and he is afraid that he's leading them home. When the hunters do catch him, they are cruel. He expects death, but they beat him until he's unconscious instead. When he wakes, he's on the floor of a sterile, secure room.

They spend weeks torturing him and asking questions about the sleuth. They taunt him with information about his father's death. They seem to forget about him for weeks at a time, and he believes he will starve before they remember him.
When they do remember, he decides it would have been better to starve.

I snatch my hands back from his face, ripping myself from the string of vivid visions. Zeke's eyes are full of concern.

"Are you okay?" he asks. He reaches for me, but I fly backward.

"Don't—please, don't touch me."

The hurt on his face is heartbreaking, but I can't let him touch me again or find the words to explain. I cannot risk seeing more. What little I've already seen of his past will scar me. To see anyone —to see my mate—treated so horribly...

"Opal?" Axel says, barging into the office. His eyes flicker between my trembling body and his brother. He takes a step toward me, a hand extended to either offer comfort or defend. I jump up and away from them like a cornered animal.

"Please..." I'm not sure what I'm begging for, but I know that I can't stand anyone touching me right now.

Like a fox, I run through the house, yank open the front door, and fly through the forest. I need to be alone. I need to be under the open sky. I need clear air in my lungs.

There's no relief. Each step I take jars me with another vision. Someone is bleeding out on the blades of grass; this plant nearly died during the last harsh winter; this flower is bending happily toward the sun's rays.

It is all just too, too much. My mind is whirling into the past and the future of everything around me, and none of the thoughts are my own.

Once I am within sight of the coven and have still found no relief, I stop running and lean against a tree. Once again, my vision blurs before I am hit with a sudden, excruciating pain. As I recover my own senses, I see a limb above me has been sawed off. I weep as I recognize the reason for this tree's pain.

I sink to the ground, sobs wracking my body as I am bombarded by visions from each blade of grass, each fallen leaf or twig, and even each worm wriggling in the dirt beneath.

Chapter Fifteen

Zeke

Telling Opal my story was harder than I thought it would be, but I thought it had gone well until she ran away. After she fled, Axel and I stood dumbfounded for a moment before he cursed.

"Shit."

"What? What is it?" I ask. His tone makes me even more concerned. "What did I do?"

"Opal has visions," he announces, as if that explains everything.

"Okay. Visions? What do you mean *visions*?"

He scrubs a hand down his face, and my heart begins to hammer in my chest.

"She told me that she sometimes catches clips of someone's past or future if she touches them. She said it was like watching a movie, but she can feel the person's emotions as if they are her own."

"Shit," I repeat my brother's earlier sentiment. I'm not worried about my own future, but I know there's not much good to see in my past. My breath catches in my chest. "Shit."

What did I show her without meaning to?

My heart constricts. I am often caught by memories of my past, but Opal should not be haunted by those same nightmares. I try to stand, but I fall back to my knees.

Needles and tubing puncture my arms. I want to rip the needles out, but I am tied to the chair so tightly that I cannot move under the binding. One takes my blood; another pumps an unfamiliar fluid into me. I don't think it's blood. It's blue and lights my veins on fire with each drop.

I grit my teeth, trying not to scream as the burning sensation follows the path of the liquid as it travels to my heart. When it reaches its destination, I am unable to take the pain. I roar.

"Serum 1-19 causes Patient B-143 pain after fifty-three seconds." A man in a white coat checks his watch before dictating this to a woman—another white coat—just outside my field of vision.

My hands clench and release as I try to gain control. I can feel my skin ripple, wanting to shift. My bear just snarls and locks himself away in my mind. I am caught between the pain of the shift being forced upon me and the pain of the shift that cannot be completed.

"It seems the beast inside Patient B-143 does not want to cooperate. Increase flow rate to thirty percent," he instructs someone behind me. The slow burn of the liquid entering my body multiplies and quickens. I begin convulsing.

I hear people shouting, but it sounds far away. The world sounds as if I'm underwater.

After what feels like an eternity, the needles and tubes are roughly ripped from my skin. I breathe a sigh of relief as the pain subsides.

"Serum 1-19 is a failure," the man says. He shows little emotion, but I can tell he's frustrated. I don't know what they are trying to achieve with these experiments, but I hope they never succeed.

Two men enter, remove my restraints, and grab under my armpits to lift me. Two guards is overkill for me these days. I don't have the strength to escape, and I don't even know how to get out of this place.

The man in the white coat stops them just before we reach the door. He stands in front of me and places a hand under my chin so that our eyes meet.

"If you want the pain to stop, all you have to do is shift."

I bare my teeth at him in defiance. Even if I could, I would never willingly shift for them.

"Pity," he says, releasing my chin and motioning for the guards to remove me. I try to keep my eyes open—try to gather any information I can—as they take me back to my cell.

I watch them drag a young girl into the same room I just left. She's only a child—no more than thirteen. I struggle, trying to escape their grip and reach her. I know what they will do to her, but I have no power to save her. The guards overpower me, and I slump back down. It isn't until I hear her first screams that I thrash in their arms. I am desperate to turn and fight—even if I know I cannot win. Someone needs to try to save that little girl, but I can't.

"Zeke..." Axel's voice breaks through the memory.

I look up into his mossy green eyes. The skin between his brows is wrinkled with concern. I open my mouth to speak, but the panic still grips me. Is this what Opal saw? Did she see something worse?

"Breathe with me," Axel says. He takes a deep breath in through his nose and releases it through his mouth. I try to match his calming pace, but it's difficult.

He helps me off the floor and into the office chair behind the desk. He crouches in front of me and studies my face.

"What brought on the panic attack?"

"I don't want her to see what I went through...she shouldn't have to see..."

My mind begins to run rampant again, and my breathing comes in shallow gasps.

"Zeke," Axel says sternly, and I snap my eyes to his. "Stay with me."

I nod. If anyone can keep me present, it's him.

"Tell me something—anything—to get my mind off this."

He nods, letting a soft smile grace his face.

"So, the other night, when they brought you back..." He pauses, clearly wondering if this is a dangerous line of thought. "Well, when I finally felt you after so long, I charged into the clearing, walked right up to Alaric, grabbed him by the shirt, and roared in his face."

"Oh, shit," I say. "And you still have your face?"

He nods.

"'Oh, shit' is right. But it's not what you're thinking. Alaric isn't the one I should've been worried about."

My brows furrow in confusion before I remember the phone conversation I had with Phoebe.

"His mate?" I ask.

"Yes. Phoebe is the sweetest woman, but she's prepared to fry anyone who hurts her family."

"Does that mean she is really as terrifying as she sounds on the phone?"

"Probably more terrifying honestly," he chuckles. "That's not the worst of it. About two seconds later, I did the same thing and threatened Darren."

"You've got a temper these days?"

"Are you aware that Darren has a mate now? Do you know who that mate is?" Axel asks, and I shake my head. "If you can believe it, Darren's mate is Phoebe's twin sister. Honestly, I am not sure which of them is scarier."

"Shit, Axel." I shake my head. "Even without two phoenixes, you couldn't take Axel and Darren on your own."

He runs a hand through his mid-length, brown hair.

"I know. I wasn't in my right mind. All I could think about was getting to you."

What I'm sure was supposed to be a funny story about my brother being a dumbass turns serious.

"I would've come to find you as soon as I could."

"Living without you has been hell. I've kept myself busy with the sleuth and running things here, but..."

"I know." I don't need him to say it. Running this sleuth may have been a one-man job when our father was alpha. Now, it's an entire enterprise.

"That's another thing."

"What is?" I question.

"Someone's taking money from the accounts. I found a bunch of transfers out of the general account, being cycled through at least a dozen accounts overseas. So far, I haven't been able to find who's doing it."

My mouth drops open. "How much money are we talking?"

He looks at me and I can tell by the look on his face that I'm not going to like the number. "Hundreds of thousands. We're nearing the million-dollar mark soon."

I let out a low whistle. "And you have no idea who's doing it? Who has access to the accounts apart from you?"

He runs his hand through his hair once more showing he's uncomfortable. "Well since you weren't here, I needed help and hired an accounting firm where one of our bears works."

I nod my head. I was always the one who was good with numbers. When Dad began grooming us for the alpha role, he separated the duties between us. I was behind-the-scenes, going over the budget and organizing schedules. Axel was supposed to take on most of the public leadership. Dad didn't want to choose between us, and we were all comfortable with the plan.

He walks around the desk and pulls out the account books, showing me all the transfers highlighted in yellow. He shows them starting about a year ago, but when I flip more pages backward, I see even smaller amounts being taken out at regular intervals.

"There's even more here than you thought." I glance up at him and watch as his brows furrow in confusion.

"What do you mean?" If you go back even further, the amounts are smaller but more frequent. Every time you made a purchase, an extra dollar or two would be transferred out at the same time. The amounts were so small, there's no wonder you missed it."

"Well shit. What do we do?"

I look up at him and smile, feeling useful and needed for the first time in a long time.

"Right now, we go check on our mate. Then, I'll start going over the books. If you know anyone who is good with computers and trustworthy, you should call them."

We begin the trek through the forest, searching for signs of which way our mate ran. I try to keep my mind off my past and what Opal may have seen. We're approaching the coven when I hear her voice. She's speaking with someone. I hear her sigh, and I can almost feel the relief in her single exhale.

When we finally catch a glimpse of her, I freeze.

There, sitting on the forest floor beside my mate, is a woman who I would recognize anywhere. She looks cleaner and healthier than the last time I saw her. Her hair is clean, but it is still long, brown, and streaked with gray. Her face is fuller, but I know those sharp cheek bones.

I may not know her name, but I know where she came from. I know it the same way I know that her eyes are a deep, muddy brown.

I will never forget those eyes.

Every time they take me from my cell, they bring me to the same room. I am not surprised, then, when they bring me to the sterile exam room. As always, they secure me with chains to a chair in the center.

Unlike any other time before, they do not immediately hook me up to any machines. Instead, they drag a woman into the room.

She walks along with them with her head held high, but it's clear she's been mistreated by them as well.

"Patient X, meet Patient B-143. Let's see if you can coax his beast out."

She turns her face to mine, her brown eyes widening as she takes in my appearance. Under her gaze, I'm momentarily embarrassed by what I must look like.

There's an aura around this woman—something that insists she should be respected, revered, and protected. Her eyes soften, and she gives me a sad smile.

She must've been taking too long because one of the men that walked in with her pushes her roughly. I instinctively try to reach out and steady her, but my hands are bound too tightly to help.

She reaches out a hand to steady herself, the soft skin of her hand making contact with mine. I watch in horror as her entire body tenses. Her muddy, brown eyes turn milky white. Seconds pass, and she begins to convulse.

"Help her," I plead. The hunters around me make no move toward her. Something is clearly wrong, but I have no way to help her.

Minutes pass before the browns of her irises begin to overtake the field of white. Her eyes lock with mine, and she lets out a gasp as they do.

The man in the white coat gives her only a moment to recover before he begins questioning.

"Well, Patient X. What can we do to bring his beast out?"

Her eyes turn to him, but her expression is cold.

"Nothing," she says with a wry chuckle. "There's nothing you can do to make him shift."

Without warning, a loud crack interrupts her. She cries out and falls to her knees before me. I raise my eyes from hers and see a younger man with an evil look on his face and a whip in one hand. The other is still suspended in the air above the woman—an open palm having knocked her to the ground.

She begins to pull herself up from the floor, using my legs as leverage.

"I'll ask you again, Patient X. What will make patient B-143 shift?"

She gives me a small wink before she turns to the man in the white coat.

"I already told you. Nothing," she says, turning to laugh in his face.

"If you manage to do it—which I doubt—he'll slaughter each and every one of you."

The same crack sounds again, and she falls into me instead of on the floor.

She lands near enough to my ear that I can I hear when she whispers.

"Don't lose hope. Stay strong. Your mate is going to need you to be strong."

I open my mouth to ask what she means, but that evil man has raised the whip above his head to strike.

She winces at the first strike, but he doesn't stop there. I thrash my arms and legs—doing anything to reach her. The skin of her back is ripped apart. There's blood on the floor and on both of us.

When the man in the white coat determines they've done enough damage, he simply raises a hand. The other man stops his onslaught.

"Well, Patient B-143, I guess you've moved to the secondary trial."

I want to ask what the fuck he means by that, but he turns on his

heel and leaves. Some guards remove the woman, who has thank-
fully passed out from pain.
The evil man who wielded the whip steps near me, and I pull at my
restraints again. Even if he's the only one I can kill, it will be
worth it.
"Congratulation." He claps me on the shoulder and gives me a
wink before walking out the door himself. "See you in round two."

"Zeke. Zeke." Once again, Axel's voice snaps me out of my memories, and I turn to look at him.

"She was there," I whisper.

"Who was where?"

"That woman sitting with Opal. She was in the facility with me."

He glances back at the woman, and I do the same. I finally realize what must have happened that day. She has the gift of sight too. She saw a vision that day, and now she's here to help Opal with hers.

Chapter Sixteen

Opal

"Opal?" A feminine voice calls, and I raise my head, blinking the tears from my eyes. I find Rayne's mother, Valerie, standing there with a concerned look on her face.

"Are you okay?" she asks, and I shake my head. She steps forward with her hands extended, but I scuttle backward.

"Please, don't," I sob, trying to keep distance between us.

"You won't get any visions when you touch me," she assures me, and my mouth drops open in shock.

"How..."

"You and I are the same." She gives me a soft smile. "I'm so sorry that I wasn't here to help you sooner."

I shake my head. "I don't understand."

"Touch me first. See that what I'm saying is true and then I will explain everything."

I reach out and use my index finger to touch her palm. Instantly, the visions fade. Even the small ones, the constant images coming from the plants around me, are replaced by static. I push my palm toward hers, desperately linking our fingers, and breathe out a sigh of relief.

"How?" I ask.

She moves to pull her hand back, but I cling to it.

She chuckles but doesn't try to take her hand away again. Instead, she sits in front of me, allowing our hands to lay gently over our knees.

"You are an oracle, Opal."

I reflexively pull back and shake my head, but the visions crowd in again.

"That's impossible. The last oracle disappeared..." I begin, and Valerie gets a soft smile on her face. "No. You can't be."

"But I am," she says with a chuckle. "And so are you. Normally, you would've been trained by now. If I had not been held in captivity, I would have found you, and you could have complete control already. If I am correct, you've been taking a potion daily that dulled your ability. Now, they are getting stronger every day. They will continue until you learn control."

"The potion didn't stop my visions," I explain. I don't know how she knows about that, but I try to ignore that fact. "I still had visions when I was taking it."

"I'm sure you did, but they were dulled. Weren't they? It was like you were watching a movie. Not like you were the person you were seeing—not like you could feel every sensation of theirs."

I nod. It's nice to talk to someone and not struggle to explain how it feels.

"How do I get control?"

She smiles encouragingly and reaches into her satchel to pull out a pair of long gloves.

"For now, you need to wear these. The visions are always stronger with skin-to-skin contact. These won't block everything, but they will help."

Reluctantly, I let go of her hand and slide the gloves onto my own. I'm not sure where she found gloves like this in Parry Sound. I pull them all the way up past my elbows, but the visions don't stop. With no skin on my hands showing, I gently reach out my bare foot and touch her. All the tension in my body releases as that blissful static begins once more.

"You were running through the forest barefoot?" she asks, raising an eyebrow. "Why on earth would you do that?" Her tone, equal parts skeptical judgement and humorous curiosity, reminds me of Rayne. It's easy to see the resemblance between mother and daughter when she's sitting in front of me with her head cocked inquisitively to the side.

I explain about the visions I saw while kissing Zeke. I tell her that I couldn't seem to stop them, and it is like they opened the floodgates to everything else.

"Did you let the vision play out to completion?" she asks, startling me. That's certainly not the question I expected.

"Think hard. Did you cut off the connection, or did it stop on its own?"

"I think it stopped on its own."

"That's good." Her tense posture relaxes at my words.

"Why?"

She reaches down, takes off her shoes and socks, and puts them on my feet as she explains.

"The vision always needs to complete itself. If you stop it too soon, you'll just end up seeing the same thing again until you see everything you're meant to."

Once the socks and shoes are on my feet, I pull my legs back to rest on the ground in front of me.

"So, you don't think I'll see anything else if I touch Zeke again?"

She contemplates my question for a moment.

"I can't be sure that you won't see anything else if you touch him, but you won't see what you just saw again. When you complete the mating with him, you won't see anything when you touch him."

"Wait. Are you saying I couldn't see visions of Axel right now? Even if I tried?"

Valerie shakes her head.

"It's a gift or curse. You won't see visions of your mates or children unless there is something extremely important that the fates want you to see."

I breathe out a sigh of relief before my mind spins back to the hurt on both Zeke and Axel's faces when I told them not to touch me. If what she's saying is true, I probably would've been fine if they had. Surely, I can explain this to them later.

"So, how do I stop the visions?"

"You don't."

"What?"

"You don't stop them. They will always come, but you can learn to control when you see them. For instance, the visions you got when your bare feet were on the ground. Those are not important visions and do not need to be seen, so you can push them to the background. Some—like the visions you saw when you touched Zeke—are important because they will help shape who you are as an oracle."

"How do I do that?"

"With practice," she says apologetically. "Lots and lots of practice."

"Okay...but in the meantime?"

"In the meantime, you keep most of your skin covered unless you're consciously practicing. Don't touch anyone or anything with your bare skin unless you're ready for a vision to come or you're touching your bonded mate."

"But...how am I supposed to bond with Zeke if I can't touch

him?" I ask sheepishly, not completely comfortable with the way the conversation is headed.

"I think you have seen everything you needed to already. The fates knew you needed to see what he went through to believe his words. There is still a chance you will see something, but I think the worst is past."

"Opal?" I hear Axel calling my name and turn to face the direction of the sound.

"Your mates are coming to make sure you're all right. Go to them. Enjoy your time with them but meet me tomorrow to begin some of your training," Valerie says, gesturing in the direction of Axel and Zeke walking toward us together.

"Thank you, I will."

With that, she stands and walks back toward the coven just as my mates reach me.

They stand steps away, looking confused and hurt. With as much grace as I can muster, I get to my feet.

"I'm sorry—" I begin.

"No, I'm sorry. I shouldn't have rushed you. I shouldn't have pushed. If I had just given you time and ..." Zeke begins. I step over to him, place my gloved hands on either side of his face, and merge my lips with his. Just like Valerie said, no visions come. There is only an overwhelming need that thrums through my body, and I deepen the kiss.

Before things go too far, he pulls back.

"Is that a yes to a second chance?" His eyes search mine.

"Yes," I say with a smile. "It's a yes."

The smile I'm rewarded with is huge.

"Can I take you somewhere tonight? Just me and you?" he asks.

"Of course, but we have to help Axel with some designs for the new island first," I tell him, and his smile gets even wider.

"Can I help? Axel told me some of the details, and I'm excited to get involved."

"Of course," I laugh, feeling lighter than I have in years. "We're already a bit behind, so we need all the help we can get."

"What happened, angel?" Axel asks, walking up behind me so that I'm sandwiched between the two.

"I had a vision when I kissed Zeke."

Zeke steps back in horror.

"What did you see?" he almost demands, but it's not out of anger. I can see the fear written all over his face.

"Nothing important," I say, closing the distance between us and giving him a soft kiss on his lips.

With Zeke on one side and Axel on the other, we walk back to their house, head straight into the kitchen, and get to work.

We work on the design for hours. It's a good thing Zeke decided to help because he and Axel make an amazing team. By the time we take a break, the designs are nearly complete. We only need the plans for each individual faction.

"Man, this is going to be so awesome," Zeke says.

"It really is. Nothing like this has been done," I agree. "Well...not that I've ever heard of."

"I guess you wouldn't have heard about it if it worked. If we do this right, we will never have to worry about hunters or needing to hide our true selves ever again," Axel adds.

Axel and Zeke are in deep conversation about some equation determining the necessary density of something when there's a gentle knock on the doorjamb.

"Sorry to interrupt. I was hoping to meet Opal." I turn to see a beautiful woman in the doorway. She's a little taller than me with long, brown hair and mossy, green eyes. The eyes are familiar enough that I know she must be the mother of my mates.

"Oh, hi!" I say, getting up from my chair and walking over to her.

Instantly, she wraps me up in a big hug. "Oh, Opal. It's so nice to finally meet you!"

After a second, I recover from the shock and wrap my arms around her.

"It's nice to meet you too."

She pulls back from me, looking me over.

"You're so beautiful. Come, let's leave the boys and have some tea."

She pulls me out of the kitchen and into a small sitting room. There is already a steaming teapot and two cups of tea waiting.

We sit and talk over the next couple of hours. Although I don't know her, conversation flows easily between us. The way her eyes sparkle as she regales me with stories of the boys shows me just how much she loves them. If she is curious about the gloves I wear, she doesn't show it.

A throat clearing from the doorway has my eyes snapping in that direction.

"Oh, Zeke. There you are." She smiles widely at the sight of him. "We were just talking about you."

He seems to blanche at that thought.

"I hope it was all good."

"Of course, it was. I was just telling Opal some of the things you and your brother got up to as children," his mom answers, and I giggle.

"Great," he mutters. "Are you ready, Opal?"

"For what?" I ask, confused.

"I hope you planned something good," his mom warns. "Go on, sweetheart. We will chat more tomorrow."

She rises and helps me to my feet. She gives me a kiss on the cheek. Like before, I tense under her touch, but the visions never come.

"Thank you so much," I respond, wrapping her in a hug before walking over to Zeke. "Are you going to tell me what you have planned?"

"Nope. You're just going to have to wait and see," he chuckles, taking my gloved hand and leading me out the door. I manage to kick off Valerie's shoes and slip on my own just before being pulled away.

Chapter Seventeen

Opal

If someone had told me last week that I would be holding hands with Zeke on our way to a surprise date, I would have said they were insane. Yet here I am. I'm in my signature yoga pants and sneakers, and I'm glad I dressed comfortably. Ever since I met these brothers, I've done so much walking. If I had worn my heels, my feet would be throbbing by now.

"Can you trust me for a few minutes?" Zeke asks. I nod, but panic hits me when he pulls out a blindfold. "It's just until we get there. Maybe five more minutes."

I turn so that he can secure the blindfold.

"Can you see anything?" he asks.

"Nope," I respond.

"Good," he says, grabbing my hands and leading me forward. Just like he promised, it's about five minutes later when we come to a stop.

"Ready?" he asks.

"As I'll ever be," I giggle. There is a small part of my brain that worries this is a trick. Would he lead me out here just to reject me again?

I push that voice aside. After hearing—and seeing—what happened to him, I understand his reasoning. Their mother, Alexa, and I talked about it during our visit. She believes we could have been fine if we'd come straight back to the sleuth, but we will never know.

As Zeke slips the blindfold from my eyes, I look around. We're by the lake, and there are fairy lights strung up from tree to tree. They look like stars twinkling in the night sky. Off to the side, there is a small cabin with a table for two set up on the front porch.

"This is beautiful, Zeke," I whisper.

"Are you hun—" he starts, but I stop his words with a soft kiss on his mouth.

This is the most romantic date I've ever had. No one has ever done anything like this for me.

"I could eat," I respond with a chuckle as I step back, and the two of us walk over to the table.

As he lifts the silver lids off each plate, I get the biggest smile on my face.

"McDonald's?"

"I'm not the best cook, so I hope you like Big Macs," Zeke responds with a shrug.

"Oh, I do!" I exclaim. I slip off the gloves—because you can't eat a Big Mac in long, elegant gloves—and dig in. I moan with the first bite. It's been so long since I had a nice, greasy burger.

"Keep making sounds like that, and we won't make it through dinner," Zeke says. I look up to meet his heated gaze. Suddenly, I want to keep making that noise just to see how far I can push him. I try to refocus on getting to know my mate instead of trying to seduce him.

"Let's play twenty questions," I suggest. "I'll go first. What is your favorite color?"

"Okay," he says with a chuckle. "Blue. What is yours?"

I ponder that for a moment. "I have so many, but honestly, it's black. Green is a close second."

"Black isn't a color; it's a shade," he laughs.

I give him a pointed look. We don't need to argue technicalities on our first actual date.

"Well, then, I guess green is my favorite color. Do you have any hobbies?"

"Hmm. Before I was taken, I loved building things. I would make tables and chairs. I loved designing furniture. Watching the designs come to life was always a thrill. What about you?" He's trying to make light of his time in captivity, but he's going to have to talk about it eventually.

"I would love to see some of the furniture you make." I choose a fry and chew it thoughtfully while I try to determine what my hobbies are. "I guess I'm still finding myself again. For a long time after you...well...just...*after*, I pretended to be someone else—someone who didn't care about anyone or anything. That person didn't have room for hobbies. When I figure it out, you'll be the first to know."

"About that, I will never be able to explain how sorry I am. If I honestly thought there was any other way, I never would have left you," he says, reaching his hand over and placing it on mine.

"It's okay. I understand your reasons now. I wish things had turned out differently, but we can't change the past." I give his hand a squeeze.

"Well," Zeke pauses after a nervous chuckle. "I was going to try really hard not to talk about that. I only made it three questions in."

"You're right. Let's change the subject again," I agree.

"How about we go for a walk on the beach," he offers.

I nod eagerly. His idea is perfect.

We hold hands and walk along the beach. We don't talk much, but it's nice to just be close to one another.

"Tell me something no one else knows about you," I say.

"Hmm. That one is hard because Axel knows just about everything about me. But..." He slides his hand through his hair. When Axel is nervous, he rubs the back of his neck, and it seems like Zeke's tell is running his hands through his hair. It's cute. "I guess —no one knows that my favorite movie of all time is *The Princess Bride*."

"Really?" The choice is a little sappier than I expected from the big, strong alpha at my side.

"Yes. Just don't tell Axel," he says, and I give him a raised eyebrow. "I'll never hear the end of it from him."

"Hmm," I threaten playfully. "I'll try, but I do sometimes forget..."

Rather than pleading with me like I expect, he begins tickling me.

We are both in fits of laughter when we land on the soft sand. With him on top of me, the tickling suddenly stops. Our playfulness instantly turns to lust. Gods, this man makes my blood boil—in a good way. After a moment of silence, our mouths find each other. Instantly, the heat turns up. I wrap my arms and legs around him, using my legs to pull his body even closer to me. Already, I can feel his erection grinding into my core.

We are a tangle of limbs on the sand as our hands roam each other's bodies. His hands—impossibly large and gentle—explore my legs and chest.

I clutch at his back, trying to get closer. It's not enough. Even though he's right on top of me, he still feels too far away. I grab his shirt and try to pull it up over his head. I need to feel his skin.

He pulls back momentarily. "Are you sure?"

"You really want to ask me that right now?" I chuckle and begin kissing the taut muscles of his neck.

"Opal," he groans, but I don't stop. I know he is trying to make sure that I'm not going to regret this. It's sweet. Right now, though, all I care about is making him mine.

I use my body weight to shift us so that I am on top of him. I continue exploring his chest and neck with my mouth, but I begin grinding myself against him. I am far from discreet, but I can feel that his need is as urgent as mine.

He grips my hips, forcing me to slow my motion.

"Opal, you need to be sure before we take this any farther."

"Are you going to reject me again?" I ask.

"What? No! Never," he exclaims.

"Then, I'm sure. Now stop talking and start stripping," I demand, removing my own shirt and revealing the embarrassingly unappealing sports bra underneath. What? I wasn't expecting today to go this way.

Zeke takes the hint and removes his shirt as I rip off my sports bra. He sucks in a breath when he realizes I'm bare. He sits up and places his mouth around one of my nipples, sucking and flicking it with his tongue.

"Zeke," I moan.

He pulls back with a growl and flips us back over so that he's on top once more.

"I've dreamed about this so many times," he whispers, breathless, as he trails kisses down my neck. He pauses at my other breast, lavishing it with the same attention as the first.

"More. I need more," I plead. In this position, I'm unable to grind on him, unable to find my release.

Zeke slowly moves down my body, kissing his way down my stomach.

"Yes," I say, willing him to go faster—to go lower.

I raise my hips, trying to push my core into his face. I want—no, need—his mouth on my pussy.

As he gets closer, a low growl rumbles from his chest, and he loses control. He rips my pants down, underwear and all, and latches onto my clit. The change is so sudden and complete that I cry out. He doesn't stop—doesn't slow. He just sucks my clit into his mouth, flicking it over and over with his tongue.

I weave my hands through his hair, pulling him closer. I wish that I could have his tongue teasing me and his cock moving inside me at the same time. I almost get my wish as he slides two fingers inside of me, pumping in and out.

"Yes. Oh, my gods, yes!" I cry out as my orgasm overtakes me.

"I forgot how sexy it is when you come," he says as he pulls his fingers out of me, licking them clean.

I lower my hands, grasping at his pants. I need them off...like...yesterday.

I get frustrated after only a few seconds.

"Off," I growl. He quickly gets to work unbuckling his belt and lowering his pants. He lines up his cock with my core and slowly pushes inside. He moans with each inch.

"I need you to move," I plead.

"Just wait a second, angel," he chuckles. "I haven't done this in eleven years. If you want it to last longer than a minute..." he begins, but I start to move my lower body against him anyway. I can't stop.

I impale myself on his cock over and over, chasing the release I can feel rising within me as his cock slides over my G-spot repeatedly.

"I'm so close," I cry, desperately trying to move faster and harder.

I try to clutch at his back, but I am unable to get a good grip unless I use my nails. As I sink them into his back, he growls loudly and begins to move—pounding in and out of me.

My power flares, and I move my hands to his shoulders. My back arches off the ground.

"Gods," I cry out as my power sinks inside him, and his teeth sink into my neck, on the opposite side of Axel's mark.

My orgasm kicks up a notch, and my legs begin to shake. The mating bond snaps into place, and it's as if I am finally full for the first time in my life. There is no hole in my soul.

He removes his teeth from my neck and laps at the newly made mate mark. I fall back, utterly spent, as Zeke collapses on top of me.

"Uh, Zeke," I rasp, as I'm crushed under his body weight. He pulls himself back up, and I suck in a breath.

"Sorry," he apologizes and removes his weight from my body.

"Opal..." He looks at me with so many emotions flitting across his face, and I worry for a moment that he regrets what we just did. "That was amazing. Honestly, I was ready to beg and grovel for the rest of my life just to be your friend. The fact that you accepted me as your mate is..."

"You don't have to say anything. I know. I forgive you for before. Like we said earlier, let's focus on the future." I sit up and kiss him on his lips.

"Okay," he says, and he helps me get dressed once more. Then, he carries me further across the beach to a small blanket set up with pillows.

"Well, this would've come in handy about ten minutes ago," I chuckle.

"It sure would've," he agrees, laying me down before snuggling in behind me.

I had been worried that our bond wouldn't snap into place because of the previous rejection, but it seems fate has deemed his reason for that to be noble enough to give us a second chance. Maybe the rejection was never truly complete because neither of us truly accepted it.

Either way, both brothers now wear a mark made by my magic. It's a small black circle surrounded by another full circle and two more that are disconnected with dots between them. It's a symbol I vaguely recognize but can't for the life of me remember. I guess it doesn't really matter. All that matters is that I am now complete; all three of us have been marked by one another.

I would love to say that I stay awake and enjoy the moment, but that would be a lie. The truth is, I fall asleep instantly, feeling completely at peace for the first time in my life.

Chapter Eighteen

Axel

Reluctantly, I leave Opal with my mother. After saying a quick goodbye and giving her a kiss, I head over to Alaric's. It surprised me that Opal forgave Zeke so easily, but it shouldn't have. She is truly an angel, and even I have to admit that Zeke took the safer of his shitty options. He's right that there was no knowing what would've happened if the hunters had caught them both.

Feeling lighter than ever, I walk up to Alaric's house.

"I hear congratulations are in order," Alaric says, coming from the side of the porch.

I accept the beer he offers me.

"Thanks. Yes, I suppose there are."

"I also heard she was talking to Zeke today," he probes. Some people say men don't gossip, but that's not true. We only gossip with the person the gossip is about—not behind their back.

"That's also true." I keep my response vague, but I know he'll ask for more details. Still, I'm not going to offer up information without him asking.

"And..." He looks at me expectantly.

"Well, it seems that she forgave him after hearing his reasons," I tell him.

"After our talk the other day, I was thinking. It does make more sense that he was trying to keep her safe. Zeke is a lot of things, but he's never been selfish. I had difficulty believing he would reject his mate without cause," Alaric leans up against the railing, sips his own beer, and looks out at the lake.

"I know," I sigh. "Knowing that he hurt my mate as well, made it difficult for me to think rationally."

"I completely understand that," Alaric chuckles. "Do you know he called me to find out what she likes."

"He did?" I ask, turning to him in surprise.

"Yup, Phoebe took the phone. She told him some things and threatened him. If he hurts her again, he'll have to deal with Phoebe." Alaric chuckles, and I join in. Now Zeke's mention of Phoebe being scary makes a whole lot more sense.

"You guys coming?" Phoebe joins us on the porch.

"Speaking of mates," Alaric says, snagging Phoebe by the waist and pulling her into him.

"Everyone is waiting for us," Phoebe says with a laugh as Alaric rubs his scruff on her neck.

"All right, that's enough of that," I laugh and walk into the house and away from the flirting couple.

As soon as I enter the house, Sarah corners me.

"Where's Opal?"

"She's with my mom right now, and then she's going on a date with Zeke," I reply. The anger on her face is palpable and expected.

"How could you let her be alone with him?" Sarah's body begins to glow purple, and I take an involuntary step back.

"Listen, Sarah, I understand how you feel about Zeke. I'm happy that you care for Opal, but it's her decision. Neither of us could tell her not to forgive him. She is her own woman."

"I know that," she growls at me. "After what he did to her, how could she want anything to do with him?"

"He had his reasons for doing what he did, and it's not my place to tell you what they are." I love that Sarah is so protective of Opal, but my mate needs to make her own decisions.

"If he hurts her..." she begins, but I cut her off.

"Trust me, I will be the first in line." I place my hand on her shoulder and let the anger slip from my body. "I honestly don't think he would do anything to hurt her now. I know Zeke is going to have to gain everyone's trust, and he knows that too. Why don't you let him tell you his reasons and then decide for yourself."

"You didn't see her before. Hell, I wasn't even there when it happened eleven years ago..."

Thankfully, Sebastyn arrives to save me.

"Axel is right, love. I had a tough time believing Zeke was the one who rejected Opal when I found out. If you knew him before, you would have too. Let's wait and talk to Opal or Zeke before jumping to conclusions."

She melts into his side with a nod, and the purple slowly fades from her body. I know Zeke will have to prove himself to Sarah, and I'm grateful that my mate found such a loyal friend.

"I just don't want her to get hurt again," Sarah says.

"None of us want that. I missed out on so much time with her because of his rejection. I am still pissed at him for it. If it were up to me, he would still be groveling for a chance with her. But Opal sat with him earlier..." She goes to interrupt, but I hold up my hand and continue. "Whatever he said made her choose to give him another chance, and we all need to respect that. If you try to get in between Opal and one of her mates, you'll push her away. Imagine if someone tried to warn you away from Sebastyn. How would you feel?"

"But Sebastyn never hurt me the way that Zeke hurt her."

"No, he didn't. But you also don't know the full story. And

until you do, you shouldn't make any rash decisions." She nods in response, and the three of us enter the office together where the rest of the group members—other than Alaric and Phoebe—are waiting.

"Hey, Axel!" Skarlyt is the first to greet us. "Opal sent us a picture of your island, and it's awesome. Have you worked on it anymore?"

"Actually…" I pull out the drawings and blueprints that Zeke and I worked on this morning. "Zeke and I drew these up. We think it's entirely possible to get this done in the time frame. But I have a few questions for you."

She looks over the papers with a smile on her face. "Such as?"

"Well, we assume it's possible but want to confirm with you…Can the witches use clay to create pipes that run through the island while we are building it so that we can set up running water?" Zeke and I would like to avoid using plastics on the island, but plumbing is non-negotiable. "If we cut down trees to build the homes, is it possible for the earth witches to help them grow back faster? If we take everything we need from Parry Sound over the next week, we are going to decimate the ecosystem here."

"Hmm…Theoretically, yes. On both accounts. I've never heard of it done before—the pipes—but I don't see why not. If we can create an island, clay pipes will be simple. As for the trees, we may not be able to get them back to the exact stage of life they are in now. We can probably get them close though." Skarlyt looks back down at the drawing, seeming confused. "What's this?"

I glance to where she is pointing.

"Oh, that's where the freshwater spring needs to go to filter water throughout the island. If you're still planning on having it in the middle of the ocean, we will need to create a freshwater spring. Unless…can you use magic to convert sea water into fresh water?"

"I didn't even think of that. Seb?" She calls her brother over.

"Is there a spell or device we can make that automatically filters salt water into fresh water?

"I don't know. But there is a spell we can place at the bottom of the spring that will automatically bring water from another source. It's like a portal, but it's always open. When the water level gets too low, it will refill with water from the source." Seb watches us both for a response.

"That could work," I say, rubbing my beard. "I also want to see if we can connect it to a waterfall that flows into a stream. That would help to purify it."

"Skarlyt, this is going to be a much bigger job than you were anticipating," Sebastyn begins, sounding wary. "I'm not sure we will have the manpower to get it done in this time frame."

"Too bad, bitches," Rayne interrupts, stepping through the door with Drake on her heels. "We need this done even sooner because our timeline just got moved up.

As one, we all turn toward her.

"What do you mean?" Alaric asks.

"Matt has been listening in on hunter conversations. They've caught on. They're planning on coming to scope out the Orillia lab in four days. So, essentially, we have three days to raid each facility and get the fuck out of here, or we have a large team waiting at Orillia and send smaller teams out to the others. Either way, four days is the most time we have."

In Rayne's flippant tone, it doesn't sound like a death sentence, but we all know it is.

"Can it be done?" Alaric asks, and everyone turns to me and Skarlyt.

"Theoretically..." she begins.

"The biggest issue will be the vampires," I look pointedly at Drake. "We need time to build something that keeps them safe from the sun."

"We can bring them into a pocket world for now." Drake's

sister, Drusilla, offers the suggestion, but she turns it toward her own mate. "If we create a pocket world on the island while it's being built, then they can stay safe during the day and help build at night. We can do that right?"

"Is it possible to make a pocket world big enough for everyone until the island is ready?" I speak up before he can respond.

"I would think so. The issue is going to be housing. The pocket world River and I created is a copy of my home from centuries ago," he says. "I don't know of anywhere big enough to house everyone."

"Wait..." Rayne begins. "Is it possible to teleport houses? You know, like you teleport people. What if all we need to do is build the island and then send all our houses over there? That would cut down the time, right?"

If it worked, that would fix everything. We would only need to focus on the main construction of the island, the water sources, and other foundational stuff. Hell, if we could teleport the entire plumbing system and everything...

"I've never tried to teleport anything like that. In theory, it should work—with enough magic that is..." Sebastyn says.

"What about the actual ground underneath each house?" I am not hopeful, but I have to ask. "Could you teleport the entire town, plumbing, and everything?"

"It would take a lot of power, and I do mean a lot." Sebastyn shares a look with Skarlyt, who then looks at Phoebe and Sophia.

"We can help with the power boost, but someone is going to have to make us cry. Like a lot," Phoebe says and Alaric growls. "Oh, come on. It's not like they're really going to hurt me. I just need to cry."

"I don't like it when you cry," he says, pulling her close to him.

"I don't know why you're getting all upset about making her cry. All we need to do is put on *A Dog's Purpose*. She and Sophia would be blubbering messes within the first hour," Rayne says with a shrug.

"Even Rayne cries at that one," Drake says with a smirk. Given the death glare that she shoots him, I'd wager that was not something she wanted to share, and I let out a little chuckle.

"What's that?" Sophia asks.

"You've never seen it?" Phoebe says. "It's a movie about this dog who has to find his purpose, and he gets reincarnated, and—" She stops herself. "Rayne is right. We will have enough tears after watching it to power up every single witch in the coven."

"Okay, so Phoebe and Sophia will be watching a movie tonight. We will need to start the island base in earnest tomorrow. I say we leave space to teleport the towns in—we will need to measure to make sure there is enough space. Seb, I need you to find a spell for that. We need something close enough that we can tweak it for our purpose." Skarlyt takes over the conversation, and we begin to plan the essentials.

The sky has turned dark, and we're still trying to figure out where to place this island. We thought that detail was already hammered out, but it turns out not everyone agreed. Most have opted to go closer to the Caribbean, but others—particularly the vampires—would prefer the shorter daylight hours of the northern hemisphere.

"If the entire coven could walk in the daylight like us," Rayne begins, "it wouldn't be an issue. But most of them don't even know that we can. If we could figure out how we are able to do it maybe—"

She is interrupted by a flash of light that reveals a beautiful blonde who has appeared inside the kitchen. Immediately, we are all on high alert. Obviously, I'm not the only one who doesn't know who she is.

"Perhaps I can shed some light on that," the blonde says, watching Rayne.

"And who the fuck are you?" Rayne asks, stepping in front of her mate in a protective manner.

The other woman waves her hand in a dismissive manner.

"You are not in any danger from me, granddaughter."

"Granddaughter?" Rayne stutters.

"Well, there's a few extra 'greats' in there I don't feel like saying, but yes. You are my granddaughter." As soon as the woman mentions the familial connection, I can see it. Like Rayne, she's a natural beauty. Although she is small in stature, she fills the room with her presence.

"Does someone want to go get my mom?" Rayne asks the witches arrayed behind her without looking away from the other woman. Skarlyt nods, blinks away, and returns seconds later with another unfamiliar woman. She's the same woman who was talking to Opal earlier, and I guess she must be Rayne's mother.

"What's going on?" she asks, turning to look at everyone before stopping, stunned, at the blonde. "Artemis?"

"At least someone knows who I am. I was beginning to wonder if you all had forgotten the gods," Artemis says with a smile.

"Wait. Artemis? As in *the* Artemis? Greek goddess of the hunt?" Rayne asks, and she nods. "But I can't be your granddaughter...I'm a descendant of Ullr, the Norse god. Right?"

She turns to her mom for answers, but the older woman just shrugs her shoulders.

"Chauvinism at its finest. You are the descendant of Skadi—the Norse *goddess* of the hunt." She makes sure to enunciate the word 'goddess' as she speaks. "The men in your family didn't want to trace their lineage back to a female god, so they replaced me with the name of the male god instead."

"Okay," Rayne prods. "You aren't Skadi though."

"We live an exceedingly long time, and—I'm sure you understand—sometimes we get bored. I have gone by many names in my long life, and Skadi is one of them," Artemis says.

"I think I need to sit down," Rayne says, and Drake pulls out a chair for her.

"You probably should. If you are struggling with that, what comes next will be worse.

Long ago there was a powerful oracle who prophesied—" Artemis begins.

"Yes. We know all about the prophecy. Andres' mother was the oracle," Rayne snaps, and Artemis shoots her a death glare. Now I know where Rayne gets it from.

"I don't know it," I speak up. I've heard bits and pieces of it but never the whole thing.

Artemis gives me a small, indulgent smile.

"As I was saying, an oracle prophesied a new enemy would awaken and bring about a time when supernaturals would need to make themselves known to defend the world." Artemis locks eyes with Andres in a challenging glare I do not understand. "Would you like to do the honors?"

Andres takes a deep breath before stepping forward. His eyes glaze over as he recalls the ancient prophecy and presents it for this new audience.

"When the daughter of the storm and the son of the moon become one;

A hunter and her prey put aside their differences;

The lost daughter of air mates the first son born of magic and fire;

A son and daughter of fire join together;

The dual natured son and the dawn cement their bond;

A new age arrives where supernatural beings will

need to come out of the shadows as a new enemy awakens."

"Some of the prophecy has already come to fruition." Artemis nods toward Sarah and Sebastyn and then Drake and Rayne. "The gods and goddesses who once gave up on this world have started waking, and they are not happy with what they see." Andres visibly flinches at her tone. "The prophecy says this enemy is new to you, but she's certainly not new to this world."

"Wait. You don't mean...?" Andres pales.

"I do, King of Dragons. She is not happy—not happy at all," Artemis responds with a smile.

"King of Dragons?" Rayne asks, narrowing her eyes at Andres. "We are definitely talking about that later. Who is *she*? Who are you two talking about?"

Thankfully, Rayne has no problem grilling the literal goddess in our midst with the questions I am sure we all want the answers to.

Artemis turns away and her eyes flash gold before a look of panic crosses her face.

"There will be time for questions later. Right now, I need every supernatural woman within your ranks in one place so I can protect them from her first attack."

"What attack?" I growl. I need to get to Opal. Zeke was supposed to take her to the cabin. Hopefully, they're still there.

"Sound the alarm. We can get everyone in the bunker," Alaric says.

"Where is this 'bunker'?" Artemis asks.

"Downstairs," Phoebe says, pointing towards the open doorway.

Artemis nods, closes her eyes for a moment, and waves her hand. Suddenly, every woman in the room is no longer present.

Everyone who is left shouts in shock and anger.

"They are in your bunker," Artemis raises her voice above the various complaints. "They are there with every other supernatural woman within a hundred miles." She sounds exasperated or bored by our slowness—not like someone who just did the impossible by teleporting every woman I know into the basement with a thought.

I rush down the stairs, needing to ensure that Opal is there. I don't know what attack Artemis is trying to protect us from, but it must be bad if a goddess is interfering.

Chapter Nineteen

Unknown

I slumber for a millennia and wake to a world I no longer recognize.

My beautiful earth. What have they done to you?

The glen I had chosen for my sleep—once filled with wildflowers and trees—is now a small garden surrounded by stone structures.

I step out of the meager, dull garden and onto the stone pathway, leaving a trail of green life erupting in my wake. Outside that garden, there is less and less green and more and more of these stone structures. The tall trees have been replaced by large buildings. The fresh, crisp air has been replaced by a thick, poison fog.

I look around, searching for my children. They were meant to look after this world while I slept. Where are the dragons who were tasked with keeping the peace? How could they have let this happen?

I step into the vale and search. Traveling through the vale is faster, and I can search for my children quickly. Everywhere I look, however, I see only one species...human. The humans have bred like rabbits and taken over my beautiful world, leaving only destruction in its place.

I can feel that it is night, but the sky is still alight. It is infected by the shining, stone structures.

I finally locate one of my children and step from the vale.

"Child, what has happened to this world?"

The vampire before me spins in shock and bares her fangs at me.

"You have no need to fear me. I wish to know what has happened to this world."

"What do you mean?" she asks.

"I have been asleep for a long time. I awoke to find this world overrun by humans."

She surprises me by laughing.

"Where are the supernatural beings who control this world?" I ask again.

"The supernaturals who—" She laughs harder. "The world belongs to the humans."

I do not let her finish. I bring my hand to her cheek and absorb her memories.

So much destruction. So much death.

"What did you just do?" she snaps and steps away.

She is too young. I need to find someone old enough to know what happened here. I step back into the vale without answering her question and resume my search.

The more I see, the more furious I become. How could the dragons let this happen? The gods have been forgotten. The humans live their puny, little lives and focus only on money. The supernatural beings—the few I find—are unaware of their true purpose and lineage.

I eventually find a shifter to question. She is not old enough to know all, but she is an elder in her sleuth. When I step from the vale, she gasps before falling to her knees.

"Goddess," she whispers, her long, gray hair spilling over her face and onto the floor.

"Rise, my child," I tell her, and she peeks up at me from under long lashes. She slowly rises to her feet, her plump body creaking and cracking as she does so.

"What has happened to my world?" I ask, and her mouth opens and closes like a fish. "You do not need to fear me. You are far too young to have caused the trouble I seek to avenge."

She nods hesitantly and reaches her hand out to me.

"I don't know everything, but I can share what I know."

As I touch her hand and close my eyes, I am assaulted by visions of the past hundred years. Beyond the span of her own lifetime, she carries the stories her own elders shared with her.

The visions make me weep. My poor, poor earth. As I see how the supernaturals abandoned the world, my fists clench, and my teeth grind.

When I step back from the woman, she shrinks under the intensity of my gaze.

"I have seen into your heart, Magdalena Garrison, and found you pure. You have nothing to fear from me."

With those words, I spin and step back into the vale, searching for a place of safety. I eventually find a place that is still green and alive, untouched by human hands, and breathe out a sigh. Of the entire world, only a small portion remains pure.

I wave my hands and, with a thought, erect a small dwelling to provide shelter for me as I begin my planning.

This will not stand. Supernatural and humankind alike—they all need to be punished.

We will see how they fare when they are no longer able to procreate. I close my eyes and let my power wash over me. I will it to spread far and wide across the planet they have corrupted.

If they cannot multiply—if they cannot constantly, mindlessly increase their numbers—my earth may stand a chance. If they repent, I may reverse this decision. If not, they will suffer for nothing.

I could wipe them all out with a single thought and rebuild, but I am a patient and merciful goddess. I will give them a chance to redeem themselves.

For now, I will watch and wait.

I admit I am rather curious to see how this plays out.

Chapter Twenty

Opal

I wake up on the beach with Zeke wrapped around me and snuggle deeper into him. After round two, we didn't bother getting dressed again. We knew there would most likely be a round three.

I think over the last few days and smile to myself. So much is true today that would have seemed impossible even a week ago.

I rub my hand over Zeke's bare arm, tracing one of his scars. I am immediately overtaken by a vision. Unlike the visions of Axel, Zeke's visions are disturbing. They feel like being caught in a nightmare. Valerie said I wouldn't have visions of Zeke after we mated, but perhaps this is something I am meant to see.

Zeke sits alone in his cell. I can hear his stomach rumbling and see his body shiver. He stills a second before the door swings open to reveal a man in a white coat with a sneer on his face.
"Ready for your interview?" he asks with a dark chuckle.
Zeke's entire body makes sounds of protest as he tries to stand. Although his body is shivering in fear, his face remains blank.

I follow along as they walk down the hallway. At first glance it looks like a doctor's office, but its true purpose becomes clear when they enter one of the exam rooms. This is a torture chamber. The shelves and hooks on the walls are filled with whips and knives.

"You know the drill," the man in the white coat says, and Zeke goes to stand by the chair and raises his hands above his head. The man secures cuffs that are hanging from the ceiling to his wrists before doing the same with the ones laying at his feet.

"Where is your pack?" he sneers. Zeke's body tenses up just before the first strike of the whip. Every inch of skin the whip touches, swells and fills with blood.

"You know, we brought in a female yesterday...Perhaps she is your mate. If you cooperate, maybe we will let her go."

Zeke's entire body freezes, and a growl rips from his chest.

The man in the white coat chuckles and continues.

"I mean, how many female bear shifters could there really be in the world?"

Zeke's entire body relaxes at his words, and he lets out a breath.

I'm ripped out of the vision and open my eyes to find myself naked in the middle of Alaric's bunker.

"What the fuck?" I say loudly, looking around me.

The bunker is filled with women. Some I recognize; some I don't.

"Opal!" Sarah cries, rushing over to me.

I grab a blanket off one of the cots and notice a lot of other women in the same predicament—butt-ass naked—doing the same.

Sarah weaves through the throngs of women to get to me, and I see some of our friends following her.

"Are you okay?" She runs her hands over my shoulders and down my arms. Visions try to overtake me, but I push them away the way Valerie taught me until the woman herself slips her hand in mine. I look down at our entwined hands and then back up to her face with a grateful smile before turning back to Sarah to answer.

"I'm not hurt, but I'm wondering why the fuck I am here and not snuggling with Zeke," I bite out. Maybe I'm a little bitter that I was taken away from my mate so soon after we found our way back to one another.

Sarah's eyebrows shoot up.

"So, you and...Zeke?" Anger laces her words. I know she's not mad at me—not really. She's just worried and being protective.

I give her a soft smile. "It's so much different than we thought, Sarah. He had his reasons. As much as I hate to admit it, they're actually really good reasons. Do you think I would've given in already if they weren't?"

"Well, no...I guess I didn't think of it like that." Sarah looks a little ashamed.

"Fucking Artemis," Rayne grumbles as she makes it to our group.

"Wait...What?" I ask.

"Oh, yeah. You missed it. Apparently, I have some psycho goddess as a great-great—I don't know how many greats—grandmother, and she just decided to pop us all down here without warning. You can't just pop into someone's kitchen with this 'I'm your grandmother' shit." Rayne seems like she's about to go off on a tangent, so I shoot Drusilla a pointed look and jerk my head toward Rayne.

"We can explain more later. Right now, we need to figure out what's going on and where all these women came from," Dru suggests, and we all nod. Rayne continues to mutter under her breath about psycho goddesses.

"Opal?" I hear Axel calling my name, and I climb up on one of the bunks to wave.

"Over here." I lift my arms as much as I can without losing the blanket. "Axel!" I yell out louder, and his eyes snap to mine.

He visibly relaxes upon meeting my eyes, and he begins to make his way over to me. The women in his path part like the red sea as he approaches, giving him a straight shot to my side.

"Thank the gods," he says as he reaches me and lifts me from the bed.

"We are not thanking goddesses," Rayne adds.

"Rayne," Dru warns as a beautiful, blonde woman approaches us with the rest of the men. She is gorgeous, and there's an other-worldly glow about her.

As their shock subsides, the other women in the bunker start panicking. Phoebe steps up, hopping on the bed that I was just on, puts her fingers in her mouth, and lets off a loud whistle.

"Hello, everyone! I'm sure you're all wondering why you're here. And...well...we aren't entirely sure. We do know that this is the safest place for you at the moment. If you would please use your bonds or phones—whatever you need—to contact your mates or family, let them know that you are currently in the bunker under the alpha house on Westwood pack land. Tell them they are more than welcome to come join you, but it's going to get crowded fast."

"Why is this the safest place for us?"

"Are we under attack?"

"I don't belong here."

Unfamiliar women begin firing off questions in rapid succession in a panic. Something about the last voice causes me to pause, and I search for the one who said she doesn't belong here. I find her without issue—she's standing on her own in a corner, looking terrified.

"Like Phoebe said, we don't have all the details yet. I promise you will know as soon as we have them." Like any good alpha, Alaric is his most reassuring when there's an emergency.

"What we do know is that there is a magical attack focused on the women of the world, and you were brought here to keep you safe." Alaric pauses and looks to Artemis for confirmation. At her nod, he continues, "It shouldn't be long." He once again looks to Artemis for direction, and she nods once more. "Then, you will all be able to return to your homes. I would ask that any leaders among you remain behind to discuss the escalating situation."

"What situation?"

"Why do we need to stay here?"

"What kind of magical attack?"

"How did you get so many of us here at once?"

Alaric speaks up again. "We will let you know as soon as we do. For now, we have young children in here who do not need to know the dangers of the world yet."

As he says the last part, we look around. There are, indeed, young girls and women holding babies among us. The group quiets down to avoid scaring them.

"We need to check on that girl who didn't belong here," I whisper to Sarah.

"Why?"

"There's just something about her. She is standing all alone, while most of the others are in groups." Sarah nods, and I lead her, Sebastyn, and Axel over to the girl, keeping a tight hold on Valerie's hand as I go. To her credit, she doesn't seem to mind and I'm very much enjoying the static in my head.

She's young, nineteen at the most, with long curly blonde—almost white—hair and bright green eyes. As we approach, her entire body tenses up and I pause, turning to Axel and Sebastyn. "You two should stay here. She's already scared enough."

I don't give them a chance to respond before grabbing Sarah's hand, and the two of us walk over.

"Hi," I say, using my most non-threatening voice.

"I don't belong here. I'm not a member of any pride or pack," she begins, her voice shaking.

"It's okay. No one here is going to hurt you." Sarah steps closer to her. She tries to shrink into the wall, but there's nowhere for her to go.

"What type of supernatural are you?" I question, and she looks confused. "If you're here with us, then you must be some type."

She looks around again, and for the first time in my life, I wish I was a shifter with the ability to scent her. As if knowing where my thoughts were headed, Samara charges in and walks right up to her.

"What are you?" Samara questions, sniffing the girl. Surprisingly, instead of being afraid, the girl scents her back and her eyes widen in surprise.

"You're a feline shifter? I didn't think there were any prides in this area. I've been alone for so long...I wish I would've known," the girl says.

"I am a mountain lion. What are you? I can only tell you're a big feline," Samara responds.

"I'm a tiger," the girl says, and we all suck in a breath.

Axel steps up, no longer worried about scaring the girl. "How long have you been in the area?" I have no idea why that would matter, but it seems to mean something to him.

The girl looks at him, fear no longer in her eyes. "Just over eleven years. My family was taken by hunters and when we were being transported..." Tears shine in her eyes as she takes a shaky breath. "My parents created a distraction long enough for me and my younger brother to escape."

"Where is your brother?" Axel looks around as if searching for the boy.

"I don't know. We had been on the run for weeks, stopping only to sleep and forage for food. Then one day we heard a noise and took off...One second, he was right behind me, and the next he was gone. It's why I've stayed in the area for so long, I was hoping to find him."

Axel's face pales at her story and I step up and snuggle into his side. He wraps his arms around me tightly. "I need to find Zeke."

"He took me to some cabin by the lake," I tell him, still unsure why this girl's story is affecting him.

"I'll be back." He drops a soft kiss on my lips and walks away. I share a confused look with Sarah and shrug. I don't know any more than she does.

"What's your name?" Samara asks.

"Meredith."

"Well, Meredith, welcome to the Westwood pack. You're not alone anymore. You will never have to be alone again. If we can, we will find your family," Samara says, pulling the young girl into her and wrapping her in a hug.

Meredith stiffens momentarily before melting into Samara, and sobs begin to wrack her body.

"I'm going to get Phoebe and Aurora," Sarah whispers. If there is anything that will put this girl at peace, it's Aurora. She has this ability to calm even the most volatile of people.

Once Sarah returns with Phoebe and Aurora, most of our group—Alaric, Sophia, Skarlyt, Lennox, and Darren—gather close. I stay back as the girls approach Meredith, gently placing Aurora in her arms.

"Where is Axel?" Alaric asks me under his breath.

"He said he needed to find Zeke. Something about this girl's story seemed to upset him," I explain.

Alaric lets out a breath. "I probably shouldn't be the one to tell you, but I don't know if either Axel or Zeke will be able to..." That gets my attention, and I turn to face him. "Their dad used to travel across Ontario rescuing lone shifters, bringing them back here, and setting them up with others of their kind." I nod, remembering what Zeke told me about their father. "Well, the last time he went out, he was searching for a young girl—a tiger shifter. He was caught by hunters and didn't make it home alive."

"Oh," I cover my mouth with my hand as the pieces slip into place. "You think she is that tiger shifter?"

"Zeke and Axel were convinced it was some kind of set up, so they never went looking for the girl." He glances over at Meredith with sad eyes. "Honestly, we all thought it must've been a set up. If I know them, they are going to feel responsible for her being alone for so long. You need to be prepared; they're going to need time to come to terms with this."

"Shit. Zeke did tell me that, but I forgot it was a tiger shifter he was looking for. There's no way they could've known."

"That's true, but they won't think like that. They worshiped their dad and the work he did. This is going to feel like a failure to them—especially since it was his last mission."

"I hope you're wrong," I tell him.

"Me too. Their lives are just beginning to look up now that you came into the picture."

I give him a soft smile, thinking about my mates. *Mates.* I didn't think I would get one mate in this life, let alone two.

I turn my attention back to Meredith, and I'm happy to find she looks much calmer with Aurora in her arms.

"I'm going to try to find out when we can leave the bunker," I say to Alaric and turn in search of Rayne and her grandmother —Artemis.

How crazy is that?

"By the way, thank you," I whisper to Valerie, raising our entwined hands. "I am sorry to drag you around."

"It's all right, Opal." She shrugs her shoulders. "I know better than most how overwhelming this many people can be."

Pulling Valerie along with me, I make my way over just as Rayne is growling at Artemis.

"You need to explain what the fuck is happening right now."

To her credit, Artemis doesn't seem fazed to be on the receiving end of Rayne's ire. Rayne is one person I would never want to piss off, but Artemis is a literal goddess. So, they may be evenly matched.

"Hey, guys," I greet them from a few steps away, trying not to startle them.

Rayne whips around on me. Her face is still filled with anger, but it softens as she recognizes me.

"Hey, Opal," she says, crossing her arms across her chest. "Are you also here to get more details about why my grandma kidnapped everyone?"

"I was just wondering..." I hesitate. "Will we be able to leave the bunker soon? I would really like to find some clothes."

"Well?" Rayne asks impatiently, turning back to Artemis.

"Soon," Artemis answers. She does not seem inclined to elaborate. She waves her hands, and I look down to find that I'm wearing a pair of harem pants, a flowy tank top, and flip flops.

I look back to Artemis in surprise.

"Uh, thank you?"

"You're welcome," she says to me before turning back to Rayne. "At least someone is grateful. Perhaps you could learn some manners from this one."

"I'll show you some manners," Rayne growls. Instantly, both Dru and I reach out to restrain her. There's no way I can match a vampire's strength, so I let Dru handle this one.

"Fine," Artemis huffs, causing her blonde hair to shake around her face. "If you insist on getting answers now, let's go somewhere quieter."

Suddenly, there's a translucent bubble around our group. It is similar to one of Sebastyn's tricks to keep a conversation private. "What do you want to know?"

"Who is attacking us? How are they attacking us? Why should we trust you?" Rayne spits out the questions.

"I cannot tell you who or how. I can tell you that you can trust me. Why else would I have jeopardized my own safety by coming to your aid?"

"You can't tell us?" Rayne demands. "Or you *won't* tell us?"

"Both. I suppose," Artemis replies simply.

"Why?" I ask softly.

"There are beings in this world that even I do not dare cross. I have already placed a target on my back by interfering here."

"Fine. You can tell me about my ancestors then," Rayne says. This turn makes my eyebrows raise in surprise. There is no way she is giving up that line of questioning that easily. She's got her plotting face on. She's not giving up on getting the answers; she's just biding her time.

"Many years ago, I met and fell in love with a human man," Artemis begins. Her eyes are far away and unfocused, but her tone is not that of a dreamy romantic. "From that love, we had four daughters. They were the best of us. We tasked them with protecting the supernatural world. They were meant to ensure that those who sought to harm others were punished. They were the first hunters."

"Like the police?" Drusilla asks.

"Exactly like that." The goddess nods. "Over the years, less and less women were born into our family. The world changed, and the men of my line decided they needed a less feminine, more violent, history. Their souls twisted, morphing them into evil beings who sought to control and destroy all those who were different from them. In the last thousand years, no one questioned their mission. No one until you, Rayne."

"Why didn't you do anything?" The judgement in Rayne's voice is thick and unmistakable. Artemis looks down, grief written across her features.

"At first, I thought there were only a few who were truly corrupt. I believed—or wanted to believe—that it would fix itself.

As you know, it didn't. By the time I was ready to step in, it was too far gone. Even if I had shown myself to them, they wouldn't have accepted the truth. They would have found a way to imprison me. I couldn't let that happen."

Rayne begins to pace before turning to Artemis. I am not sure if her anger is abating or increasing.

"Do you know what they've done to the people they've captured? Do you have any idea how many lives you could've saved? Dru was held captive for years because you didn't step in. You could've stopped all of this. Go visit the building in the clearing north of here. There are people still recovering from the destruction you've caused." Tears are streaming down her face as she storms away.

"I'll go after her," Dru says, leaving me and Valerie alone with Artemis.

"Even gods and goddesses make mistakes," Artemis whispers.

"Do they? You're supposed to be better than us." I pause. I am not Rayne; I know it is not my place to berate a god. "Rayne was the one who found Drusilla imprisoned in that shed. It's going to take a while for her to come to terms with this."

"Artemis," Valerie begins, and the goddess turns to look at her. There are tears shining in their eyes. "She will come around."

The certainty in her voice has me thinking that she must've seen it in a vision. Perhaps I'll ask her later.

Artemis nods at Valerie and then me before blinking away.

"Let's go find your mates," Valerie whispers, and I nod.

I do not completely understand what's going on here, but I let Valerie pull me toward the opening of the bunker as I review what I just learned.

Chapter Twenty-One

Zeke

I snap awake, jolting myself out of a nightmare. As usual, I'm drenched in sweat, breathing heavily, and in a panic. I glance around, seeing the lake in front of me and a blanket beneath me.

Suddenly, the events of last night—or tonight, I guess, based on the lack of light still in the sky—come back to me. A smile forms on my face as I think of Opal, but I do not see her when I look around. A quick touch of the blanket tells me she hasn't been here for a while.

"Opal?" I call out, standing up and searching for her. I use my nose to follow her scent. As I draw away from the blanket where we slept, her scent fades. It's like she simply vanished. That's not possible. Is it?

As the minutes tick by, I begin to panic. What if the hunters found me again and took her? What if she regretted last night and left of her own free will?

I pace back and forth—from the little path by the cabin and back to the beach—trying to decide what I should do.

"Zeke?" I hear Axel call out. "Are you here?"

"Is Opal with you?" I respond as he steps through the trees.

"No, but she's safe."

"Where is she?" I demand, grabbing him by the shirt, unable to control myself.

"Calm down," Axel says, removing my hands from his shirt. "She's safe at the pack house."

"How the fuck did she get to the pack house?"

"That is a long story," he says.

"It's a long walk back to Alaric's, so we have time."

Axel nods, and we begin to walk through the trees.

"Well, apparently the old gods are real. Artemis popped up during our meeting today..."

"Wait. Artemis—like? You mean like Zeus, Hera, Gaia. Those gods?" I ask, my mouth open in shock.

"Yes, exactly. Apparently, Rayne is the descendant of Artemis."

"Wait, who's Rayne?" I ask.

"I forgot. There are a few people you haven't met yet. Rayne is a hunter—"

As soon as the word is out of his mouth, I stop dead in my tracks and a large growl rips out of me.

"She *was* a hunter. She's the one who led the charge on the Orillia facility. She set everyone there free. Besides, she's mated to Drake."

"You mean the old Drake? Vampire Drake?" Axel nods. "How is that possible? Why would the gods be so cruel after what happened to his sister."

"Well, that's another thing...Remember when Drusilla escaped, and she said a hunter helped her?"

"Yeah...You mean this Rayne was that hunter?"

He nods again.

"Anyway, Artemis showed up in the middle of our meeting with a warning about some attack on the women of the world. She waved her hands and every supernatural woman in the area was teleported to the bunker under Alaric's house."

Wow. Who knew the gods were real? I mean, I knew that they must've been real at some point, but I assumed they were more like supernaturals with extreme gifts that had died out over time. The fact that they are living beings is a lot to take in, and the fact that they are so incredibly powerful is daunting. Axel said Artemis teleported hundreds—if not thousands—of people with a wave of her hands.

"That's a lot of power," I say. Axel nods in agreement.

"There's more..."

"What? How is there more than that?" I ask.

"Well, when Artemis brought all the women in, it was really all the women ..."

"What does that mean?"

"There was a young tiger shifter," he spits out the words in a rush, and I stop dead in my tracks.

"How young?"

"She's only about nineteen. She said her family was taken by hunters over eleven years ago. Her parents helped her and her little brother escape, but then she lost him a couple weeks later. She's been alone ever since, trying to stay in the area in case her brother returned."

"You think—you think she's the one?" I ask, and I'm terrified to know the answer. As much as I want him to say no, I have a feeling that's not the truth. If she's real, it's my fault she's been all alone all this time.

"I do."

My stomach drops at his words.

"It's *our* fault," he stops my next words with a growl. "Not just you. We both agreed that it was fake intel."

"I said it first, Axel. How has she survived on her own all these years?"

"It doesn't matter who said it first, we agreed. Not just me and you either. The other leaders also agreed it was most likely a trap."

He is trying to reassure me, but it is in vain. I know he's feeling just as bad as I am.

"Opal's going to hate me," I mutter under my breath. Gods, I just got her back. What am I going to do?

"There is no way she will hate you. She may look at us differently, but she won't hate us."

"You can't know that," I say. I have already pushed my luck with her too far.

"Just watch and see."

We break through the trees once more in front of the pack house.

Opal is standing on the porch with a group of women and a young girl with white hair when we arrive. As soon as she sees us, she races off the porch and into my arms. Axel gives us a moment before joining.

"I'm so sorry. I was worried you would think I ran off on you when you woke up," she whispers.

"Never, angel," I tell her, placing a soft kiss on her hair.

She tilts her head up and captures my lips with hers. I let my tongue slip out and lick the seam of her lips. They part easily to allow me access. Our kiss quickly turns heated, and I can scent her arousal almost immediately.

"We're not alone," Axel groans, and we quickly part.

"To be continued," I whisper to Opal, sending her a wink.

Suddenly, my heart drops. That is, if she will still want me after.

"Both of you?" She looks between Axel and me. I glance at my brother and give him a nod which he returns.

"Yes, angel, both of us."

Her cheeks flush a rosy red and her arousal increases, making Axel and I groan in response.

We walk toward the steps, and the woman who banished me from the pack is glaring at me. If what Axel explained is true, this is Opal's friend. This is Sarah, and she is the one who I will need to win over.

Before we reach the group, Alaric comes bounding down the steps.

"Zeke!" He greets me, pulling me away from Opal and in for a hug.

"It's been a long time," I say.

"Too long! But we have other things to talk about tonight," he says as he pulls back and clasps me on the tops of my arms.

Opal steps up and wraps her arm around my waist as we walk up the stairs.

"I'll be inside in a minute," I say. She looks at me in confusion. "I just want to talk to Sarah first."

"Be nice," Opal growls at her friend, who raises her hands in defense. She goes up on her toes and gives me a peck on the cheek before turning and walking inside.

"I just wanted to let you know that I will do anything in my power to ensure that Opal never gets hurt again," I tell her.

"I appreciate you saying that, but it's not what I want to hear."

"What do you want to hear?" I question.

"I want to know your reasons for rejecting Opal in the first place. Axel seems to think you were justified, but he said it was not his place to tell me."

I gesture to the bench along the house for us to sit down.

"I was running from the hunters when I found Opal the first time. I had been running for almost two weeks straight, trying desperately to stay one step ahead of them." I take a deep breath and wonder how many times I'm going to have to repeat this story. "I tried to run away from Opal before she knew I was there, but my bear wouldn't let me. He was enthralled and took over. I allowed myself to get lost in her for a moment before I realized I had to fight my bear for control before he could mark her. I knew the hunters were on my trail, and I can only imagine what they would have done to her just for being a witch...let alone what they would do if they knew we were bonded mates. So, I took control, rejected her, and ran."

I pause and look her in the eyes. I can see that she's still skeptical, so I continue.

"Not even two hours later, the hunters caught up to me. They didn't kill me like I thought they would. They kept me in that facility for eleven years. It was hard enough getting through that myself. If Opal had been taken as well..." A shudder flows through me at the thought. "I wouldn't have survived. You may not like me, and you don't have to. I love your friend and would never intentionally be the cause of any of her pain."

She nods at me in response, looking back out to the forest for a few long moments. She pauses for so long that I wonder if she's going to respond at all.

"You know, I don't exactly know what I was expecting you to say, but that wasn't it. You protected her the only way that you knew how, and—as much as I want to hate you for hurting her in the first place—I understand why."

"Thank you," I tell her.

Her opinion means a lot to Opal, and so it means a lot to me too.

"You don't have to thank me. Just keep her happy and safe."

I close my eyes momentarily and let out a shaky breath.

"I am afraid I'm going to lose her again after tonight."

"After finding out that you didn't go after Meredith when your dad died?" she asks, and I look at her in shock. "Alaric told Opal about it after Axel left to find you. She was worried that something upset him."

I nod at her in understanding. "Yeah, because of that..."

"Opal isn't upset with you at all. She doesn't believe you were at fault, and neither do I. The way Alaric explained it, your sleuth agreed the information was false."

Gods, I hope everything she is saying is the truth. Her words should alleviate my stress, but the pit in my stomach is still there.

"Thank you for saying that."

She places her hand on my shoulder. "Don't let the guilt fester. If you need to apologize to Meredith, then do that. All guilt does is twist your insides up, and it'll be your loved ones who suffer."

"That's easier said than done, but I will do my best," I promise.

"That's good enough for me. Let's head inside before Opal and Seb come to see if I've killed you yet." She laughs as she gets up to walk inside.

"Yet?" I call after her.

I follow her inside, searching the faces gathered around me. Some I recognize from my past, and some are new. They all display various emotions upon greeting me: happiness, sadness, understanding. The worst is pity. I don't want people to feel bad for me because I was held captive. I survived that horrid place. I fought to keep my hope. I fought hard to stay alive while I was there. Their pity seems to lessen that effort.

"It's not pity, you know," Drusilla says, walking up to me. If anyone knows this struggle, it's her.

"What is it?" I whisper back.

"It's empathy."

"That's the same thing," I argue.

"It's not. I thought so too. I thought everyone was looking at me thinking 'poor Drusilla.' Really, they were more awe-struck that I survived. Just because someone shows you compassion doesn't mean they think any less of you."

I nod as if I understand, but I don't. Pity and empathy are the same thing. She can dress it up to make it sound pretty, but it doesn't change anything.

I make my way over to Opal and Axel, taking a seat and

pulling Opal into my lap. She snuggles in as the rest of the group talks.

"Where is Artemis?" the woman beside Alaric—I assume from the look they share this is Phoebe—says.

"Gone. Hopefully, she won't come back." This comes from another woman who is standing close to Drake. That means this is the infamous Rayne. I really need to get Axel to introduce me to everyone...

"If what she said is true, we are in her debt," Skarlyt argues. Rayne just scoffs.

"Artemis or no Artemis, we need to be ready for more surprises like today. The sooner we get this island ready the better," Alaric jumps in. "Everyone go home, get some sleep, and we will meet back here first thing in the morning."

With that, I pick up Opal and carry her right out the door and toward the woods. I don't wait for Axel; I know he'll catch up. Besides, my anxiety makes it miserable to be around so many people at once.

"Where are we going?" Opal asks.

"We're going to the cabin I brought you to earlier. There's a room inside with a bed big enough for all three of us. I figured you wouldn't want your first night alone with both of us to be under the same roof as our mother," I chuckle.

"No, definitely not," she agrees and tilts her head, beginning to kiss up and down my neck.

Time for me to pick up speed—the sooner I can get us there, the sooner we can start.

Chapter Twenty-Two

Opal

As we're walking, I start placing small kisses up and down Zeke's neck. I know it's wrong to tease him, but I can't help it. Since that display earlier, my entire body has been on fire.

"Angel, you're killing me," he groans as he speedwalks through the forest. Instead of stopping, I place my mouth on his neck and suck hard, massaging his skin with my tongue. "I'll stop right here and give you something else to suck on," he threatens, but he doesn't stop or slow his pace.

I twist my body, clinging to him with my arms around his neck, and place a leg on either side of his thick torso. In this new position, I can lower and raise myself to grind against his growing bulge.

This time he does stop, placing his hands firmly under my ass and pulling me back to look into my eyes. "Seriously, angel. We can do this right here, or you can wait five minutes until we're inside. Your choice."

I contemplate this for a second but ultimately decide to wait until we get inside.

"Ugh. Fine. I'll wait," I pout, and he chuckles before moving again. I have nothing against a romantic interlude in the forest, but I don't want anyone to interrupt us—especially if Axel catches up.

As soon as he takes the steps up to the cabin, I seal my mouth to his and slip my tongue through his lips with a moan. I paw at his back, desperately trying to get closer to him.

"Take this off," I demand, pulling away from him.

"So impatient, angel," he chides, placing me on the counter. Slowly, he reaches down, grasping the hem of his shirt, and lifts it. Each second that he draws out the reveal of his tattooed and sculpted torso is pure torture.

"Zeke," I plead. He raises a brow at me and continues removing his shirt. His muscled torso is now on full display, and my core throbs with need. Goddess, this man is sexy.

Not willing to wait any longer, I jump down from the counter and rush toward him, prepared to undress him myself. He chuckles and steps back, but he finally pulls his shirt over his head.

I place my hands on his firm chest muscles as I reach him, slowly tracing my way down to the well-defined "V" at the bottom. My hands wander, and I admire all the incredible artwork on his skin as I go. My fingers slip into his waistband, and his breath hitches. I slide my hands along the band, inching them downwards, only to have his hands stop mine.

"Not yet, angel. I removed my shirt; it's only fair for you to take yours off too." I groan in displeasure. I don't want slow right now; I want hard and fast.

I grip the bottom of my shirt and rip it over my head before unclasping my bra and letting it slip off.

"Gods, you're so beautiful," he whispers. He places his hands on my waist and moves them upward until he's palming each breast. He rubs his thumbs over my nipples, and it's my turn to go breathless as a moan slips from between my lips.

"You're so responsive. I love that," he says as he moves his head down to take one of my nipples in his mouth. There's something about the compliment that makes my heart hammer in my chest. I arch my back, allowing him better access while trying to move my core closer to him.

"I see you've started without me." Axel's voice comes from the door, and I freeze in panic. What if he isn't comfortable with this? What if he doesn't want to share me? We have already talked about the fact that they are both my mates, but we haven't discussed any of the sexual stuff that comes along with that. Goddess, what if I just fucked up?

"Stop. I can see your mind racing over there, but I'm definitely not upset," he says as he stalks toward us. Seamlessly, Zeke moves around me so that he's now at my back as Axel presses into my front. "I'm the exact fucking opposite actually." When Axel dips his head down to capture my lips, I lose all control.

With a moan, I wrap my arms around his neck and return his kiss with a fierceness I am unfamiliar with before lifting myself up and wrapping my legs around his waist. Zeke moves with me, sliding his hands around to fondle my exposed breasts while kissing up and down my neck.

I grind myself on Axel with all the strength I have, moving up and down faster and faster.

"Not yet," Axel growls out, gently removing me and placing me on the ground. Unlike Zeke, he removes his shirt in one smooth motion. He doesn't make me wait, and my body vibrates with the need to be closer to him. If Zeke wasn't at my back, holding me in place with kisses across my neck and shoulders, I would be.

"To the bedroom," Axel orders, and Zeke lifts me again. He carries me to the other room and places me gently on the bed.

I pop up onto my elbows to watch them. I am breathless and uncertain, but I cannot deny my excitement.

"How is this going to work?" I ask.

"You're going to do as we say, angel," Zeke begins in a tone that promises so much. "And you're going to trust us to make sure you feel good. Can you do that?"

I bite my lip and nod. Holy shit, this is really happening.

"Good girl," Axel growls, and the words make a desperate warmth pool in my stomach. He moves toward the bed and deftly slips my pants and underwear off in one go. He glides a long, cool finger along my core, and I can't help but arch up into his touch.

"So wet. Is that all for us?"

Again, words utterly escape me, so I nod.

"Zeke, take off your pants and lay on the bed. I think our angel here needs you underneath her." Axel lifts me from the bed and merges his mouth with mine as Zeke takes up his position. One brother sets me down and releases me as the other lowers me down onto his impressive cock. With each incredible inch, another moan slips out of me as he reaches spots inside me I have never felt before. Axel kneels before me where I'm straddling his brother backward and latches onto my clit.

Zeke begins to move his hips up and down as much as he can while Axel sucks and flicks at my clit with his tongue. The dual sensation quickly brings me to climax with a scream of pleasure. My pussy tightens around Zeke's enormous member as my pleasure builds. Although I cannot see his face, his moans tell me he's enjoying the feeling of being inside me just as much as I am. Axel doesn't stop though. He continues the assault with his tongue until I'm crying out for him once more.

As he stands, I grip the waistband of his jeans. I quickly pull his giant cock free before eagerly taking him into my mouth.

"I thought you were going to do as we say?" Axel groans out.

I pull away for a second.

"Oh, I'm sorry. Did you want me to stop?" I ask as my brain finally allows me some coherent thoughts. As if to punctuate my joke, Zeke grips my hips tightly and thrusts up into me hard, making me gasp. With my mouth open, Axel takes the opportunity

Bound by Fate

to slip his cock back into it. Suddenly, both of my mates are pounding in and out of me in a delicious rhythm.

I place my hands on Axel's hips, urging him to slow and deepen his motions. I want a moment to savor the taste of him. I pop him out of my mouth and lick him from base to tip once, finding the deep vein pulsing along the bottom of his cock before I return to lavish the head with extra attention.

My core begins to flutter with my impending release, and I pull my mouth from Axel's cock with a throaty scream. I cannot support myself any longer, and I dive forward in ecstasy. Axel's hand slides expertly down my body and circles my clit, extending my orgasm until I feel Zeke pulse inside me with his own release.

Without warning, I am lifted into Axel's arms. I groan as Zeke removes his impressive length from me. I am breathless and awash in the sensations of pleasure all around me. Axel wraps my legs around him and, without warning, slips inside of me. I am so wet and ready for him that he can sheath himself into me without preamble, and he exhales his pleasure into my neck. I brace my hands on his shoulders and use my little strength to raise and lower myself onto him. In this position, his cock drags along my G-spot with each thrust. I grind against him with all my might. I feel as if any more pleasure in this moment could kill me, but I chase the euphoria anyway.

I worry for just a moment that we are neglecting Zeke, but then I feel him behind me. His lips are at my neck, and his hands wander across my hips and thighs before stopping to cup my ass. One hand grips my thigh, pulling me even farther open for his brother's thrusting. The other hand moves between us, toward my puckered hole, and I tense against him.

"One day soon, angel," Zeke's whisper is honey against my skin. "Soon, you'll take us both at the same time. You'll like that, won't you?" His finger slowly circles my hole before pushing in slightly.

I gasp in shock at this new invasion. Zeke goes no further though, and I relax against him. Soon, I am luxuriating in the feeling of him sliding his finger in and out in time with Axel's thrusts.

I lift my head and capture Axel's mouth with mine. As my orgasm hits, he swallows down my screams with a moan of his own. Zeke's finger slips from my ass, and his strong hands grip my hips. He supports me, holding me in place as Axel pounds in and out of me like a man on a mission.

My core clenches Axel's cock tighter, milking him of his own release. As one, we collapse on the bed drenched in sweat.

For a moment, I am breathless, my body continuing to spasm on the rumpled bed.

"Was that all right, angel?" Zeke asks. He is on his side, propped up on one elbow and studying my face.

"That was..." I'm once again at a loss for words. "It was..."

"Incredible," Axel provides, and I nod. I see both of my mates smile as my eyes begin to drift closed.

I feel the bed dip and then something wet across my exposed core. I open my eyes a crack to see Zeke cleaning up the evidence of our love making. He steps away with a smile as he meets my gaze.

His release came earlier, so he is already more alert than Axel and me. I curl into Axel, relishing the warmth of him as I drift inexorably toward sleep. There is another dip in the bed as Zeke climbs in behind me and drapes an arm over my side.

I don't know what the gods were thinking by giving me two mates. If every time is going to be like that, I owe someone big time.

Maybe I should ask Artemis who I should send the gift basket to.

* * *

When I wake up the next morning, I reach out for my two mates and come up empty on either side.

"Zeke? Axel?" I call out. Seconds later, Axel opens the door to check on me.

"We were going to let you sleep," he says, coming over to give me a kiss. I run my fingers through his hair and pull him on top of me, deepening the kiss.

"Angel," Zeke says from the doorway, and I remove my mouth from Axel's to look over at him. My body is absolutely buzzing with need. He must see the look on my face because he groans. "I'm going to finish making breakfast. You need to help her with that, Axe." He reluctantly tears his gaze away and shuts the door behind him.

"Woke up feeling needy, did we?" Axel jokes, but he slides down my body and swipes his tongue up my core.

"Yes!" I cry out my answer. As he flicks my clit over and over, my only thought is 'Goddess, this man knows how to eat pussy'...and he's all mine.

When he slips two of his long, large fingers inside me, my orgasm overtakes my body, and my legs begin to shake. As soon as the tremors start to slow, he flips me over. Axel is pressing the head of his cock inside me, and I push up against the rumpled bed, anxious to meet him.

"Gods, you feel so good. So—fucking—perfect."

He thrusts in and out of me hard and fast, bringing us both to climax within minutes.

"I don't think I'm ever going to get enough of this," I whisper as he slips from me.

"Me neither, angel," he says as he places a soft kiss on my head. "But we have other things to do today."

"We do?" I question.

"Yes, we said we would help with the island, remember?"

"Do we have to?" I whine as I turn to face him.

221

He chuckles. "Unfortunately."

With a groan and a nod, I get up and walk to the bathroom.

"I'm going to hop in the shower."

"Okay, angel. I'll go help Zeke with breakfast," he says as he leaves the bedroom.

I hop in the shower, but my core is still throbbing with need. Slowly, I move my hands down my body to explore my need. I don't understand how I can still be so horny after Axel just woke me up. As I slowly circle my clit, increasing the speed and pressure, the shower curtain moves and Zeke—already naked—steps in.

"Need some help, angel?" he asks, and he moves his hand to replace my own. Within seconds, I can feel my release building. I place my foot on the side of the tub, lining myself up with his cock. Without prompting, Zeke slams into me. He removes his hand and backs me up against the wall. His mouth smashes into mine, and he thrusts in and out of me.

The feeling of him slamming deep into me is delicious, and I slow him down to savor it. He supports me as I circle my hips, putting pressure on my clit with his body. Soon, we are both moaning out our releases once more.

Now that I finally feel sated, we wash up in the now-cold water and prepare for our day. I hope we get through it quickly so I can have some more of that later.

Chapter Twenty-Three

Axel

I walk into the kitchen to find Zeke trying and failing to concentrate on breakfast.

"Opal's going for a shower...She might need some help if you're up for it," I tell him with a wink.

He looks at me with wide eyes before turning and running to the bedroom. I let out a small chuckle and shake my head as I begin salvaging the breakfast. Luckily, only the bacon suffered from his inattention. I prefer mine extra-crispy anyway.

By the time they're done with their lovemaking—I mean shower—I have a big spread laid out on the counter.

"This looks delicious," Opal says as she walks into the kitchen and gives me a soft kiss.

"Hey! I started it," Zeke pouts, but we both shoot him a look. "What? I did!"

"You burnt the bacon," I say, pointing to the evidence.

"You like it burnt!" he argues, and Opal laughs at us.

"I don't," she says, and we both turn to her in horror.

"How do you like your bacon, then?" Zeke asks.

"I like my bacon soft and chewy," she responds, digging

through the pile of bacon to retrieve the softest pieces. She won't find many.

"What?" Zeke shrieks and places his hand on his chest in a dramatic way.

She slaps his shoulder playfully before loading the rest of her plate and sitting down. Zeke and I wait until she's started eating. Shifters can eat—like a lot—and we want to make sure she gets whatever she needs before we start. With full plates and growling stomachs, we sit down on either side of her.

"This really is delicious, Axel. Thank you," she says between mouthfuls.

"Anything for you, angel," I say, placing a kiss on her head.

A ringing sound comes from my jacket where it is hanging by the door, and I rush over to answer it.

"Hello?"

"Hey, Axel. It's Alaric. Have you watched or listened to the news today?"

"Uh...no. I don't usually pay attention to the news."

"Well, I think you should," he says, and I turn to Zeke and Opal.

"Can one of you turn on the news?"

Opal quickly pulls out her phone, opening the browser to find a news outlet.

She sucks in a breath, and her eyes go wide as she reads the headline. I walk over to stand behind her and read it for myself.

Breaking news—global pandemic reported as pregnant women across the globe suffer unexplained miscarriages.

"Miscarriages?" I growl into the phone.

What the fuck is this? How can this be a pandemic?

"Apparently, all the pregnant women on earth lost their babies last night..." Alaric explains, sadness lacing his voice.

"And Phoebe?" I ask.

"She's fine," he sighs. "Thank the gods. She's fine. The other pregnant women in our pack are also all right. You might want to reach out to the sleuth to check on your own."

"I'm going to do that right now. We'll be over at your place in a bit," I say, just before hanging up with him.

"Did Phoebe?" Opal asks, her eyes are wide and concerned.

I rub my hands up and down her arms like I am trying to warm her.

"No. All the women in the pack seem to be fine."

"That must've been the attack Artemis was protecting us from."

I nod at her, having come to the same conclusion.

"It makes sense. I'm going to text Mom and ask her to get in touch with the pregnant women in the sleuth just to make sure."

"I'll call her," Zeke offers and takes my phone to the other room. I nod my thanks.

"I wanted to have more time with just the three of us this morning, but after this..." I begin.

"We need to get moving. This may not be the only attack. The sooner we are safe on the island, the better," Opal finishes, jumping up and clearing away the dishes.

With three of us, it doesn't take long to clean up the mess from breakfast. We easily slip into a familiar rhythm with each other, and we seem to anticipate each other's movements. Our celebratory mood from before is gone though, and we all silently go through the motions of getting ready to leave.

"Do you think it will be done in time?" Opal asks, fear ringing in her voice as we step out onto the porch.

"I don't know, angel. But we're going to try," Zeke responds, pulling her into a hug as I lock up.

Giving myself a mental shake, I walk up behind her and sandwich her between the two of us. We might not have much time available right now, but we can spare a few minutes to comfort our mate. I share a look with Zeke over her head.

We need to figure out how to keep her safe, he says through the bond.

I nod.

We will, I respond. I can't promise she won't come to any harm, but I can promise we will do everything we can to keep her safe. That includes building this island in record time.

After a moment, Zeke steps back and places his hand under Opal's chin and raises her eyes to meet his.

"We really need to go, angel."

Again, she nods and steps out of my embrace. The three of us begin our trek to Alaric's. We had hoped for an exciting day of building an island together, but it has turned somber. Hunters are now the least of our worries. If we have incurred the wrath of a god or goddess, there is nowhere on earth we will be able to hide from them. I'm not even sure the island will be able to keep us safe.

"Opal!" Samara calls out as we breach the tree line, and Opal takes off running to embrace her friend.

"Are you okay? The baby?" Opal asks anxiously, placing her hand on her friend's stomach.

"The baby is fine. It seems like whatever Artemis did the other night kept us safe. Everyone else though—all the humans—"

"I know," Opal responds.

"You must be Zeke," Samara says, stepping back from Opal and offering her hand to my twin.

"I am."

"I'm Samara. It's nice to meet you. It's good to see you again, Axel."

"You too, Samara," I pipe in. "The girls missed you at breakfast the other day."

"Yeah..." she begins sheepishly. "The mornings aren't great for me; I've been really sick. Honestly, the nights aren't great either. Trevan says it's normal because our types of magic combining can be 'volatile.'"

I nod sympathetically and pretend to understand, but I don't. I haven't been around anyone who is pregnant other than shifters with shifter mates, so I don't know how that works. I suppose it's something I should investigate now. If Opal wants to carry our cubs, we will need to figure out how our separate magics will merge. I've only ever heard about children who take after one or the other parent, but Samara's comment has me wondering if that is always the case.

"Come on," Samara says, leading us inside. "Everyone is waiting."

The mood of the group assembled inside isn't much better than our own. There are worried looks plastered on everyone's faces.

Alaric walks over, greeting both Zeke and I with a handshake and Opal with a small hug.

"After you left last night, Phoebe pointed out that some introductions are in order." I look at him in confusion. He gestures toward Zeke, and I catch his meaning. Zeke hasn't been around for the last eleven years, so there are quite a few people he hasn't met yet. We take a moment to make the necessary introductions, but I can't imagine my brother will be able to remember everyone's name at once. Our group of friends has quickly expanded.

"So, let's get to business. What is the plan for today?" Alaric steps up to a whiteboard he has hung up on the wall and takes the lid off a marker. "Witches?" he asks Skarlyt.

"All the earth witches are coming with us to begin construction on the island. The rest will be gathering supplies. They'll collect food, medicine, and whatever else we will need until we can get the island to be self-sustainable."

Alaric nods, writing it down on the board.

"Lions?" he asks Trixie.

"We are going travelling to all the lumberyards within driving distance to get as many construction materials as we can. The rest will be packing up our homes, getting ready to move."

Once again, Alaric nods and writes it down before turning to Drake.

"Vampires?"

"They'll be sleeping for most of the day, but we have scheduled mass blood shipments over the next two evenings, and we have a large group of volunteers for construction. They'll pick up wherever the day's crew leaves off."

Alaric then looks at me.

"And the bears?"

"I briefly spoke with my crews last night. They are gathering all the necessary tools to begin construction as soon as we're able. The rest will be gathering food and supplies. I had a few volunteers gather some livestock as well. They'll house them at their ranches until the island is ready," I supply.

Nodding, Alaric turns and writes that down too.

"The pack is preparing to storm the laboratories. Each able-bodied shifter is gathering weapons." We all look at him in shock, but he continues. "I know we don't usually use weapons, but we need to get this done quickly. With this new threat—"

He's cut off by Sebastyn teleporting into the room.

"Where have you been?" Skarlyt asks the question like her brother has missed his curfew again.

"Sophia woke me up first thing," Sebastyn explains, looking exhausted. "She was worried about Blaze and the others in the Amazon after last night's attack."

"Shit," Skarlyt curses. "I didn't even—"

"You've had a lot to worry about, Skar." Sebastyn cuts her off. "I dropped them off, but I warned them they'd have to stay until I can help with the island."

"Them?" Phoebe asks.

"Yeah. Darren wasn't going to let her go alone."

"Okay. Let's get to work. The ones with the hardest job by far are the witches, so let's help them with whatever we can," Alaric says, and we break apart.

"Are you two coming with us?" Skarlyt asks, and I look at Zeke. One of us should stay behind to handle the sleuth.

Surprisingly, it's Zeke who speaks up.

"I'm going to stay and help the sleuth prepare. Axel should go with you to ensure the foundation is strong."

"Are you sure?" I ask.

He nods. "Yes. It's time I step up and help you with the sleuth."

"Thank you," I tell him. For the first time in eleven years, the burden isn't entirely on me. I don't need to feel as if I need to be in two places at once. When Zeke and I are a team, we can be in two places at once.

"Be good, angel," he says, stepping up to give Opal a brief kiss.

"Always," she responds, earning a snort from the rest of the women.

It seems there are some things we still have to learn about our mate...

"Ready?" Skarlyt turns to us after giving Lennox a quick kiss as well, and we nod. She clasps our hands and teleports us onto a boat in the middle of the ocean. The wind is strong, and it blows sprays of water on our faces, making Opal shiver. I wrap my arms around her and look out to the water. There are dozens of boats floating in a circle. They are all quickly filling with witches.

"Okay, everyone. We're going to start right here," Skarlyt yells out and raises her palms. I look out toward the water and watch in awe as a small patch of dirt forms. As each witch raises her hands, the patch of dirt grows. Not only is it spreading, but I can see that it's getting thicker under the water as well.

"This is amazing," I whisper—more to myself than anyone else —but I'm shushed all the same.

As the earthen circle grows, the boats are pushed back. Soon, I'm staring at an actual island. It's not as big as we need it to be, but it's an incredible start.

"What do you think you're doing?" Artemis calls out from behind us, shocking everyone on our boat.

Skarlyt turns to her.

"We're making an island. What does it look like?"

"Why are you making an island? Don't you have much bigger things to worry about? You know...like how we're going to appease a very pissed off deity," Artemis challenges.

Skarlyt places her hands on her hips. "In order to focus on that, we need to be safe. We need this island so we can begin planning for the future."

"And what are you planning to do with a hunk of dirt floating in the middle of the ocean?"

"We are going to build here," Skarlyt answers. "If we can find a way to teleport our homes here, we will. If not, we are prepared to build a new home here."

"Well, then..." Artemis glances at the drawings of the island Skarlyt has taped to the wall of the boat. There are similar copies in every boat for the witches to reference. "If you're set on it, let me help you speed up the process."

I watch as an island materializes before us. It is the island exactly how I designed it—complete with our homes and full-grown forests as far as the eye can see.

"Seriously?" Skarlyt balks at her display of power.

"What? You needed it done, and it's done," Artemis says, looking at Opal and I as if Skarlyt is crazy.

"Yes but..." Skarlyt begins.

"I think what Skar is trying to say is thank you," Opal chimes in.

"That's not—" Opal throws her hand over Skarlyt's mouth quickly to stop her from continuing.

"Did you bring everyone here?" I ask, and Artemis turns to me excitedly.

"Yes! Come, come. Let me show you." Another wave of her hands brings the three of us to the roof of a large tower that over-looks absolutely everything.

It's beautiful. Apart from a few small beaches, the island is surrounded by large cliffs. The forested areas are vast, and rivers snake through them. The largest river begins in a waterfall that is stunning.

The more I look around, the more I see...I spot Alaric's home surrounded by the other pack homes, the coven's village, Trixie's pride, my sleuth, and even the large triage structure the witches built for the rescued supernaturals.

"Fabulous, isn't it? Some of my best work. Everything is done: plumbing, electricity, fresh water, crops, livestock—everything you need to survive here. It's a perfect replica of your home."

"Replica?" I ask, and she nods.

"Yes. I thought it might attract unwanted attention if hundreds of homes actually disappear, so I just copied them."

We nod at her, trying to hide our awe.

"And now the *pièce de résistance*." Once again, Artemis waves her hands, and we land at the bottom of the tower we're in. From this angle, it's clear it is a temple of some sort.

The goddess leads us inside, and I realize that's exactly what this is. A temple of worship for—you guessed it—Artemis.

She leads us to a door at the back of the temple.

"Through here," she commands as she steps back from us.

We look at each other in question but step forward anyway. As I look around, I recognize where I am: I'm back in Parry Sound.

"How the fuck?" I question as I look around.

"This is a portal to the island."

We look at Artemis in shock once again.

"I'm not sure a portal is the best idea," I say carefully. I'm not interested in calling the choices of a goddess who just created an entire island with a thought into question. "If the hunters figured this out, they could just walk through."

Artemis clucks her tongue.

"I'm not stupid. The portal is linked to intent. If the person stepping through means the inhabitants of the island no harm, they will be allowed to proceed...If there is the slightest desire to harm, they will simply open the door and walk into a cabin."

"What the fuck just happened?" Skarlyt is the first to recover.

"I don't know," Opal responds. "Let's head back to the island and find everyone else. I think we need help figuring this one out."

"Good idea," I say, wrapping my arm around her shoulder and guiding us back through the door. We walk into the temple, and I get a good look around this time. It's exactly how Greek temples for the gods look in pictures, but this one is brand new.

We find most of our friends standing at the large doorway of the temple with their mouths hanging open. I wonder how to explain the impossible things we just witnessed. Hopefully, they believe us.

Honestly, they kind of have to since the evidence is under our feet.

Chapter Twenty-Four

Zeke

I could tell that Axel was surprised by my offer to handle the alpha duties for the sleuth. Hell, I surprised myself. I have been mulling it over for the last few days, but I wasn't sure if it was something I would actually do. When I knew one of us would have to stay and handle the fallout from last night, I didn't think. I just reacted.

But now, as I'm walking up to the house and the shifters gathered on the lawn, I'm not sure I made the right decision. Most nod their head at me in greeting, but others turn to whisper to the person next to them. They are no doubt wondering why I'm here instead of my brother. There was a time when no one would have been able to tell the difference between us, but I have lost a lot of muscle mass during my years of captivity. It's easy to tell us apart right now.

I walk up the steps and take a deep breath before turning to face the crowd.

"I know you're probably confused why I'm here instead of Axel..." I see a lot of nodding heads, so I continue. "Axel is currently helping the witches create a safe haven for us. They are building an island where we are free to be ourselves. Where we no longer have to live in fear of the hunters or humans finding out about us."

"What about our lives here? Our jobs? Friends?" one person calls out, and I take another deep breath.

"I understand why you would be concerned about leaving here, but we need to think about the sleuth. The hunters as well as other forces..." I pause, wondering how much I should tell them.

"Are we under attack again? Is that what happened to the women?" another voice rings out.

I nod. "Yes, we are." Whispers and panic begin to rise, so I hold up my hand again. "We don't have all the information, but I will tell you what we know so far. You should know that our allies raided a facility not far from here last week. During that raid, I was rescued—along with a lot of others—from a laboratory. At that place, hunters would take us to experiment on and torture." Gasps ring out from the crowd. "During that raid, they discovered evidence of five other facilities just like that across Canada. Collectively, the other faction leaders are planning to raid them and rescue the supernaturals there as well. Before we can do that, we need a safe place for us. The hunters will want revenge for an attack this big, and we need to protect ourselves. I understand we're asking a lot of you...to leave your homes, your lives. But I promise you it's the only way for now."

I wait for some of the murmurs to die out before continuing.

"As for the events of last night...There was an attack on the world—not just supernaturals. It seems some of the old gods and goddesses are walking amongst us once more and aren't pleased. The attack last night was by a particularly powerful deity. We aren't sure what he or she wants or how to fix it, but we can only assume this will not be the last attack."

"Are we going to lose our babies too?" a heavily pregnant woman cries out.

"We've been reassured that every woman in the bunker last night was safe from the attack..."

Suddenly, the ground trembles and throws me to the side. When I stand and regain my balance, I notice a few things. The weather that was once sunny with the sun directly above us has turned grey, and the once calm wind is now whipping through the trees. The scent of home I have grown accustomed to is gone. There is only salty sea air.

"What's happening?"

"Why do I smell the ocean?"

"Where are we?"

The questions fire out at the same time, making it hard to distinguish them. I only know one thing: we're no longer in Ontario.

"Please calm down," I call out, and the crowd quiets. "The witches were trying to find a way to teleport the entire community when I left them this morning. Perhaps they found a way. For now, please go home and make notes of who is here and who is not. We need to ensure that everyone is accounted for. I will go find out what has happened."

Luckily, everyone turns to do as I asked without complaint, and I let out a sigh. That went better than I thought it would.

"What's going on, Zeke?" My mom asks, fear plastered on her face.

I meet her eyes, trying to hide the fear I know is shining back in my own.

"I honestly don't know."

She nods and heads inside, probably heading straight for the kitchen. She cooks when she's scared or stressed.

Axel? I reach out through our bond but get nothing but static.

I walk inside the house and pick up the landline phone, dialing his number quickly. As I bring the phone to my ear there's nothing, no dial tone, no ringing, nothing.

I begin to pace and try reaching out to Axel again.

What's going on?

Zeke? Axel says.

Thank the gods. What happened? Where are you? I let some of the panic slip through our bond and feel him send reassurances back to me.

Artemis created the island for us. Is everyone in the sleuth here?

I have them making a list to account for everyone. I am trying to keep them busy. It looks like everyone is here. Our houses are even here. Where's Opal?

Good thinking. She's here. We're both back on the island and will head to you now. I feel the pride he has for me flow through our bond, and I puff out my chest a little under the compliment.

Okay I'll tell Mom. She's stress-cooking, I say and get a chuckle back before he cuts off the connection. I look around at the buildings and homes that surround the house. Everything is the same as it was. Even the trees look the same. Did Artemis really teleport our entire village here? Is there anything that goddess can't do? Why won't she use her power to help in the real fight?

"Hey, Mom?" I call out as I head into the kitchen. I find her elbow deep in dough, making her famous biscuits.

"Did you find out anything?" she asks, stopping her pounding to look at me. I nod and tell her what Axel just told me. She visibly relaxes at my words, showing just how afraid she was.

"So now what?" she asks, and I scrub a hand down my face.

"I'm not sure. Axel will know more when he gets here."

She nods, and I walk over, take the dough, and knead it for her. Between the familiar scent and sensation, I'm transported back to my childhood. To a safe place.

Whenever I was angry or stressed, she would pull me into the kitchen.

I can still remember her talking me through whatever emotion I was feeling.

"It's natural for you to get angry or scared, Zeke. Everyone feels these emotions, but we need to learn when to act on them and when to tamp them down."

My argument was always the same. If everyone feels like this, why can't I just punch them in the face? Surely, they would understand.

"Instead, we punch the dough," she said, laughing. "It doesn't talk back and can take the pain."

She would always emphasize that point by pounding her fist into the dough over and over, leaving me curious just who she pictured in that dough.

Silently, the two of us beat the dough. I picture the hunters when I punch the dough. The guards. The man in the white coat. The woman who kept his notes. Before long, the image morphs into my own face. I punch it harder for hurting Opal...for hurting my mom...for hurting Axel. By the time I'm done, I'm breathing heavily, and sweat is lacing my brow.

"I'd hate to be whoever you just pictured there," my mom chuckles.

"It was more than one someone..." I begin, and then I turn to her. "You know, Mom, I always wondered. Who did you picture when you punched the dough like that?"

She sighs heavily, wiping her forehead with the back of her hand.

"For a long time, it was a few of the other women in the sleuth who made plays for your father when they thought I wasn't look-ing. Now, it's a mixture of nondescript hunters and, mostly..." tears begin to pool in her eyes as she looks at me. "Mostly, I see your father, and I punch him as hard as I can for leaving me. For leaving us." I reach out and wrap my arms around her. "I know it wasn't his fault. It's just hard not to blame him for leaving. He could've skipped that mission. He should have skipped that mission. There was no tiger...just hunters," she sobs into my chest.

"Mom, I have to tell you something." She steps back and looks at me, confusion plain on her face. "About the tiger shifter...it turns out she was real. She was transported to the bunker last night with the rest of the women."

"What?" she exclaims. "You mean..." I nod. "That poor girl. She was out there alone all this time?"

I wrap my arms around her once more, both of us indulging in a moment of weakness. We give ourselves a moment to feel the guilt that has been weighing on our shoulders.

"We'll make it right. We're going to help her find her brother," I decree as I step back. My mom nods her head in agreement, and we make quick work of the biscuits.

While waiting for them to bake, I head down the hallway to Axel's office and pull out the books for the sleuth's accounts.

Even though we're on this island, we'll still need money eventually. If I can figure out where the missing money has gone and make some smart investments, we may have a sizable sum when—if—we return to civilization.

I pour over the books, taking note of important transactions and dates. If I can give them to Opal's brother Matt, he can hack into the cameras in the accounting firm's building so we can see who was making the transfers. Theoretically. I guess I'm not sure if any of that is actually possible.

When I'm finished writing the dates and times, I begin making a list of what needs to be done to keep us connected to the real world. We need cell phone towers and solar panels to start. The gas lines transferred over, but with no source for them, they shouldn't work.

I begin to wonder if Artemis moved all our homes here or simply made a copy of them. If our homes are still there in Parry Sound, we could still tap into the lines there with that portal idea

Sebastyn brought up. The more I think about it, the better it sounds. Hell, even if it's not a copy, we could probably make a portal on either side from somewhere else.

The oven bell dings, and I walk back into the kitchen as Axel and Opal walk through the door.

Chapter Twenty-Five

Opal

"Zeke reached out through our bond. We should probably head over to the sleuth," Axel says with his arms around me as we watch our friends walk in and out of the portal.

"This is so freaking cool," Phoebe announces.

"It would be cooler if a certain goddess would come explain what the fuck she was thinking," Rayne yells at the sky, as if that will summon Artemis for her.

I chuckle a little as we approach the group.

"We're going to the sleuth to get a head count and make sure no one was left behind," Axel says.

"Good idea. We should probably do the same," Alaric agrees.

"We can meet here tonight to plan our next move," Axel suggests, and everyone nods.

We turn to walk away, but Rayne calls me back.

"I almost forgot; Matt wanted me to give you this." She hands me a satellite phone which immediately begins ringing.

"Thanks," I say to her as I press the answer button.

"Hey, Matt."

"I'm glad you're safe."

"Of course, I'm safe. Why wouldn't I be?" I question with a chuckle.

"Oh, I don't know. An all-powerful goddess just waved her hands and created an island out of nothing, and then teleported several structures millions of miles away...Is it so far-fetched for me to worry you might've been left behind or that your particles didn't go back together quite right when you landed? You do have all your fingers and toes, right?"

I wiggle my toes and look down at my fingers to make sure before I answer.

"Fingers and toes are accounted for. I'm fairly sure she technically just made a copy of everything—not teleported."

"I don't think that's any more reassuring."

"I'm assuming you have another reason for calling..."

He scoffs. "Other than making sure my big sister still has all of her extremities?"

"Matt," I warn. There's always something more with him.

"Okay, fine. I hate that I wasn't there to see it. How cool was it? Explain it from the beginning. Don't leave anything out."

The geekiness of my brother astounds me, and I bark out a laugh. I tell him all about it anyway. I start from the moment Artemis showed up until now. To say he's in awe would be an understatement. I think Artemis just got her first follower.

"I can't wait to meet her," he says, and I groan.

"Unless she plans on helping us with the hunters or this mysterious enemy, she should stay away. Rayne is beyond pissed. If I were you, I'd make myself scarce when she gets back to the lab," I tell him.

"Oh, believe me, I already am. I locked myself away in the control room after the first time I walked in on her and Drake using the chains hanging from the ceiling..." I can hear him shudder through the phone.

"Okay...Thanks for that visual."

"Hey, at least you didn't see it firsthand."

"True. Axel and I are heading to the sleuth to get a head count and make sure no one was left behind," I tell him, ready to be done with this conversation. It's one thing to get all the details from Rayne about her sexcapades, but it's another thing entirely to hear about them from my little brother.

"Oh, good idea. I'll also do a satellite scan of Parry Sound to see if anything looks different."

"Thanks, Matt. That would be great. Let us know if you find anything."

"Will do," he says and then hangs up. No 'I love you, big sis.' Not even a goodbye.

"Well, that was rude," I say, staring at the phone.

"What was rude?" Axel asks.

"He hung up without saying goodbye," I say, looking up at him.

He lets off a chuckle. "Most men aren't particularly good at phone etiquette. What did he want?"

"He wanted to hear all about how Artemis created the island and to gush about how amazing she is."

He just nods. "Sounds about right."

"What do you mean by that?" I say, narrowing my eyes at him.

He raises his hands in defense. "Just that your brother strikes me as the type of guy who would find this interesting."

I think about it for a moment. "Are you calling my brother a geek?"

He gets a panicked look on his face, which tells me that is exactly what he was doing. I let him sweat it for several seconds before smiling at him.

"Don't worry. He totally is a geek. He's such a big geek that even though he is a witch and has magic, he still wishes he could go to a school like Hogwarts."

Axel relaxes at my words, bringing my hand to his lips and placing a kiss on my knuckles.

"We have the Westwood Academy," he offers, and I nod.

"Yes, but apparently, it's not 'magical' enough for him," I say with a laugh.

We begin to walk through the dense forest. I'm not even sure whose territory we are in right now. Even though everything is the same, it is also wildly, impossibly different. My internal compass is completely off.

"Do you know where we're going?" I ask.

"Of course, I do. The sleuth is this way," he says, pointing in the direction we're walking.

"How do you know that?"

He taps his finger on his nose. Of course. Shifter senses.

"So, what happens now?" I ask, trying to eat up the silence of our walk.

"What do you mean?"

"I mean, we had planned to spend days building this island. Now that it's done..."

He nods his head, understanding my question now.

"Well, I suppose we'll settle into our new home for the next few days until we're ready to go after the hunters."

"How will it all work? Our new home—Will I take turns sleeping in each of your beds? Will I have my own room where you take turns coming in to sleep with me?" I begin to rifle off questions, and he chuckles. "These are reasonable questions, Axel."

He raises my hand to his lips once more, placing a soft kiss on it.

"I'm not laughing at you, angel. I promise. The three of us will share a room. We will have to do some renovations, maybe extend it so that our room can be far away from my mother's...That is, if you're okay with her living with us. After my dad..." He pales a bit as if I would say no to that.

"Of course, I don't have a problem with her living with us. She's amazing. But I do agree that we should make her bedroom as far away from ours as possible...Otherwise there will be some interesting topics to discuss over breakfast," I chuckle.

He relaxes and laughs along with me. "Yes, I suppose there would be."

"But, really, you two are okay with the three of us sleeping in the same bed? I didn't get a chance to ask either of you last night if being together—the three of us—bothered either of you."

He stops and turns me to face him, raising my chin with his hand. "Let me alleviate your stress about that right now. Zeke and I have had our entire lives to discuss what our life would be like when we found our mate. We always assumed we would share a bed with her unless she wanted something different. When it comes to sharing you, there is no jealousy. All we see when you're with the other is another person making you laugh or bringing you pleasure. We also know there will be times when you want to be alone with one of us, and that's okay too.

"I know that this is new to you, and you'll need to figure out how to navigate the relationship with two mates...But you don't need to worry about Zeke and me. We've been preparing for you our entire lives. We share very well," he says with a wink, sending sparks to my core.

"Really?" I ask, and he nods, bringing his lips down to meet mine.

"Really. Now let's get home so Zeke can tell you the same thing," he says, and we begin walking again.

As we finally reach an opening in the trees, I glance around. Every single building looks exactly how it was back home, right down to the small bushes planted outside the pack house.

I nod, and we continue up the steps into the alpha house. My new home.

"Something smells amazing," I call out as we walk straight to the kitchen.

"I hope you like biscuits," Alexa says, bringing me a tray of warm, buttered biscuits.

I snatch one and quickly throw it in my mouth, moaning loudly as it melts in my mouth.

"Oh, my gods," I say, covering my mouth with my hand to hide the food inside.

"Good?" Zeke asks as he walks over and places a kiss on the side of my head. I just nod and grab another one off the plate, making everyone chuckle.

"So?" Alexa says, looking at Axel.

"What?" he questions.

She rolls her eyes at him. "What do we do now?"

"Now, we eat these biscuits," he says, grabbing one for himself.

She slaps him on the shoulder. "You know what I mean."

He swallows down his biscuit and nods.

"Opal and I were just talking about that. For now, we settle into our new normal and prepare as much as we can for the upcoming raids on the other laboratories."

"And the tiger shifter?" Alexa asks.

Axel's eyes shoot to her then Zeke in panic.

"I had to tell her. She told me she envisions Dad's face when she's making the dough," Zeke says. I do not understand this explanation, but Axel seems to.

"Really?" Axel asks, turning to face his mom.

She nods sullenly. "I blamed him for leaving us. I also believed that it was fake intel."

Axel gets up from his spot, walking over to his mom and wrapping his arms around her.

"It's okay. We didn't know," he reassures her.

She pushes back out of his arms.

"That girl was out there alone for years. How can we fix that?"

Axel looks at Zeke and then me. All three of them feel responsible for Meredith being out there alone, but it was not their fault.

"You'll be there for her if she needs it. You apologize if you feel you must, and you move forward. It is not your fault. None of you are to blame. You went there to search for your father, right?" I ask, looking at Zeke and Axel. They both nod. "Did you find Meredith? No. You didn't. She was hiding. Even if you believed she was there, you likely wouldn't have found her. Right now, she's safe. She's with Samara, and they are doing the feline bonding thing. I've talked to Samara already and she knows to bring her here to talk with you when she's ready."

They each nod as the phone rings.

"Hello?"

"Hey, Opal. It's Alaric. Is Axel there?"

"One sec," I say, handing the phone over to Axel. He walks out of the room with it at his ear.

"Are you two okay now?" I ask Alexa and Zeke.

"Yes. What you said makes a lot of sense. I still feel responsible for that girl being out there for so long. Hopefully, we can find her brother," she says just as Axel comes back in.

"We already did. That was Alaric. Turns out Meredith's mother and brother were in the group that they rescued from Orillia."

"And her father?" I ask. Axel shakes his head. "Well at least most of the family is together. They can begin to heal together."

"I'll be right back. I'm just going to go check in with the sleuth to see if we're missing anyone," Axel says, turning and walking out with a little more pep in his step than earlier. I guess he needed Meredith to have something good come out of this.

Zeke and I begin to clean up the kitchen while Axel goes to check in with the sleuth, and Alexa excuses herself to move her things to the large, furnished basement. She claims she'll need more privacy now that we are all going to be living here. I snort out a laugh.

While she's gone, I question Zeke about the sharing that Axel and I talked about on the way here, and he assures me everything Axel told me is true. Neither of them feel any jealousy toward one another. In fact, he says he finds it appealing to see me with his twin.

It seems like even thinking about it turns him on because he props me up on the counter and starts kissing the ever-living fuck out of me. His tongue snakes into my mouth, demanding attention, as his hands grip my hips and pull me closer to him so I can feel just how much it turns him on.

A low growl snaps me out of my lust, and we turn toward Axel in the doorway. Now that I've talked with Zeke, I know that the look on his face isn't anger. It's desire.

I beckon him closer.

"The sleuth?" I ask, needing to get it out of the way.

"Accounted for," he grinds out.

"Goo—" I don't even get to finish the word as his mouth descends on mine.

I think I'm going to enjoy getting used to my new normal if this is what it's going to be.

Chapter Twenty-Six

Axel

I t's been twenty-four hours of living on the island, and life is good. When Artemis said that she made an exact replica, she truly did. Zeke showed me his list of questions to ask her, but it turns out we don't need her to answer them.

Given that we still have hot water, gas for our stoves, and hydro lines, it's pretty safe to say that she made a portal connecting us to our homes in Parry Sound. She even added the farmlands that I had drawn on the map for us to farm our own food. We can't expect the witches to run around the island going from farm to farm helping the crops grow—or maybe we can. I write that down on my list of things to ask Skarlyt. With most of our members now without a job, they will all be looking for something to take up their time.

I eye the satellite phone, debating whether I make the call to Matt now or not. Zeke and I discussed looping him in and having him help us with finding out who is stealing from us. I argued that he's got enough on his plate right now, but Opal assured me that he's probably begging for things to keep him busy.

I sigh and pick up the phone, dialing his number.

"Opal?" He answers.

"No," I chuckle. "It's Axel."

"Axel?" He asks confused for a moment before panicking. "Is my sister, okay?"

"She's fine," I say, standing up out of my big chair and pacing around the room. "I was calling to ask for your help."

"My help?"

I rub the back of my neck, a little uncomfortable having this conversation over the phone.

"Yeah. I found out that someone has been taking money from our accounts, and I was hoping you could help find out who."

There's some shuffling of papers on the other end.

"I'll be right there," he says, hanging up the phone and leaving me standing in my office staring down at the phone.

"Matt!" I hear Opal yell from the living room and rush out of the office, down the hallway, and stop dead in my tracks. At the front door, Opal is hugging her brother tightly.

I watch as her body stiffens in his arms. He steps back, looking at her with concern. I know without looking that her eyes have gone white. She's being overtaken by a vision. I make a mental note to remind her to get ahold of Valerie to continue her training.

She steps back with a gasp, looking up at her brother as I step up behind her.

"What was that?" Matt asks, concern all over his face.

I ignore his question and focus on my mate.

"Are you okay?" She has tears lining her eyes as she looks up at me and then back at her brother.

"You need to be careful," she warns him.

His mouth opens and closes like a fish.

"I still don't know what that was."

"You remember my sight?" she asks him, and he nods.

"Yes, but *that* was not like any other time I've seen you get a vision."

I wrap my arms around her waist, pulling her back to me recognizing that she's uncomfortable by the stiffness of her shoulders.

"Well, apparently, the reason we couldn't find out anything about it was because I am an oracle, and it's not just an extra gift."

"But..." he begins and then his brows furrow. "What did you see?"

She shakes her head. "I can't tell you."

"What do you mean?" he asks, in an agitated tone.

I know he's not really mad at her, but tears line her eyes anyway as she sinks into me. I guide her toward the couch as I talk.

"We don't know much about how this works. She gets visions. Sometimes she can share what she sees; other times she can't."

He nods along with my words like he's understanding.

"Wait. You said *oracle?*" he asks as he takes a seat on the love seat across from us.

"Yes. That's what Valerie said, right?" I ask, looking down at Opal.

"She said that potion Vivian had me taking dulled my visions and that I was supposed to have started my training when I was twelve. She was imprisoned in the facility, so she couldn't train me."

"Is there anything you can tell me?"

She shakes her head. "Not really. I can say that you need to be careful."

"Well, that's not ominous at all."

She scrunches up her nose in thought.

"I know. There are some things you've been doing recently, and you need to cover your tracks better."

His mouth flies open, and his face pales. It's clear he has some idea what she's talking about. I let it go for now. If it's something that she wants to talk to me about later, she will.

Seeing that the conversation is not going anywhere, I clear my throat.

"How did you get here anyway?"

Matt shakes his head, clearing his thoughts. "I called Sebastyn. He was going to bring me right inside, but I thought it would be better if I didn't pop in the middle of your living room."

Opal chuckles, the tension she was just holding leaches from her body, and I breath out a sigh.

"Now that you know where we live, you can come anytime," she says before turning back to me. "If that's all right."

I place a soft kiss on her temple. "Of course, angel. This is your home now too."

Matt smiles at his sister. "I think I'll stick to using the door. I wouldn't want to pop in at an inconvenient time."

He shudders at the thought of interrupting the two of us—or worse the three of us—and I let off a chuckle of my own.

He claps his hands together.

"All right. You said you have an issue with your accounts."

I nod my head and get up from the couch.

"I'll make some snacks," Opal supplies, getting up and making her way into the kitchen where I can hear my mom greet her happily.

Matt grabs his backpack from the door and follows me into my office where he quickly makes himself at home. He pulls out his laptop, a small satellite dish, and some other electronics I'm unfamiliar with.

Once he's set up, he looks up at me expectantly.

"Well, what have we got?"

With that, I pull up a chair next to him—since he's already sitting in mine—and begin to explain.

"At first, I thought it only went back a few months, but Zeke went through the books when he got home and found transfers going back years. They were never big amounts, but they've grown exponentially."

His fingers fly over the keyboard, and I watch him go through a series of screens.

"Okay, I'm in. When did the transfers start?" he asks, and my mouth gapes open. I didn't even give him the account number or name of the company.

"Uh..." I say, reaching over and rummaging through the papers on the desk. I can't find Zeke's notes.

"When was the last transfer?" he asks, and I quickly grab up the most recent account book and read it.

"Ten days ago."

His fingers tap away some more.

"And you have a member of your sleuth working there?"

"Yes. Arthur Masters."

"Okay." He pauses, scrolling through a bunch of pages on his screen. None of them make any sense to me, but they must mean something to him. "It looks like all the transfers were made from his computer."

I heave out a sigh.

"That's not what I wanted to hear." I stand up and begin pacing.

"Let me check the cameras first."

A few more clicks, and I go to stand behind him as Opal walks in the room.

"Anyone hungry?" she asks, her beautiful, blue eyes shining with love, and I don't have the heart to tell her I have no appetite after the news I just got.

Instead, I nod my head and walk over to take the plate of sandwiches from her. "Thanks, angel."

Matt, in his own little world, glances up as I place the plate next to him, quickly swipes one, and takes a large bite.

"Okay, cameras are up. Now, we watch."

I stare at the screen, watching as Arthur walks into an office that must be his before he's joined by another man. A few minutes later, Arthur walks out, but the balding man that had joined him remains for another ten minutes. When he leaves the office, Matt pauses the video and zooms in on his face.

"Do you recognize him?" Matt asks, and I move closer to the screen to get a better look. His round belly hangs over the top of his tightly fitted pants, and his huge smile shows crooked teeth.

"I've never seen that man in my life," I confidently answer.

"Okay, then," Matt says, closing the window and pulling up the accounting firm's website. He scrolls through the pages until he finds a picture of the man under the employee page. The name Jason Webber captions the photo.

Now that he has a name to work with, Matt works quickly. He pulls up another program with a black screen and blue writing, and a window pops up showing Jason Webber's life story.

"It seems like this guy is a compulsive gambler and owes a lot of bad people a lot of money." After a few more clicks, Matt is looking at his bank records. They show multiple transfers in and out—far more than he was taking from me. "It looks like the sleuth isn't the only client he's taking money from."

My mind whirls as I watch Matt. The things he's able to do with just a few taps on a keyboard and clicks of a mouse makes me look at him in a new light. Honestly, it's a little scary.

I watch as he sends copies of all the false transfers to the CEO of the accounting firm and then anonymously sends the same to the newspaper in Parry Sound. It's been less than an hour, and Matt has effectively destroyed this guy's life.

I glance over at Opal. She is also in awe of her brother. It doesn't seem she knew the extent of what he could do either.

"There. I transferred all your accounts from their company over to me. Not only will I not steal your money, but I will also duplicate any investments I make using your own."

"What do you mean?"

He sighs, looking up from his laptop for the first time.

"I have a lot of investments, and they generally turn a pretty good profit. I have purchased a program that will duplicate any investments I make on my account so that yours will do the same. You're not going to be hurting for money any time soon."

My mouth gapes open, and I share a look with Opal who smirks. Guess she knew about this part of what he does.

"I also took the liberty of sending everything he was doing to his boss, the cops, and the newspaper. He's going to have a hard time finding a way to pay off his debts, and that company is probably going to go under real soon with the amount of money they're going to have to pay back to their clients."

"Shit. I should go tell Arthur."

I give Opal a kiss on the head as I walk by before mind-linking Arthur to meet me at the house.

It only takes a few minutes before he comes striding up to the porch where I'm waiting. He looks nervous.

"Thanks for coming so quickly," I say, sticking my hand out for him to shake.

"Of course, Alpha. I was hoping to talk to you anyway."

"What did you want to talk to me about?" I ask and watch as he hops from foot to foot with nervousness.

"Well, you see..." he begins, and I nod, encouraging him to continue. "Some of us don't really know what to do on the island and were wondering..."

"Yes?" I probe, not understanding what he's getting at.

"Well, some of us were hoping to move back to Parry Sound so that we could continue going to our jobs and such." He spits the words out fast, and I smile as I gesture for him to take a seat on one of the chairs.

"I know our move here was sudden. If some of you wish to continue working in Parry Sound, we will figure out a way you can do so without you having to live there without protection." He opens his mouth to protest, but I hold up my hand. "Make no mistake—we need the protection this island offers. Not only from the attack the other night, but also from the hunters. We do have a portal that goes back and forth, and I will discuss setting up a guard rotation with the other faction leaders. That way our members can go to and from Parry Sound when they like. If it was *your* job that you wanted to go back to…" He nods. "I'm sorry to say that you won't have a job for much longer."

His mouth flies open. "What do you mean?"

I sigh and tell him everything I've learned about Jason Webber.

A growl rumbles in his chest. "I knew there was something fishy about him. He was always such a sleaze ball. I'm so sorry, Axel. I swear, if I had known…"

I wave my hand.

"There was no way that you could've predicted that a human at your firm was going to steal money from us."

He nods but still has a guilty look on his face.

"Besides, I do have a few other things I would like to talk to you about." I hadn't planned on singling anyone out to do this. I was going to put it out to the entire sleuth and look for volunteers, but I can tell Arthur needs a purpose.

"Anything."

"I know that there are a lot of us who are now out of work because of the move, but there's also a lot of things that we need in order to make this island self-sufficient."

"What do you mean?"

"Well, for one thing, we need a census done so that we know how many members we have, then we need someone to crunch the numbers and figure out how much food we need to survive. Sure, we could just go through the portal and get groceries when we want, but I know that the other faction leaders would like to make this our permanent home and a haven for other supernaturals in the future."

He nods, an excited glint in his eyes.

"We will need a dairy farm, a mill, and we need to rotate the crops so that we're not growing the same thing on each one..."

I cut him off with a chuckle.

"Exactly. I am going to have all the other factions assign a member to do the same, and all of you can work as a team. We will also need to think of the vampires and figure out a way to set up a blood bank on the mainland."

"Of course." He pulls a notebook out of his back pocket and scribbles down some notes.

"You can recruit whoever you think you'll need to help you."

"Thank you." He nods and waves as he quickly hurries away, leaving me on the porch smiling. Well, that's one thing off my list. A bunch of things actually.

We found out who was stealing money and will probably get most of it back, I've recruited help to ensure the island is sustainable and helped give some of my sleuth members purpose.

"All right, I'm headed over to Valerie's for training," Opal says as she and Matt step out the front door.

"Do you want me to come with you?" I ask, snagging her by the waist before she can get too far, placing a kiss on her lips.

"No. Matt's going to walk me before heading back to Orillia," she says, going up on her toes to place a soft kiss on my lips.

I watch from the front porch as they walk away with his arm around her shoulder and hers around his waist.

Do you think we should plan a mating ceremony? I ask my brother through our link.

His answer is instant. *Yes.*

Then get over here and let's get planning. If we can, I'd like to get it done tonight.

On my way.

I pick up the phone to call Alaric first. Once I know he's on board, I call Skarlyt, Sarah, and Rayne to enlist their help.

Chapter Twenty-Seven

Opal

After saying goodbye to Axel, Matt and I begin to make our way to Valerie's house in a comfortable silence. Since that night where we talked and watched movies, it almost feels like I have my little brother back. He's not that little anymore. His arm is bulky and feels like it weighs a million pounds as it rests across my shoulders.

I reach over and pull one of his suspenders, making it crack against his chest. He jerks away.

"What was that for?"

I shrug my shoulders. "I just felt like it."

"Oh, really," he says right before he charges at me, his hands out in tickling position and I start to run, squealing in delight the entire way. His long legs make short work of catching up to me.

"I really missed you, Matty," I whisper from the ground when he finally stops tickling me.

"I missed you too, Opal. Don't do anything like that again," he says, and I nod sullenly. I wish I could go back in time and change everything.

I dust myself off after he helps me up, and I turn to him.

"You understood what I meant about being careful, right?" I ask. To say that I was surprised my geeky baby brother is moonlighting as an online vigilante is a gross understatement, but that wasn't all I saw. The people he goes after are not good people.

He nods. "I do, and I promise I will be more careful."

"How did you start doing that anyway?" I ask, too curious to help myself.

"When you left..." he begins, and I feel a pang of regret. He must notice because he slings his arm around my shoulders again. "When you left, I got angry. I was angry at you, angry at Mom and Dad, angry at myself, and I started acting out. I started pushing people away, wanting to hurt them the way I was hurting."

"I'm sorry, Matty. I never meant..."

He waves me off. "I know you didn't. Knowing your story now, I don't blame you. I wish you would've felt comfortable talking to me about it, but I understand why you did what you did. Anyway, Mom and Dad recognized what I was doing too, so they enrolled me in some computer courses on coding. They thought having something to focus on would help."

"And it did, right?" I ask. He is still doing it a decade later, so that's something.

"Yes," he chuckles. "Just not the way they thought. They believed I would start coding and maybe go into video game design or something like that, but I met some people in the course who taught me to help the little guy. It started with this bully at school who just wouldn't leave us alone, so we hacked into his cameras at home hoping to get incriminating or embarrassing footage of him. What we saw..." He shudders, and I squeeze my arm around his waist.

"His dad was abusing him. It was—merciless. He was careful to not leave bruises, but once we knew...I had to do something. A few of us decided to teach his dad a lesson. We combed through his digital files until we hit the holy grail. He was taking bribes from multiple criminals to turn a blind eye to certain suspicious activity. Not a huge deal for some people. For the Chief of Police? It wasn't a good look for him."

"So, what did you do?" I ask, enthralled by the story.

"We took copies of absolutely everything we could get our hands on, including a redacted video of him beating his son, and sent it to the Crown attorney and a couple of judges we found who weren't dirty. Side note: a lot of judges are dirty. It took less than twenty-four hours. He was arrested, his son was placed with his grandparents, and the Deputy Chief of Police was named the Interim Chief."

"Did you look into him too?"

"We did. We wanted to make sure that we didn't help put someone even worse in a position of power. Thankfully, the worst thing he had was a couple of unpaid parking tickets."

"So, now that's what you do? You find bad guys and destroy them online?"

"Destroy is kind of a harsh word. We have a listing up on the dark web as well as on our Supernatural Online Network offering our services. We don't have a set fee. We accept whatever someone can pay. Once we find the dirt, we send it on to someone who we know will actually take action against it."

"That's really cool."

"It is. I'd love to show you sometime."

"I'd like that," I say as we walk up to my old house—Valerie's new home."

"I'll catch up with you soon," he says, leaning down and placing a soft kiss on the top of my head.

"I love you, Matty," I whisper. He whispers it back before teleporting away—probably back to Drake and Rayne.

"Opal," Valerie exclaims as she opens the front door.

"Hey Val," I respond as I walk up the steps.

"I'm glad you're here. We're going on a field trip today."

My steps falter. "A field trip?"

She nods, excitement written all over her face.

"Skarlyt met someone and came over to ask if I could get a read on her, but my powers are fading. I thought this would be the perfect opportunity for you to try and force a vision."

"But..." I begin, my mouth gaping open in shock. "You think I'm ready for that?"

She claps her hands together. "Of course, you are. I'll be there beside you the whole time. If you get bombarded with visions, you can just reach out and touch me."

I nod. "I had a vision when I touched Matt this morning."

"How did it go?" she asks, gesturing for me to take a seat on her couch.

"It was weird feeling the emotions of my baby brother, but what I saw was also scary and concerning."

"Do you feel comfortable sharing what it was?"

I shake my head.

"I can't explain it, but somehow I know that I can't."

She nods. "That is how it is. You will instinctively know what you can share."

Next thing I know, Skarlyt is popping into the living room right in front of us.

"What the fuck?" I exclaim, and both Skarlyt and Val cackle. "You scared the shit out of me."

"I live to please," Skarlyt snarks, and I wave her away.

"Did you tell her?" Skarlyt asks.

Val shakes her head. "No, I didn't get the chance."

My gaze ping pongs between the two. "Tell me what?"

"Remember the vision you had of Kayne?"

My eyes snap to hers before sliding to Val.

"She knows?" I whisper, and both women immediately begin laughing.

"I had a vision of Kayne using magic in wolf form too," Valerie states, and I release some of the tension I was holding onto.

"I met someone recently who seems to be the same as Kayne, and I was hoping Valerie could try and get a vision to confirm it. She seems to believe you're the better one for this."

"Who?"

"Her name is Ester. She recently mated with Ethan, one of the pack members." I nod along as if I know who either of those people are.

Skar grips my hand with her left and Valerie's with her right and, without warning, teleports us to a house on pack land.

A red-haired man with pale, freckled skin and big, brown eyes opens the door. He's maybe nineteen or twenty.

"Hi, Skar."

"Ethan, these are the friends I was telling you about. Valerie and Opal," she says, each of us waving when she says our names.

"Are you sure this is safe?" he whispers, and my metaphorical hackles rise. If his mate is like Kayne, he's right to be nervous. Now that we're on the island, she should be safe. Especially if Artemis put the protection spell over it.

"I trust these two with my own secret. Believe me, I wouldn't put Ester in danger," Skarlyt says, and her words must hit home because Ethan visibly relaxes. He opens the door wider and invites us inside.

As soon as we walk in, I see a beautiful, young woman with black, curly hair, big, brown eyes, and porcelain skin. My feet move on their own toward her. I hear the three people behind me talking, but I can't understand anything that they're saying. There is something pulling me toward this girl, urging me to touch her.

"It's okay, Opal. Follow your instincts." I hear Valarie say, and I search the girl's brown eyes.

"May I touch you?" I ask. Her eyes go wide with fear, and she glances behind me. Whatever she sees there must placate her because she gives me a nod.

No further prompting needed, I reach out my hands, placing one on her forehead and another on her heart. I am instantly sucked into a vision. It feels like I'm in a car, and the radio station keeps changing before a song can start. It's like many visions are fighting for dominance at once.

A woman who can only be Ester's mother sits beside a man. She has the same dark hair and eyes as her daughter, but hers is pin straight. Ester's curls must have come from her father. He holds her mother's hand, looking up at her through auburn curls.

"We're really having a baby?" he asks, and I feel his excitement through the vision.

"A girl," she says, and I watch with fascination as his face pales even further.

The vision shifts forward to the night of Ester's birth. Both parents are huddled together with their baby swaddled in a pink blanket in their arms.

"It's not possible." This comes from a woman standing at the edge of the bed. Her words are coated in fear.

"I don't understand it either, High Priestess, but it's true," Ester's mother states.

"What do we do?" her father pipes in, and all three shake their heads.

"Tell no one. Hide her," the High Priestess demands.

The next visions come in quick succession. Each one is the same, yet different. The couple run away with their newborn baby. They are found and attacked, while they search for safety and find none. Finally, with no other options, they admit defeat. They finally stop in Thunder Bay and pay the rest of their savings to a witch. They ask her to use blood magic to bind their baby girl so that she can't access her wolf or magic. As soon as the deed is done, they make their way across Ontario and land in Parry Sound.

I feel their heartbreak through the vision, and I can feel tears streaking down my own face.

"We have to go," he says to her.

"Just one more minute," she pleads, sobs wracking her body.

"One more," he agrees, wrapping his arms around his mate and their baby girl. They whisper their love to her, their hopes for her future.

I watch as they place the baby on the steps of the Fire Department before ringing the bell. They watch from the shadows as a kind-looking man picks their daughter up, cradles her with love, and shuts the door behind him.

The images speed and change.

Ester is a young girl, wondering why no one wants her. She cries herself to sleep, wishing for a mom and dad.

Ester is a teenager, angry and acting out. She causes trouble with the families who take her in because she wants them to love her even if she is trouble. She curses the mom and dad that left her.

Ester is a young adult. She ages out of foster care before finding a family she could be a part of.

As soon as my eyes open, I place a palm on either side of her face.

"They loved you so much," I whisper.

Tears flood her eyes. "What?"

"Your parents. They loved you so much. They did the only thing they knew would keep you safe. They gave you away, hoping and praying that you would be loved the way you deserved."

"But why?" Ester sobs.

"They were being hunted. You were not safe. I'm assuming it's because of what you are. You survived because they sacrificed the thing they loved most—you."

Her head falls to my shoulders as sobs wrack her body. I wrap my arms around her, rubbing her back soothingly.

"Are they—?" she asks, pulling her head up to look into my eyes.

I close my eyes, trying to focus on the unspoken question, but all I get is static.

"I don't know," I sigh and turn to look back at Valerie, hoping she can step in and get the vision when I can't.

"If you can't see it, we're not meant to know," she says, and Ester's sobs begin anew. "Not yet anyway," she adds quietly, but I catch it. She does know something; she just can't share it.

We spend the next hour talking to and consoling Ester before leaving her with her mate.

When we land back at Valerie's, we find Rayne and Sarah waiting in the kitchen.

"What are you two doing here?" I ask.

"We're here to get you ready," Sarah says, and I look between all the women surrounding me.

"Get me ready? Ready for what?"

"Your surprise," Rayne pipes in, guiding me to a chair. She sounds a little too excited for me to be totally confident about whatever is happening next. She pulls my hair down from the ponytail I've been wearing all day and begins brushing.

By the time they are done with me, I look like an angel. I'm in a flowy, white dress. A flower crown sits atop my perfect, blonde curls. My make-up—much to Rayne's displeasure—is soft and simple.

Although they have yet to reveal the surprise waiting for me, I have a few guesses.

My friends lead me through a path in the woods. I walk barefoot, enjoying my connection to the nature around us.

"What is—" I exclaim as we walk through the tree line.

In the distance, I see the little cabin where we were all together for the first time. The fairy lights are still strung between the trees, and there are now benches lining either side of an aisle that leads to the beach.

Once, this view looked out on a familiar lake. Now, it is ocean waves and salt spray that assault my senses. There is a bright quarter moon shining down.

At the end of that aisle, my mates wait proudly in matching pairs of beige khakis and white dress shirts at the edge of the ocean. Sarah and Rayne lead me toward them. I immediately wrap my small arms around them, struggling to reach around them both at once.

"This is amazing," I whisper.

"Anything for you, angel," Zeke replies. Axel places a soft kiss on the top of my head.

A throat clears behind us, and we turn to see Skarlyt smirking and Alaric chuckling.

"Ready?" he asks. I glance at my mates and nod.

"Yes."

"We have come together tonight to celebrate the mating of Opal to Zeke and Axel," Alaric begins, raising his voice and assuming the formality of a human wedding ceremony. Skarlyt scoffs.

"We have been brought together today in front of the Mother to join these three together as a mated triad," Skarlyt continues loudly.

"Do you, Opal, take Zeke as your bonded mate?" Skarlyt asks.

I don't hesitate.

"I do."

"Do you also take Axel as your bonded mate and accept your rightful place as luna at his side?"

My heart skips a beat at this responsibility. When I accepted the mating bond, I hadn't really been thinking about what it would mean to be mated to an alpha. I look up into his mossy green eyes for confirmation and know that I can do anything with this man at my side.

"I do."

"Do you promise to guide and protect the sleuth from this day forward until your dying breath?"

"I do." My words are thick with emotion as I answer and tears spring to my eyes.

"Finally, do you reaffirm your pledge to me, Skarlyt Moon, as your coven leader?"

"I do," I repeat.

"Do you, Zeke, take Opal as your bonded mate?" Alaric asks, and Zeke looks down at me.

"Always."

I smile at his answer.

Was it only a few weeks ago that this seemed so impossible?

"Do you recognize Axel as your alpha and Skarlyt as your coven leader?"

Zeke's eyes flit to Axel and then Skarlyt.

"I do."

"Do you, Axel, take Opal as your mate and luna?" Alaric asks.

"I do," he responds, looking into my eyes.

"Do you pledge your allegiance to me as the leader of your mate's coven?" Skarlyt asks, mischief lining her eyes.

"I do," he replies, sounding less certain of this promise than the others.

"Then, before the Mother and these witnesses, we declare you a mated triad," Skarlyt says, clapping her hands together.

I turn to Axel, running my hands up his chest before linking them behind his neck and pulling his mouth down to mine in a heated kiss. It's over far too soon, but he's not my only mate.

I turn and do the same to Zeke. I feel Axel press his front up against my back, sandwiching me between them. A moan slips out of my mouth as I consider the possibilities, and Axel chuckles.

"You're ours now, angel. Forever and always," he whispers into my ear.

"Forever and always," I parrot as I release Zeke's lips.

Epilogue

Breanne

The door to my room opens, and I'm greeted by my puppet master. Richard is the man who pulls all my strings. He's also the reason I finally have a room with a bed. He's the reason my daily torture has stopped.

Even now, the thought of all the things he's made me do makes me sick to my stomach. I've slaughtered so many of my own kind in his name, but I know it was either their lives or mine. I remember the faces of each person I've cut down for him. I remember the way their eyes widen when they realize I'm about to strike them down, the look of betrayal that settles in their eyes as I go in for the kill...

A shudder runs through me at the thought, and I turn to look at him.

"I have a new mission for you, *Breanne.*"

I give a slight nod, showing him I'm listening. I know better now than to say it aloud. He believes I should be seen and not heard. He believes I am a weaker species, and I don't mean because I am a vampire. I hope not all the women in Richard's life are treated like I am.

"It seems one of the hunters from the Orillia faction has gone rogue, and the facility there has been sending some concerning reports. We told them we would be there in four days to check on the situation, but we're sending you in now."

He gets an evil glint in his eyes as he tells me the plan.

"You will track down the rogue hunter and report back on the situation at the facility..."

Excitement blooms in my chest at the knowledge that I'll be so close to home. Maybe I can see my family. Maybe they'll be able to help me finally escape. I try to hide the excitement I'm feeling, but I must not have hidden it well enough. I stiffen as a metal prod presses into the side of my neck.

"Now, now," Richard says. "No getting any ideas. Remember I can end you with the touch of a button."

My shoulders slump. Richard loves to remind me of the collar I wear around my neck. I'm not even sure what's in it. All I know is that they injected me with different substances over and over, day after day, for the first few years I was here until they found something that sets my blood on fire and makes me feel like I'm burning from the inside.

"Who is the hunter?" I ask.

Richard chuckles. The evil glint blooms in his eyes once more.

"Her name is Rayne. Apparently, she's been consorting with an old friend of yours ..."

My brows furrow in confusion.

"I believe you called her Dru."

At his mention of Drusilla, I suck in a breath.

"That can't be. She was taken when I was."

Surely, he's wrong. Dru would've found me if she escaped...

He shakes his head.

"It seems the incompetence of the Orillia faction runs deep. She was able to escape years ago. She ran back to her coven to hide and cower like the vermin she is."

The knowledge that Drusilla has been free for years and hasn't found me yet sends a pang of hurt through my chest, but I tamp it down. At least one of us is safe.

"Now, what is your mission?" Richard asks.

I look at him in the eyes as I recite my mission.

"Go to the Orillia facility, hunt down the rogue hunter, and report back to you on the situation at the facility."

"Good, dog," he says as he leads me out the door, ready to send me on my mission.

I'm never happy to do Richard's bidding, but at least this is just a recon mission. It helps that I'll be tracking hunters instead of other supernaturals.

Honestly, if this rogue hunter got the drop on me and put me out of my misery, it wouldn't be the worst thing in the world.

* * *

Want more from the Westwood Pack?
Of course, you do!
Information about Book 8, Blood Magic here:
https://fdfairauthor.wixsite.com/website

About the Author

F.D. Fair is the author of the Westwood Pack Series. As an avid reader of Paranormal Romance Novels for the past 20 years, she turned her love of everything paranormal into steamy True Mate novels with a twist.

F.D. Fair lives and works in southern Ontario, Canada and

spends her time when she is not working or writing with the loves of her life—Her husband and 3 boys.

She is as weird as they come but is proud of it. Embracing her weirdness makes for some great stories.

Sign up for FD Fair's Newsletter:
https://dashboard.mailerlite.com/forms/76323/
5809623843156931o/share

Make sure to stalk her...

Instagram:
https://www.instagram.com/f.d.fairauthor
Facebook:
https://www.facebook.com/profile.php?id=100071688648516
Goodreads:
https://www.goodreads.com/author/show/21734156.F_D_Fair
Twitter:
https://twitter.com/FdFair
Bookbub:
https://www.bookbub.com/authors/f-d-fair

More from Foundations

D. Thomas Jerlo

~Fantasy~

GET IT HERE: https://www.dthomasjerlo.com/

A best-selling and award nominated author of fantasy and paranormal, D. Thomas Jerlo's novels hook unsuspecting readers into worlds of mage'ic and refuses to let them go until that last page is read.

Imprisoned for over a thousand years by the Diveneans of old, Lord Balthazar covets one thing: his freedom. Using his minion, Isafel, and an evil imp spawn called Ilio, they will search Etharia for the one thing that will set their master free and bring chaos to the lands—the Kruthos Key.

With underlords scheming to take the throne and demons roaming freely throughout the land, it's a race against time. But one Divenean still lives, and with the help of an ex-General there may be hope left.

But is it enough?

Foundations Book Publishing

Our mission is to exceed the expectations of our authors and the reading community with an uncompromising commitment to quality, individualism and personal pride. We measure our success one book at a time.

You can find more great works in multiple genres including Romance, Literary Fictions, Thrillers, Suspense, Young Adult, and more!

Visit us at FoundationsBooks.net